LANDOU

Ruskin Bond is known for his signature simplistic and witty writing style. He is the author of several bestselling short stories, novellas, collections, essays and children's books; and has contributed a number of poems and articles to various magazines and anthologies. At the age of twenty-three, he won the prestigious John Llewellyn Rhys Prize for his first novel, *The Room on the Roof*. He was also the recipient of the Padma Shri in 1999, Lifetime Achievement Award by the Delhi Government in 2012, and the Padma Bhushan in 2014.

Born in 1934, Ruskin Bond grew up in Jamnagar, Shimla, New Delhi and Dehradun. Apart from three years in the UK, he has spent all his life in India, and now lives in Landour, Mussoorie, with his adopted family.

RUSKIN BOND
LANDOUR BAZAAR

Published by
Rupa Publications India Pvt. Ltd 2018
7/16, Ansari Road, Daryaganj
New Delhi 110002

Sales centres:
Allahabad Bengaluru Chennai
Hyderabad Jaipur Kathmandu
Kolkata Mumbai

Copyright © Ruskin Bond 2018

This is a work of fiction. Names, characters, places and incidents are either the product of the author's imagination or are used fictitiously and any resemblance to any actual person, living or dead, events or locales is entirely coincidental.

All rights reserved.
No part of this publication may be reproduced, transmitted, or stored in a retrieval system, in any form or by any means, electronic, mechanical, photocopying, recording or otherwise, without the prior permission of the publisher.

ISBN: 978-93-5304-146-5

First impression 2018

10 9 8 7 6 5 4 3 2 1

Printed at Parksons Graphics Pvt.Ltd., Mumbai.

This book is sold subject to the condition that it shall not, by way of trade or otherwise, be lent, resold, hired out, or otherwise circulated, without the publisher's prior consent, in any form of binding or cover other than that in which it is published.

CONTENTS

Introduction	vii
Sita and the River	1
Voting at Barlowganj	28
A Song of Many Rivers	37
Cold Beer at Chutmalpur	53
Time Stops at Shamli	59
The Story of Madhu	99
Tales of Old Mussoorie	104
Dust on the Mountain	112
A Walk through Garhwal	131
Bus Stop, Pipalnagar	141
Once You Have Lived with Mountains	169
The Night Train at Deoli	172
A Hill Station's Vintage Murders	178
The Blue Umbrella	182
A Long Walk for Bina	204
A Face in the Dark	227
Landour Bazaar	230

INTRODUCTION

I have spent a lifetime in the mountains. And if I had to do it all over again, I would still choose to spend my life here.

I live in Landour, above Mussoorie. This is the Garhwal Himalaya and the people who live on these mountain slopes in the mist-filled valleys have long since learned humility, patience, and a quiet resignation. Deep in the crouching mist lie their villages, while climbing the mountain slopes are forests of rhododendron, spruce, and deodar, soughing in the wind from the ice-bound passes. Pale women plough, they laugh at the thunder as their men go down to the plains for work; for little grows on the beautiful mountains in the dry seasons. This landscape is typical of Garhwal, one of India's most northerly regions with its massive snow ranges bordering on Tibet. Although thinly populated, it does not provide much of a living for its people. Most Garhwali cultivators are poor, some are very poor. And yet these are cheerful people, sturdy and with wonderful powers of endurance. Somehow they manage to wrest a precarious living from the unhelpful soil.

These mountains and these people have stood the test of time like no other. And I have always been grateful to them, for it is because of them that I have never run out of stories to tell. One may get a writer's block while living in big cities, but not in small-town India. There may be fewer people living in these towns than in the cities, but they have certainly provided me with plenty of tales.

In this collection, I have put together some of my best fiction and non-fiction works that the mountains have inspired me to write. For if you cannot come up here, I hope these stories will at least give you a glimpse into our lives. Included here are some of my novellas such as 'Sita and the River', 'Time Stops at Shamli', 'The Blue Umbrella', and 'A Long Walk for Bina'; along with some anecdotal tales like 'Cold Beer at Chutmalpur', 'A Walk through Garhwal', and 'Voting at Barlowganj'; fiction that includes 'Dust on the Mountain' and 'The Night Train at Deoli'; and some essays such as 'Tales of Old Mussoorie' and 'A Hill Station's Vintage Murders', and many more.

My favourite thing while living up here are the nights. Walking home at midnight in Landour can be quite eventful as it makes one aware of the silent life in the trees and bushes, of the wild animals on the prowl, and to the calls of nightjars, owls, and other birds that live by night. However, the Landour Bazaar of my title is a little different today from what it was twenty years ago, when I wrote that particular essay. Cars, motorcycles, and trucks have taken the place of mules and rickshaws, and the poor pedestrian has a hard time negotiating his way through all the traffic.

With this collection I hope to create a charming little portrait of our life in the hills, where we live in a quiet, unhurried manner and at our own pace. And I hope that it would inspire you to come visit us too someday.

Ruskin Bond

SITA AND THE RIVER

In the middle of the big river, the river that began in the mountains and ended in the sea, was a small island. The river swept round the island, sometimes clawing at its banks, but never going right over it. It was over twenty years since the river had flooded the island, and at that time no one had lived there. But for the last ten years a small hut had stood there, a mud-walled hut with a sloping thatched roof. The hut had been built into a huge rock, so only three of the walls were mud, and the fourth was rock.

Goats grazed on the short grass which grew on the island, and on the prickly leaves of thorn bushes. A few hens followed them about. There was a melon patch and a vegetable patch.

In the middle of the island stood a peepul tree. It was the only tree there.

Even during the Great Flood, when the island had been under water, the tree had stood firm.

It was an old tree. A seed had been carried to the island by a strong wind some fifty years back, had found shelter between two rocks, had taken root there, and had sprung up to give shade and shelter to a small family; and Indians love peepul trees, especially during the hot summer months when the heart-shaped leaves catch the least breath of air and flutter eagerly, fanning those who sit beneath.

A sacred tree, the peepul: the abode of spirits, good and bad.

'Don't yawn when you are sitting beneath the tree,' Grandmother used to warn Sita. 'And if you must yawn, always snap your fingers in front of your mouth. If you forget to do that, a spirit might jump down your throat!'

'And then what will happen?' asked Sita.

'It will probably ruin your digestion,' said Grandfather, who wasn't much of a believer in spirits.

The peepul had a beautiful leaf, and Grandmother likened it to the body of the mighty god Krishna—broad at the shoulders, then tapering down to a very slim waist.

It was an old tree, and an old man sat beneath it.

He was mending a fishing net. He had fished in the river for ten years, and he was a good fisherman. He knew where to find the slim silver Chilwa fish and the big beautiful Mahseer and the long-moustached Singhara; he knew where the river was deep and where it was shallow; he knew which baits to use—which fish liked worms and which liked gram. He had taught his son to fish, but his son had gone to work in a factory in a city, nearly a hundred miles away. He had no grandson; but he had a granddaughter, Sita, and she could do all the things a boy could do, and sometimes she could do them better. She had lost her mother when she was very small. Grandmother had taught her all the things a girl should know, and she could do these as well as most girls. But neither of her grandparents could read or write, and as a result Sita couldn't read or write either.

There was a school in one of the villages across the river, but Sita had never seen it. There was too much to do on the island.

While Grandfather mended his net, Sita was inside the hut, pressing her Grandmother's forehead, which was hot with fever.

Grandmother had been ill for three days and could not eat. She had been ill before, but she had never been so bad. Grandfather had brought her some sweet oranges from the market in the nearest town, and she could suck the juice from the oranges, but she couldn't eat anything else.

She was younger than Grandfather, but because she was sick, she looked much older. She had never been very strong.

When Sita noticed that Grandmother had fallen asleep, she tiptoed out of the room on her bare feet and stood outside.

The sky was dark with monsoon clouds. It had rained all night, and in a few hours it would rain again. The monsoon rains had come early, at the end of June. Now it was the middle of July, and already the river was swollen. Its rushing sound seemed nearer and more menacing than usual.

Sita went to her grandfather and sat down beside him beneath the peepul tree.

'When you are hungry, tell me,' she said, 'and I will make the bread.'

'Is your grandmother asleep?'

'She sleeps. But she will wake soon, for she has a deep pain.'

The old man stared out across the river, at the dark green of the forest, at the grey sky, and said, 'Tomorrow, if she is not better, I will take her to the hospital at Shahganj. There they will know how to make her well. You may be on your own for a few days—but you have been on your own before...'

Sita nodded gravely; she had been alone before, even during the rainy season. Now she wanted Grandmother to get well, and she knew that only Grandfather had the skill to take the small dugout boat across the river when the current was so strong. Someone would have to stay behind to look after their few possessions.

Sita was not afraid of being alone, but she did not like the look of the river. That morning, when she had gone down to fetch water, she had noticed that the level had risen. Those rocks which were normally spattered with the droppings of snipe and curlew and other waterbirds had suddenly disappeared.

They disappeared every year—but not so soon, surely?

'Grandfather, if the river rises, what will I do?'

'You will keep to the high ground.'

'And if the water reaches the high ground?'

'Then take the hens into the hut, and stay there.'

'And if the water comes into the hut?'

'Then climb into the peepul tree. It is a strong tree. It will not fall. And the water cannot rise higher than the tree!'

'And the goats, Grandfather?'

'I will be taking them with me, Sita. I may have to sell them to pay for good food and medicines for your grandmother. As for the hens, if it becomes necessary, put them on the roof. But do not worry too much'—and he patted Sita's head—'the water will not rise as high. I will be back soon, remember that.'

'And won't Grandmother come back?'

'Yes, of course, but they may keep her in the hospital for some time.'

◆

Towards evening, it began to rain again—big pellets of rain, scarring the surface of the river. But it was warm rain, and Sita could move about in it. She was not afraid of getting wet, she rather liked it. In the previous month, when the first monsoon shower had arrived, washing the dusty leaves of the tree and bringing up the good smell of the earth, she had exulted in it, had run about shouting for joy. She was used to it now, and indeed a little tired of the rain, but she did not mind getting wet. It was steamy indoors, and her thin dress would soon dry in the heat from the kitchen fire.

She walked about barefooted, barelegged. She was very sure on her feet; her toes had grown accustomed to gripping all kinds of rocks, slippery or sharp. And though thin, she was surprisingly strong.

Black hair, streaming across her face. Black eyes. Slim brown arms. A scar on her thigh—when she was small, visiting her mother's village, a hyaena had entered the house where she was sleeping, fastened on to her leg and tried to drag her away, but her screams had roused the villagers and the hyaena had run off.

She moved about in the pouring rain, chasing the hens into a shelter behind the hut. A harmless brown snake, flooded out of its hole, was moving across the open ground. Sita picked up a stick, scooped the snake up, and dropped it between a cluster of rocks. She had no quarrel with snakes. They kept down the rats and the frogs. She wondered how the rats had first come to the island—probably in someone's boat, or in a sack of grain. Now it was a job to keep their numbers down.

When Sita finally went indoors, she was hungry. She ate some dried peas and warmed up some goat's milk.

Grandmother woke once and asked for water, and Grandfather held the brass tumbler to her lips.

◆

It rained all night.

The roof was leaking, and a small puddle formed on the floor. They kept the kerosene lamp alight. They did not need the light, but somehow it made them feel safer.

The sound of the river had always been with them, although they were seldom aware of it; but that night they noticed a change in its sound. There was something like a moan, like a wind in the tops of tall trees and a swift hiss as the water swept round the rocks and carried away pebbles. And sometimes there was a rumble, as loose earth fell into the water.

Sita could not sleep.

She had a rag doll, made with Grandmother's help out of bits of old clothing. She kept it by her side every night. The doll was someone to talk to, when the nights were long and sleep elusive. Her grandparents were often ready to talk—and Grandmother, when she was well, was a good storyteller—but sometimes Sita wanted to have secrets, and though there were no special secrets in her life, she made up a few, because it was fun to have them. And if you have secrets, you must have a friend to share them with, a companion of one's own age. Since there were no other children on the island, Sita shared her secrets with the rag doll whose name was Mumta.

Grandfather and Grandmother were asleep, though the sound of Grandmother's laboured breathing was almost as persistent as the sound of the river.

'Mumta,' whispered Sita in the dark, starting one of her private conversations. 'Do you think Grandmother will get well again?'

Mumta always answered Sita's questions, even though the answers could only be heard by Sita.

'She is very old,' said Mumta.

'Do you think the river will reach the hut?' asked Sita.

'If it keeps raining like this, and the river keeps rising, it will reach the hut.'

'I am a little afraid of the river, Mumta. Aren't you afraid?'

'Don't be afraid. The river has always been good to us.'

'What will we do if it comes into the hut?'

'We will climb onto the roof.'

'And if it reaches the roof?'

'We will climb the peepul tree. The river has never gone higher than the peepul tree.'

As soon as the first light showed through the little skylight, Sita got up and went outside. It wasn't raining hard, it was drizzling, but it was the sort of drizzle that could continue for days, and it probably meant that heavy rain was falling in the hills where the river originated.

Sita went down to the water's edge. She couldn't find her favourite rock, the one on which she often sat dangling her feet in the water, watching the little Chilwa fish swim by. It was still there, no doubt, but the river had gone over it.

She stood on the sand, and she could feel the water oozing and bubbling beneath her feet.

The river was no longer green and blue and flecked with white, but a muddy colour.

She went back to the hut. Grandfather was up now. He was getting his boat ready.

Sita milked the goat. Perhaps it was the last time she would milk it.

◆

The sun was just coming up when Grandfather pushed off in the boat. Grandmother lay in the prow. She was staring hard at Sita, trying to speak, but the words would not come. She raised her hand in a blessing.

Sita bent and touched her grandmother's feet, and then Grandfather pushed off. The little boat—with its two old people and three goats—riding swiftly on the river, moved slowly, very slowly, towards the opposite bank. The current was so swift now that Sita realized the boat would be carried about half a mile downstream before Grandfather could get it to dry land.

It bobbed about on the water, getting smaller and smaller,

until it was just a speck on the broad river.

And suddenly Sita was alone.

There was a wind, whipping the raindrops against her face; and there was the water, rushing past the island; and there was the distant shore, blurred by rain; and there was the small hut; and there was the tree.

Sita got busy. The hens had to be fed. They weren't bothered about anything except food. Sita threw them handfuls of coarse grain and potato peelings and peanut shells.

Then she took the broom and swept out the hut, lit the charcoals burner, warmed some milk and thought, 'Tomorrow there will be no milk...' She began peeling onions. Soon her eyes started smarting and, pausing for a few moments and glancing round the quiet room, she became aware again that she was alone. Grandfather's hookah pipe stood by itself in one corner. It was a beautiful old hookah, which had belonged to Sita's great-grandfather. The bowl was made out of a coconut encased in silver. The long winding stem was at least four feet in length. It was their most valuable possession. Grandmother's sturdy Shisham-wood walking stick stood in another comer.

Sita looked around for Mumta, found the doll beneath the cot, and placed her within sight and hearing.

Thunder rolled down from the hills. BOOM—BOOM—BOOM...

'The gods of the mountains are angry,' said Sita. 'Do you think they are angry with me?'

'Why should they be angry with you?' asked Mumta.

'They don't have to have a reason for being angry. They are angry with everything, and we are in the middle of everything. We are so small—do you think they know we are here?'

'Who knows what the gods think?'

'But I made you,' said Sita, 'and I know you are here.'

'And will you save me if the river rises?'

'Yes, of course. I won't go anywhere without you, Mumta.'

Sita couldn't stay indoors for long. She went out, taking Mumta with her, and stared out across the river, to the safe land on the other side. But was it safe there? The river looked much wider now. Yes, it had crept over its banks and spread far across the flat plain. Far away, people were driving their cattle through waterlogged, flooded fields, carrying their belongings in bundles on their heads or shoulders, leaving their homes, making for the high land. It wasn't safe anywhere.

She wondered what had happened to Grandfather and Grandmother. If they had reached the shore safely, Grandfather would have to engage a bullock cart, or a pony-drawn carriage, to get Grandmother to the district town, five or six miles away, where there was a market, a court, a jail, a cinema and a hospital.

She wondered if she would ever see Grandmother again. She had done her best to look after the old lady, remembering the times when Grandmother had looked after her, had gently touched her fevered brow and had told her stories—stories about the gods: about the young Krishna, friend of birds and animals, so full of mischief, always causing confusion among the other gods; and Indra, who made the thunder and lightning; and Vishnu, the preserver of all good things, whose steed was a great white bird; and Ganesh, with the elephant's head; and Hanuman, the monkey-god, who helped the young Prince Rama in his war with the King of Ceylon. Would Grandmother return to tell her more about them, or would she have to find out for herself?

The island looked much smaller now. In parts, the mud banks had dissolved quickly, sinking into the river. But in the middle of the island there was rocky ground, and the rocks would never crumble, they could only be submerged. In a space in the middle of the rocks grew the tree.

Sita climbed into the tree to get a better view. She had climbed the tree many times and it took her only a few seconds to reach the higher branches. She put her hand to her eyes to shield them from the rain, and gazed upstream.

There was water everywhere. The world had become one vast river. Even the trees on the forested side of the river looked as though they had grown from the water, like mangroves. The sky was banked with massive, moisture-laden clouds. Thunder rolled down from the hills and the river seemed to take it up with a hollow booming sound.

Something was floating down with the current, something big and bloated. It was closer now, and Sita could make out the bulky object—a drowned buffalo, being carried rapidly downstream.

So the water had already inundated the villages further upstream. Or perhaps the buffalo had been grazing too close to the rising river.

Sita's worst fears were confirmed when, a little later, she saw planks of wood, small trees and bushes, and then a wooden bedstead, floating past the island.

How long would it take for the river to reach her own small hut?

As she climbed down from the tree, it began to rain more heavily. She ran indoors, shooing the hens before her. They flew into the hut and huddled under Grandmother's cot. Sita thought it would be best to keep them together now. And having them with her took away some of the loneliness.

There were three hens and a cock bird. The river did not bother them. They were interested only in food, and Sita kept them happy by throwing them a handful of onion skins.

She would have liked to close the door and shut out the swish of the rain and the boom of the river, but then she would have no way of knowing how fast the water rose.

She took Mumta in her arms, and began praying for the rain to stop and the river to fall. She prayed to the god Indra, and, just in case he was busy elsewhere, she prayed to other gods too. She prayed for the safety of her grandparents and for her own safety. She put herself last but only with great difficulty.

She would have to make herself a meal. So she chopped up some onions, fried them, then added turmeric and red chilli powder and stirred until she had everything sizzling; then she added a tumbler of water, some salt, and a cup of one of the cheaper lentils. She covered the pot and allowed the mixture to simmer.

Doing this took Sita about ten minutes. It would take at least half an hour for the dish to be ready.

When she looked outside, she saw pools of water amongst the rocks and near the tree. She couldn't tell if it was rain water or overflow from the river.

She had an idea.

A big tin trunk stood in a corner of the room. It had belonged to Sita's mother. There was nothing in it except a cotton-filled quilt, for use during the cold weather. She would stuff the trunk with everything useful or valuable, and weigh it down so that it wouldn't be carried away, just in case the river came over the island.

Grandfather's hookah went into the trunk. Grandmother's walking stick went in too. So did a number of small tins containing the spices used in cooking—nutmeg, caraway seed, cinnamon, coriander and pepper—a bigger tin of flour and a tin of raw sugar. Even if Sita had to spend several hours in the tree, there would be something to eat when she came down again.

A clean white cotton shirt of Grandfather's, and Grandmother's only spare sari also went into the trunk. Never mind if they got stained with yellow curry powder! Never mind if they got to smell of salted fish, some of that went in too.

Sita was so busy packing the trunk that she paid no attention to the lick of cold water at her heels. She locked the trunk, placed the key high on the rock wall, and turned to give her attention to the lentils. It was only then that she discovered that she was walking about on a watery floor.

She stood still, horrified by what she saw. The water was oozing over the threshold, pushing its way into the room.

Sita was filled with panic. She forgot about her meal and everything else. Darting out of the hut, she ran splashing through ankle-deep water towards the safety of the peepul tree. If the tree hadn't been there, such a well-known landmark, she might have floundered into deep water, into the river.

She climbed swiftly into the strong arms of the tree, made herself secure on a familiar branch, and thrust the wet hair away from her eyes.

◆

She was glad she had hurried. The hut was now surrounded by water. Only the higher parts of the island could still be seen—a few rocks, the big rock on which the hut was built, a hillock on which some thorny bilberry bushes grew.

The hens hadn't bothered to leave the hut. They were probably perched on the cot now.

Would the river rise still higher? Sita had never seen it like this before. It swirled around her, stretching in all directions.

More drowned cattle came floating down. The most unusual things went by on the water—an aluminium kettle, a cane chair, a tin of tooth powder, an empty cigarette packet, a wooden slipper, a plastic doll…

A doll!

With a sinking feeling, Sita remembered Mumta.

Poor Mumta! She had been left behind in the hut. Sita, in her hurry, had forgotten her only companion.

Well, thought Sita, if I can be careless with someone I've made, how can I expect the gods to notice me, alone in the middle of the river?

The waters were higher now, the island fast disappearing.

Something came floating out of the hut.

It was an empty kerosene tin, with one of the hens perched on top. The tin came bobbing along on the water, not far from the tree, and was then caught by the current and swept into the river. The hen still managed to keep its perch.

A little later, the water must have reached the cot because the remaining hens flew up to the rock ledge and sat huddled there in the small recess.

The water was rising rapidly now, and all that remained of the island was the big rock that supported the hut, the top of the hut itself and the peepul tree.

It was a tall tree with many branches and it seemed unlikely that the water could ever go right over it. But how long would Sita have to remain there? She climbed a little higher, and as she did so, a jet-black jungle crow settled in the upper branches, and Sita saw that there was a nest in them—a crow's nest, an untidy platform of twigs wedged in the fork of a branch.

In the nest were four blue-green, speckled eggs. The crow sat on them and cawed disconsolately. But though the crow was miserable, its presence brought some cheer to Sita. At least she was not alone. Better to have a crow for company than no one at all.

Other things came floating out of the hut—a large pumpkin;

a red turban belonging to Grandfather, unwinding in the water like a long snake; and then—Mumta!

The doll, being filled with straw and wood-shavings, moved quite swiftly on the water and passed close to the peepul tree. Sita saw it and wanted to call out, to urge her friend to make for the tree, but she knew that Mumta could not swim—the doll could only float, travel with the river, and perhaps be washed ashore many miles downstream.

The tree shook in the wind and the rain. The crow cawed and flew up, circled the tree a few times and returned to the nest. Sita clung to her branch.

The tree trembled throughout its tall frame. To Sita it felt like an earthquake tremor; she felt the shudder of the tree in her own bones.

The river swirled all around her now. It was almost up to the roof of the hut. Soon the mud walls would crumble and vanish. Except for the big rock and some trees far, far away, there was only water to be seen.

For a moment or two Sita glimpsed a boat with several people in it moving sluggishly away from the ruins of a flooded village, and she thought she saw someone pointing towards her, but the river swept them on and the boat was lost to view.

The river was very angry; it was like a wild beast, a dragon on the rampage, thundering down from the hills and sweeping across the plain, bringing with it dead animals, uprooted trees, household goods and huge fish choked to death by the swirling mud.

The tall old peepul tree groaned. Its long, winding roots clung tenaciously to the earth from which the tree had sprung many, many years ago. But the earth was softening, the stones were being washed away. The roots of the tree were rapidly losing their hold.

The crow must have known that something was wrong, because it kept flying up and circling the tree, reluctant to settle in it and reluctant to fly away. As long as the nest was there, the crow would remain, flapping about and cawing in alarm.

Sita's wet cotton dress clung to her thin body. The rain ran down from her long black hair. It poured from every leaf of the tree. The crow, too, was drenched and groggy.

The tree groaned and moved again. It had seen many monsoons. Once before, it had stood firm while the river had swirled around its massive trunk. But it had been young then.

Now, old in years and tired of standing still, the tree was ready to join the river.

With a flurry of its beautiful leaves, and a surge of mud from below, the tree left its place in the earth, and, tilting, moved slowly forward, turning a little from side to side, dragging its roots along the ground. To Sita, it seemed as though the river was rising to meet the sky. Then the tree moved into the main current of the river, and went a little faster, swinging Sita from side to side. Her feet were in the water but she clung tenaciously to her branch.

◆

The branches swayed, but Sita did not lose her grip. The water was very close now. Sita was frightened. She could not see the extent of the flood or the width of the river. She could only see the immediate danger—the water surrounding the tree.

The crow kept flying around the tree. The bird was in a terrible rage. The nest was still in the branches, but not for long... The tree lurched and twisted slightly to one side, and the nest fell into the water. Sita saw the eggs go one by one.

The crow swooped low over the water, but there was nothing it could do. In a few moments, the nest had disappeared.

The bird followed the tree for about fifty yards, as though hoping that something still remained in the tree. Then, flapping its wings, it rose high into the air and flew across the river until it was out of sight.

Sita was alone once more. But there was no time for feeling lonely. Everything was in motion—up and down and sideways and forwards. 'Any moment,' thought Sita, 'the tree will turn right over and I'll be in the water!'

She saw a turtle swimming past—a great river turtle, the kind that feeds on decaying flesh. Sita turned her face away. In the distance, she saw a flooded village and people in flat-bottomed boats but they were very far away.

Because of its great size, the tree did not move very swiftly on the river. Sometimes, when it passed into shallow water, it stopped, its roots catching in the rocks; but not for long—the river's momentum soon swept it on.

At one place, where there was a bend in the river, the tree struck a sandbank and was still.

Sita felt very tired. Her arms were aching and she was no longer upright. With the tree almost on its side, she had to cling tightly to her branch to avoid falling off. The grey weeping sky was like a great shifting dome.

She knew she could not remain much longer in that position. It might be better to try swimming to some distant rooftop or tree. Then she heard someone calling. Craning her neck to look upriver, she was able to make out a small boat coming directly towards her.

The boat approached the tree. There was a boy in the boat who held on to one of the branches to steady himself, giving his free hand to Sita.

She grasped it, and slipped into the boat beside him.

The boy placed his bare foot against the tree trunk and

pushed away.

The little boat moved swiftly down the river. The big tree was left far behind. Sita would never see it again.

◆

She lay stretched out in the boat, too frightened to talk. The boy looked at her, but he did not say anything, he did not even smile. He lay on his two small oars, stroking smoothly, rhythmically, trying to keep from going into the middle of the river. He wasn't strong enough to get the boat right out of the swift current, but he kept trying.

A small boat on a big river—a river that had no boundaries but which reached across the plains in all directions. The boat moved swiftly on the wild waters, and Sita's home was left far behind.

The boy wore only a loincloth. A sheathed knife was knotted into his waistband. He was a slim, wiry boy, with a hard flat belly; he had high cheekbones, strong white teeth. He was a little darker than Sita.

'You live on the island,' he said at last, resting on his oars and allowing the boat to drift a little, for he had reached a broader, more placid stretch of the river. 'I have seen you sometimes. But where are the others?'

'My grandmother was sick,' said Sita, 'so Grandfather took her to the hospital in Shahganj.'

'When did they leave?'

'Early this morning.'

Only that morning—and yet it seemed to Sita as though it had been many mornings ago.

'Where have you come from?' she asked. She had never seen the boy before.

'I come from...' he hesitated, '...near the foothills. I was in my boat, trying to get across the river with the news that one of the villages was badly flooded, but the current was too strong. I was swept down past your island. We cannot fight the river, we must go wherever it takes us.'

'You must be tired. Give me the oars.'

'No. There is not much to do now, except keep the boat steady.'

He brought in one oar, and with his free hand he felt under the seat where there was a small basket. He produced two mangoes, and gave one to Sita.

They bit deep into the ripe fleshy mangoes, using their teeth to tear the skin away. The sweet juice trickled down their chins. The flavour of the fruit was heavenly—truly this was the nectar of the gods! Sita hadn't tasted a mango for over a year. For a few moments she forgot about the flood—all that mattered was the mango!

The boat drifted, but not so swiftly now, for as they went further away across the plains, the river lost much of its tremendous force.

'My name is Krishan,' said the boy. 'My father has many cows and buffaloes, but several have been lost in the flood.'

'I suppose you go to school,' said Sita.

'Yes, I am supposed to go to school. There is one not far from our village. Do you have to go to school?'

'No—there is too much work at home.'

It was no use wishing she was at home—home wouldn't be there any more—but she wished, at that moment, that she had another mango.

Towards evening, the river changed colour. The sun, low in the sky, emerged from behind the clouds, and the river changed slowly from grey to gold, from gold to a deep orange, and then, as the sun went down, all these colours were drowned in the river, and the river took on the colour of the night.

The moon was almost at the full and Sita could see across the river, to where the trees grew on its banks.

'I will try to reach the trees,' said the boy, Krishan. 'We do not want to spend the night on the water, do we?'

And so he pulled for the trees. After ten minutes of strenuous rowing, he reached a turn in the river and was able to escape the pull of the main current.

Soon they were in a forest, rowing between tall evergreens.

◆

They moved slowly now, paddling between the trees, and the moon lighted their way, making a crooked silver path over the water.

'We will tie the boat to one of these trees,' said Krishan. 'Then we can rest. Tomorrow we will have to find our way out of the forest.'

He produced a length of rope from the bottom of the boat, tied one end to the boat's stern and threw the other end over a stout branch which hung only a few feet above the water. The boat came to rest against the trunk of the tree.

It was a tall, sturdy toon tree—the Indian mahogany—and it was quite safe, for there was no rush of water here; besides, the trees grew close together, making the earth firm and unyielding.

But the denizens of the forest were on the move. The animals had been flooded out of their holes, caves and lairs, and were looking for shelter and dry ground.

Sita and Krishan had barely finished tying the boat to the tree when they saw a huge python gliding over the water towards them. Sita was afraid that it might try to get into the boat; but it went past them, its head above water, its great awesome length trailing behind, until it was lost in the shadows.

Krishan had more mangoes in the basket, and he and Sita sucked hungrily on them while they sat in the boat.

A big sambur stag came thrashing through the water. He did not have to swim; he was so tall that his head and shoulders remained well above the water. His antlers were big and beautiful.

'There will be other animals,' said Sita. 'Should we climb into the tree?'

'We are quite safe in the boat,' said Krishan. 'The animals are interested only in reaching dry land. They will not even hunt each other. Tonight, the deer are safe from the panther and the tiger. So lie down and sleep, and I will keep watch.'

Sita stretched herself out in the boat and closed her eyes, and the sound of the water lapping against the sides of the boat soon lulled her to sleep. She woke once, when a strange bird called overhead. She raised herself on one elbow, but Krishan was awake, sitting in the prow, and he smiled reassuringly at her. He looked blue in the moonlight, the colour of the young god Krishna, and for a few moments Sita was confused and wondered if the boy was indeed Krishna; but when she thought about it, she decided that it wasn't possible. He was just a village boy and she had seen hundreds like him—well, not exactly like him; he was different, in a way she couldn't explain to herself...

And when she slept again, she dreamt that the boy and Krishna were one, and that she was sitting beside him on a great white bird which flew over mountains, over the snow peaks of the Himalayas, into the cloud-land of the gods. There was a great rumbling sound, as though the gods were angry about the whole thing, and she woke up to this terrible sound and looked about her, and there in the moonlit glade, up to his belly in water, stood a young elephant, his trunk raised as he trumpeted his predicament to the forest—for he was a young elephant, and he was lost, and he was looking for his mother.

He trumpeted again, and then lowered his head and listened. And presently, from far away, came the shrill trumpeting of another elephant. It must have been the young one's mother, because he gave several excited trumpet calls, and then went stamping and churning through the flood water towards a gap in the trees. The boat rocked in the waves made by his passing.

'It's all right now,' said Krishan. 'You can go to sleep again.'

'I don't think I will sleep now,' said Sita.

'Then I will play my flute for you,' said the boy, 'and the time will pass more quickly.'

From the bottom of the boat he took a flute, and putting it to his lips, he began to play. The sweetest music that Sita had ever heard came pouring from the little flute, and it seemed to fill the forest with its beautiful sound. And the music carried her away again, into the land of dreams, and they were riding on the bird once more, Sita and the blue god, and they were passing through clouds and mist, until suddenly the sun shot out through the clouds. And at the same moment, Sita opened her eyes and saw the sun streaming through the branches of the toon tree, its bright green leaves making a dark pattern against the blinding blue of the sky.

Sita sat up with a start, rocking the boat. There were hardly any clouds left. The trees were drenched with sunshine.

The boy Krishan was fast asleep in the bottom of the boat. His flute lay in the palm of his half-open hand. The sun came slanting across his bare brown legs. A leaf had fallen on his upturned face, but it had not woken him, it lay on his cheek as though it had grown there.

Sita did not move again. She did not want to wake the boy. It didn't look as though the water had gone down, but it hadn't risen, and that meant the flood had spent itself.

The warmth of the sun, as it crept up Krishan's body, woke him at last. He yawned, stretched his limbs, and sat up beside Sita.

'I'm hungry,' he said with a smile.

'So am I,' said Sita.

'The last mangoes,' he said, and emptied the basket of its last two mangoes.

After they had finished the fruit, they sucked the big seeds until these were quite dry. The discarded seeds floated well on the water. Sita had always preferred them to paper boats.

'We had better move on,' said Krishan.

He rowed the boat through the trees, and then for about an hour they were passing through the flooded forest, under the dripping branches of rain-washed trees. Sometimes they had to use the oars to push away vines and creepers. Sometimes drowned bushes hampered them. But they were out of the forest before noon.

Now the water was not very deep and they were gliding over flooded fields. In the distance, they saw a village. It was on high ground. In the old days, people had built their villages on hilltops, which gave them a better defence against bandits and invading armies. This was an old village, and though its inhabitants had long ago exchanged their swords for pruning forks, the hill on which it stood now protected it from the flood.

The people of the village—long-limbed, sturdy Jats—were generous, and gave the stranded children food and shelter. Sita was anxious to find her grandparents, and an old farmer who had business in Shahganj offered to take her there. She was hoping that Krishan would accompany her, but he said he would wait in the village, where he knew others would soon be arriving, his own people among them.

'You will be all right now,' said Krishan. 'Your grandfather will be anxious for you, so it is best that you go to him as soon as you can. And in two or three days, the water will go down and you will be able to return to the island.'

'Perhaps the island has gone forever,' said Sita.

As she climbed into the farmer's bullock cart, Krishan handed her his flute.

'Please keep it for me,' he said. 'I will come for it one day.' And when he saw her hesitate, he added, his eyes twinkling, 'It is a good flute!'

◆

It was slow going in the bullock cart. The road was awash, the wheels got stuck in the mud, and the farmer, his grown son and Sita had to keep getting down to heave and push in order to free the big wooden wheels. They were still in a foot or two of water. The bullocks were bespattered with mud, and Sita's legs were caked with it.

They were a day and a night in the bullock cart before they reached Shahganj; by that time, Sita, walking down the narrow bazaar of the busy market town, was hardly recognizable.

Grandfather did not recognize her. He was walking stiffly down the road, looking straight ahead of him, and would have walked right past the dusty, dishevelled girl if she had not charged straight at his thin, shaky legs and clasped him around the waist.

'Sita!' he cried, when he had recovered his wind and his balance. 'But how are you here? How did you get off the island? I was so worried—it has been very bad these last two days...'

'Is Grandmother all right?' asked Sita.

But even as she spoke, she knew that Grandmother was no longer with them. The dazed look in the old man's eyes told her as much. She wanted to cry, not for Grandmother, who could suffer no more, but for Grandfather, who looked so helpless and bewildered; she did not want him to be unhappy. She forced back her tears, took his gnarled and trembling hand, and led him down the crowded street. And she knew, then, that it would be on her shoulder that Grandfather would have to lean in the years to come.

They returned to the island after a few days, when the river was no longer in spate. There was more rain, but the worst was over. Grandfather still had two of the goats; it had not been necessary to sell more than one.

He could hardly believe his eyes when he saw that the tree had disappeared from the island—the tree that had seemed as permanent as the island, as much a part of his life as the river itself. He marvelled at Sita's escape. 'It was the tree that saved you,' he said.

'And the boy,' said Sita.

'Yes, and the boy.'

She thought about the boy, and wondered if she would ever see him again. But she did not think too much, because there was so much to do.

For three nights they slept under a crude shelter made out of jute bags. During the day, she helped Grandfather rebuild the mud hut. Once again, they used the big rock as a support.

The trunk which Sita had packed so carefully had not been swept off the island, but the water had got into it, and the food and clothing had been spoilt. But Grandfather's hookah had been saved, and, in the evenings, after their work was done and they had eaten the light meal which Sita prepared, he would smoke with a little of his old contentment, and tell Sita about other floods and storms which he had experienced as a boy.

Sita planted a mango seed in the same spot where the peepul tree had stood. It would be many years before it grew into a big tree, but Sita liked to imagine sitting in its branches one day, picking the mangoes straight from the tree, and feasting on them all day. Grandfather was more particular about making a vegetable garden and putting down peas, carrots, gram and mustard.

One day, when most of the hard work had been done and the new hut was almost ready, Sita took the flute which had been given to her by the boy, and walked down to the water's edge and tried to play it. But all she could produce were a few broken notes, and even the goats paid no attention to her music.

Sometimes, Sita thought she saw a boat coming down the river and she would run to meet it; but usually there was no boat, or if there was, it belonged to a stranger or to another fisherman. And so she stopped looking out for boats. Sometimes she thought she heard the music of a flute, but it seemed very distant and she could never tell where the music came from.

Slowly, the rains came to an end. The flood waters had receded, and in the villages people were beginning to till the land again and sow crops for the winter months. There were cattle fairs and wrestling matches. The days were warm and sultry. The water in the river was no longer muddy, and one evening Grandfather brought home a huge Mahseer fish and Sita made it into a delicious curry.

◆

Grandfather sat outside the hut, smoking his hookah. Sita was at the far end of the island, spreading clothes on the rocks to dry. One of the goats had followed her. It was the friendlier of the two, and often followed Sita about the island. She had made it a necklace of coloured beads.

She sat down on a smooth rock, and, as she did so, she noticed a small bright object in the sand near her feet. She stooped and picked it up. It was a little wooden toy—a coloured peacock—that must have come down on the river and been swept ashore on the island. Some of the paint had rubbed off, but for Sita, who had no toys, it was a great find. Perhaps it would speak to her, as Mumta had spoken to her.

As she held the toy peacock in the palm of her hand, she thought she heard the flute music again, but she did not look up. She had heard it before, and she was sure that it was all in her mind.

But this time the music sounded nearer, much nearer. There was a soft footfall in the sand. And, looking up, she saw the boy, Krishan, standing over her.

'I thought you would never come,' said Sita.

'I had to wait until the rains were over. Now that I am free, I will come more often. Did you keep my flute?'

'Yes, but I cannot play it properly. Sometimes it plays by itself, I think, but it will not play for me!'

'I will teach you how to play it,' said Krishan.

He sat down beside her, and they cooled their feet in the water, which was clear now, reflecting the blue of the sky. You could see the sand and the pebbles of the riverbed.

'Sometimes the river is angry, and sometimes it is kind,' said Sita.

'We are part of the river,' said the boy. 'We cannot live without it.'

It was a good river, deep and strong, beginning in the mountains and ending in the sea. Along its banks, for hundreds of miles, lived millions of people, and Sita was only one small girl among them, and no one had ever heard of her, no one knew her—except for the old man, the boy, and the river.

VOTING AT BARLOWGANJ

I am standing under the deodars, waiting for a taxi. Devilal, one of the candidates in the civic election, is offering free rides to all his supporters, to ensure that they get to the polls in time. I have assured him that I prefer walking but he does not believe me; he fears that I will settle down with a bottle of beer rather than walk the two miles to the Barlowganj polling station to cast my vote. He has gone to the expense of engaging a taxi for the day just to make certain of lingerers like me. He assures me that he is not using unfair means—most of the other candidates are doing the same thing.

It is a cloudy day, promising rain, so I decide I will wait for the taxi. It has been plying since 6 a.m., and now it is ten o'clock. It will continue plying up and down the hill till 4 p.m. and by that time it will have cost Devilal over a hundred rupees.

Here it comes. The driver—like most of our taxi drivers, a Sikh—sees me standing at the gate, screeches to a sudden stop, and opens the door. I am about to get in when I notice that the windscreen carries a sticker displaying the Congress symbol of the cow and calf. Devilal is an Independent, and has adopted a cock bird as his symbol.

'Is this Devilal's taxi?' I ask.

'No, it's the Congress taxi,' says the driver.

'I'm sorry,' I say. 'I don't know the Congress candidate.'

'That's all right,' he says agreeably; he isn't a local man and has no interest in the outcome of the election. 'Devilal's taxi will be along any minute now.'

He moves off, looking for the Congress voters on whose behalf he has been engaged. I am glad that the candidates have had to adopt different symbols; it has saved me the embarrassment of turning up in a Congress taxi, only to vote for an Independent. But the real reason for using symbols is to help illiterate voters know whom they are voting for when it comes to putting their papers in the ballot box. All through the hill station's mini-election campaign, posters have been displaying candidates' symbols—a car, a radio, a cock bird, a tiger, a lamp—and the narrow, winding roads resound to the cries of children who are paid to shout, 'Vote for the Radio!' or 'Vote for the Cock!'

Presently my taxi arrives. It is already full, having picked up others on the way, and I have to squeeze in at the back with a stout lalain and her bony husband, the local ration-shop owner. Sitting up front, near the driver, is Vinod, a poor, ragged, quite happy-go-lucky youth, who contrives to turn up wherever I happen to be, and frequently involves himself in my activities. He gives me a namaste and a wide grin.

'What are you doing here?' I ask him.

'Same as you, Bond Sahib. Voting. Maybe Devilal will give me a job if he wins.'

'But you already have a job. I thought you were the games-boy at the school.'

'That was last month, Bond Sahib.'

'They kicked you out?'

'They asked me to leave.'

The taxi gathers speed as it moves smoothly down the

winding hill road. The driver is in a hurry; the more trips he makes, the more money he collects. We swerve round sharp corners, and every time the lalain's chubby hands, covered with heavy bangles and rings, clutch at me for support. She and her husband are voting for Devilal because they belong to the same caste; Vinod is voting for him in the hope of getting a job; I am voting for him because I like the man. I find him simple, courteous and ready to listen to complaints about drains, street lighting and wrongly assessed taxes. He even tries to do something about these things. He is a tall, cadaverous man, with paan-stained teeth; no Nixon, Heath or Indira Gandhi; but he knows that Barlowganj folk care little for appearances.

Barlowganj is a small ward (one of four in the hill station of Mussoorie); it has about 1,000 voters. An election campaign has, therefore, to be conducted on a person-to-person basis. There is no point in haranguing a crowd at a street corner; it would be a very small crowd. The only way to canvass support is to visit each voter's house and plead one's cause personally. This means making a lot of promises with a perfectly straight face.

The bazaar and village of Barlowganj crouch in a vale on the way down the mountain to Dehra. The houses on either side of the road are nearly all English-looking, most of them built before the turn of the century. The bazaar is Indian, charming and quite prosperous: tailors sit cross-legged before their sewing machines, turning out blazers and tight trousers for the well-to-do students who attend the many public schools that still thrive here; halwais—potbellied sweet vendors—spend all day sitting on their haunches in front of giant frying pans; and coolies carry huge loads of timber or cement or grain up the steep hill paths.

Who was Barlow, and how did the village get his name? A search through old guides and gazetteers has given me no clue. Perhaps he was a revenue superintendent or a surveyor, who came striding up from the plains in the 1830s to build a hunting lodge in this pleasantly wooded vale. That was how most hill stations began. The police station, the little Church of the Resurrection, and the ruined brewery were among the earliest buildings in Barlowganj.

The brewery is a mound of rubble, but the road that came into existence to serve the needs of the old Crown Brewery is the one that now serves our taxi. Buckle and Co.'s 'Bullock Train' was the chief means of transport in the old days. Mr Bohle, one of the pioneers of brewing in India, started the 'Old Brewery' at Mussoorie in 1830. Two years later he got into trouble with the authorities for supplying beer to soldiers without permission; he had to move elsewhere.

But the great days of the brewery business really began in 1876, when everyone suddenly acclaimed a much-improved brew. The source was traced to Vat 42 in Whymper's Crown Brewery (the one whose ruins we are now passing), and the beer was retasted and retested until the diminishing level of the barrel revealed the perfectly brewed remains of a soldier who had been reported missing some months previously. He had evidently fallen into the vat and been drowned and, unknown to himself, had given the Barlowganj beer trade a real fillip. Apocryphal though this story may sound, I have it on the authority of the owner of the now defunct *Mafasalite Press* who, in a short account of Mussoorie, wrote that 'meat was thereafter recognized as the missing component and was scrupulously added till more modern, and less cannibalistic, means were discovered to satiate the froth-blower'.

Recently, confirmation came from an old India hand now living in London. He wrote to me reminiscing of early days in the hill station and had this to say:

> Uncle Georgie Forster was working for the Crown Brewery when a coolie fell in. Coolies were employed to remove scum etc. from the vats. They walked along planks suspended over the vats. Poor devil must have slipped and fallen in. Uncle often told us about the incident and there was no doubt that the beer tasted very good.

What with soldiers and coolies falling into the vats with seeming regularity, one wonders whether there may have been more to these accidents than met the eye. I have a nagging suspicion that Whymper and Buckle may have been the Burke and Hare of Mussoorie's beer industry.

But no beer is made in Mussoorie today, and Devilal probably regrets the passing of the breweries as much as I do. Only the walls of the breweries remain, and these are several feet thick. The roofs and girders must have been removed for use in other buildings. Moss and sorrel grow in the old walls, and wildcats live in dark corners protected from rain and wind.

We have taken the sharpest curves and steepest gradients, and now our taxi moves smoothly along a fairly level road which might pass for a country lane in England were it not for the clumps of bamboo on either side.

A mist has come up the valley to settle over Barlowganj, and out of the mist looms an imposing mansion, Sikander Hall, which is still owned and occupied by the Skinners, descendants of Colonel James Skinner who raised a body of Irregular Horse for the Marathas. This was absorbed by the East India Company's forces in 1803. The cavalry regiment is still known as Skinner's Horse, but of course it is a tank regiment now. Skinner's troops called him 'Sikander' (a corruption of both Skinner and Alexander), and that is the name his property bears. The Skinners who live here now have, quite sensibly, gone in for keeping pigs and poultry.

The next house belongs to the Raja of K but he is unable to maintain it on his diminishing privy purse, and it has been rented out as an ashram for members of a saffron-robed sect who would rather meditate in the hills than in the plains. There was a time when it was only the sahibs and rajas who could afford to spend the entire 'season' in Mussoorie. The new rich are the industrialists and maharishis. The coolies and rickshaw-pullers are no better off than when I was a boy in Mussoorie. They still carry or pull the same heavy loads, for the same pittance, and seldom attain the age of forty. Only their clientele has changed.

One more gate, and here is Colonel Powell in his khaki bush shirt and trousers, a uniform that never varies with the seasons. He is an old shikari; once wrote a book called *The Call of the Tiger*. He is too old for hunting now, but likes to yarn with me when we meet on the road. His wife has gone home to England, but he does not want to leave India.

'It's the mountains,' he was telling me the other day. 'Once the mountains are in your blood, there is no escape. You have to come back again and again. I don't think I'd like to die anywhere else.'

Today there is no time to stop and chat. The taxi driver, with a vigorous blowing of his horn, takes the car round the last bend, and then through the village and narrow bazaar of Barlowganj, stopping about a hundred yards from the polling stations.

There is a festive air about Barlowganj today, I have never seen so many people in the bazaar. Bunting, in the form of rival posters and leaflets, is strung across the street. The tea shops are doing a roaring trade. There is much last-minute canvassing, and I have to run the gamut of various candidates and their agents. For the first time I learn the names of some of the candidates. In all, seven men are competing for this seat.

A schoolboy, smartly dressed and speaking English, is the first to accost me. He says: 'Don't vote for Devilal, sir. He's a big crook. Vote for Jatinder! See, sir, that's his symbol—the bow and arrow.'

'I shall certainly think about the bow and arrow,' I tell him politely.

Another agent, a man, approaches, and says, 'I hope you are going to vote for the Congress candidate.'

'I don't know anything about him,' I say.

'That doesn't matter. It's the party you are voting for. Don't forget it's Mrs Gandhi's party.'

Meanwhile, one of Devilal's lieutenants has been keeping a close watch on both Vinod and me, to make sure that we are not seduced by rival propaganda. I give the man a reassuring smile and stride purposefully towards the polling station, which has been set up in the municipal schoolhouse. Policemen stand at the entrance, to make sure that no one approaches the voters once they have entered the precincts.

I join the patient queue of voters. Everyone is in good humour, and there is no breaking of the line; these are not film stars we have come to see. Vinod is in another line, and grins proudly at me across the passageway. This is the one day in his life on which he has been made to feel really important. And he *is*. In a small constituency like Barlowganj, every vote counts.

Most of my fellow voters are poor people. Local issues mean something to them, affect their daily living. The more affluent can buy their way out of trouble, can pay for small conveniences; few of them bother to come to the polls. But for the 'common man'—the shopkeeper, clerk, teacher, domestic servant, milkman, mule driver—this is a big day. The man he is voting for has promised him something, and the voter means to take the successful candidate up on his promise. Not for another five years will the same fuss be made over the local cobblers, tailors and laundrymen. Their votes are indeed precious.

And now it is my turn to vote. I confirm my name, address and roll number. I am down on the list as 'Rusking Bound', but I let it pass: I might forfeit my right to vote if I raise any objection at this stage! A dab of marking-ink is placed on my forefinger—this is so that I do not come round a second time—and I am given a paper displaying the names and symbols of all the candidates. I am then directed to the privacy of a small booth, where I place the official rubber stamp against Devilal's name. This done, I fold the paper in four and slip it into the ballot box.

All has gone smoothly. Vinod is waiting for me outside. So is Devilal.

'Did you vote for me?' asks Devilal.

It is my eyes that he is looking at, not my lips, when I reply in the affirmative. He is a shrewd man, with many years' experience in seeing through bluff. He is pleased with my reply, beams at me, and directs me to the waiting taxi.

Vinod and I get in together, and soon we are on the road again, being driven swiftly homewards up the winding hill road.

Vinod is looking pleased with himself; rather smug, in fact. 'You did vote for Devilal?' I ask him. 'The symbol of the cock bird?'

He shakes his head, keeping his eyes on the road. 'No, the cow,' he says.

'You ass!' I exclaim. 'Devilal's symbol was the cock, not the cow!'

'I know,' he says, 'but I like the cow better.'*

I subside into silence. It is a good thing no one else in the

---

*In spite of Vinod's defection, Devilal won 1974.

taxi has been paying any attention to our conversation. It would be a pity to see Vinod turned out of Devilal's taxi and made to walk the remaining mile to the top of the hill. After all, it will be another five years before he gets another free taxi ride.

A SONG OF MANY RIVERS

1
Suswa River

When I look down from the heights of Landour to the broad Valley of the Doon far below, I can see the little Suswa river, silver in the setting sun, meandering through fields and forests on its way to its confluence with the Ganga.

The Suswa is a river I knew well as a boy, but it has been many years since I took a dip in its quiet pools or rested in the shade of the tall spreading trees growing on its banks. Now I see it from my windows, far away, dream-like in the mist, and I keep promising myself that I will visit it again, to touch its waters, cool and clear, and feel its rounded pebbles beneath my feet.

It's a little river, flowing down from the ancient Siwaliks and running the length of the valley until, with its sister river the Song, it slips into the Ganga just above the holy city of Haridwar. I could wade across (except during the monsoon when it was in spate) and the water seldom rose above the waist except in sheltered pools, where there were shoals of small fish.

There is a little-known and charming legend about the Suswa and its origins, which I have always treasured. It tells us that the Hindu sage, Kasyapa, once gave a great feast to which all the gods were invited. Now Indra, the god of rain, while on his way to the entertainment, happened to meet 60,000 'balkhils' (pygmies) of the Brahmin caste, who were trying in vain to cross a cow's footprint filled with water—to them, a vast lake!

The God could not restrain his amusement. Peals of thunderous laughter echoed across the hills. The indignant Brahmins, determined to have their revenge, at once set to work creating a second Indra, who should supplant the reigning God. This could only be clone by means of penance, fasting and self-denial, in which they persevered until the sweat flowing from their tiny bodies created the 'Suswa' or 'flowing waters' of the little river.

Indra, alarmed at the effect of these religious exercises, sought the help of Brahma, the creator, who taking on the role of a referee, interceded with the priests. Indra was able to keep his position as the rain god.

I saw no pygmies or fairies near the Suswa, but I did see many spotted deer, cheetal, coming down to the water's edge to drink. They are still plentiful in that area.

2
The Nautch Girl's Curse

At the other end of the Doon, far to the west, the Yamuna comes down from the mountains and forms the boundary between the states of Himachal and Uttarakhand. Today, there's a bridge across the river, but many years ago, when I first went across, it was by means of a small cable car, and a very rickety one at that.

During the monsoon, when the river was in spate, the only way across the swollen river was by means of this swaying trolley, which was suspended by a steel rope to two shaky wooden platforms on either bank. There followed a tedious bus journey, during which some sixty-odd miles were covered in six hours.

And then you were at Nahan, a small town a little over 3,000 feet above sea level, set amids hill slopes thick with sal and shisham trees. This charming old town links the subtropical Siwaliks to the first foothills of the Himalayas, a unique situation.

The road from Dagshai and Shimla runs into Nahan from the north. No matter in which direction you look, the view is a fine one. To the south stretches the grand panorama of the plains of Saharanpur and Ambala, fronted by two low ranges of thickly forested hills. In the valley below, the pretty Markanda river winds its way out of the Kadir valley.

Nahan's main street is curved and narrow, but well-made and paved with good stone. To the left of the town is the former Raja's palace. Nahan was once the capital of the state of Sirmur, now part of Himachal Pradesh. The original palace was built some three or four hundred years ago, but has been added to from time to time, and is now a large collection of buildings mostly in the Venetian style.

I suppose Nahan qualifies as a hill station, although it can be quite hot in summer. But unlike most hill stations, which are less than two hundred years old, Nahan is steeped in legend and history.

The old capital of Sirmur was destroyed by an earthquake some seven to eight hundred years ago. It was situated some twenty-four miles from present day Nahan, on the west bank of the Giri, where the river expands into a lake. The ancient capital was totally destroyed, with all its inhabitants, and apparently no record was left of its then ruling family. Little remained of the ancient city, just a ruined temple and a few broken stone figures.

As to the cause of the tragedy, the traditional story is that a nautch girl happened to visit Sirmur, and performed some wonderful feats. The Raja challenged the girl to walk safely over the Giri on a rope, offering her half his kingdom if she was successful.

The girl accepted the challenge. A rope was stretched across the river. But before starting out, the girl promised that if she fell victim to any treachery on the part of the Raja, a curse would fall upon the city and it would be destroyed by a terrible catastrophe.

While she was on her way to successfully carrying out the feat, some of the Raja's people cut the rope. She fell into the river and was drowned. As predicted, total destruction came to the town.

The founder of the next line of the Sirmur Raja came from the Jaisalmer family in Rajasthan. He was on a pilgrimage to Haridwar with his wife when he heard of the catastrophe that had immolated every member of the state's ancient dynasty. He went at once with his wife into the territory, and established a Jaisalmer Raj. The descent from the first Rajput ruler of Jaisalmer stock, some seven hundred years ago, followed from father to son in an unbroken line. And after much intitial moving about, Nahan was fixed upon as the capital.

The territory was captured by the Gurkhas in 1803, but twelve years later they were expelled by the British after some severe fighting, to which a small English cemetery bears witness. The territory was restored to the Raja, with the exception of the Jaunsar Bawar region.

Six or seven miles north of Nahan lies the mountain of Jaitak, where the Gurkhas made their last desperate stand. The place is worth a visit, not only for seeing the remains of the Gurkha fort, but also for the magnificent view the mountain commands.

From the northernmost of the mountain's twin peaks, the whole south face of the Himalayas may be seen. From west to north you see the rugged prominences of the Jaunsar Bawar, flanked by the Mussoorie range of hills. It is wild mountain scenery, with a few patches of cultivation and little villages nestling on the sides of the hills. Garhwal and Dehra Dun are to the east, and as you go downhill you can see the broad sweep of the Yamuna as it cuts its way through the western Siwaliks.

3
Gently Flows the Ganga

The Bhagirathi is a beautiful river, gentle and caressing (as compared to the turbulent Alaknanda), and pilgrims and others have responded to it with love and respect. Lord Shiva released the waters of Goddess Ganga from his locks, and she sped towards the plains in the tracks of Prince Bhagirath's chariot.

> He held the river on his head
> And kept her wandering, where
> Dense as Himalaya's woods were spread
> The tangles of his hair.

Revered by Hindus and loved by all, Goddess Ganga weaves her spell over all who come to her. Some assert that the true Ganga (in its upper reaches) is the Alaknanda. Geographically, this may be so. But tradition carries greater weight in the abode of the Gods, and traditionally the Bhagirathi is the Ganga. Of course, the two rivers meet at Devprayag, in the foothills, and this marriage of the waters settles the issue.

I put the question to my friend Dr Sudhakar Misra, from whom words of wisdom sometimes flow; and true to form, he answered: 'The Alaknanda is Ganga, but the Bhagirathi is Ganga-ji.'

She issues from the very heart of the Himalayas. Visiting Gangotri in 1820, the writer and traveller Baillie Fraser noted: 'We are now in the centre of the Himalayas, the loftiest and perhaps the most rugged range of mountains in the world.'

Here, at the source of the river, we come to the realization that we are at the very centre and heart of things. One has an almost primaeval sense of belonging to these mountains and to this valley in particular. For me, and for many who have been here, the Bhagirathi is the most beautiful of the four main river valleys of Garhwal.

The Bhagirathi seems to have everything—a gentle disposition, deep glens and forests, the ultravision of an open valley graced with tiers of cultivation leading up by degrees to the peaks and glaciers at its head.

At Tehri, the big dam slows down Prince Bhagirath's chariot. But upstream, from Bhatwari to Harsil, there are extensive pine forests. They fill the ravines and plateaus, before giving way to yew and cypress, oak and chestnut. Above 9,000 feet the deodar (*devdar*, tree of the gods) is the principal tree. It grows to a little distance above Gangotri, and then gives way to the birch, which is found in patches to within half a mile of the glacier.

It was the valuable timber of the deodar that attracted the adventurer Frederick 'Pahari' Wilson to the valley in the 1850s. He leased the forests from the Raja of Tehri, and within a few years he had made a fortune. From his horse and depot at Harsil, he would float the logs downstream to Tehri, where they would be sawn up and despatched to buyers in the cities.

Bridge-building was another of Wilson's ventures. The most famous of these was a 350-feet suspension bridge at Bhaironghat, over 1,200 feet above the young Bhagirathi where it thunders through a deep defile. This rippling contraption was at first a source of terror to travellers, and only a few ventured across it.

To reassure people, Wilson would mount his horse and gallop to and fro across the bridge. It has since collapsed, but local people will tell you that the ghostly hoof beats of Wilson's horse can still be heard on full moon nights. The supports of the old bridge were massive deodar trunks, and they can still be seen to one side of the new road bridge built by engineers of the Northern Railway.

The old forest rest houses at Dharasu, Bhatwari and Harsil were all built by Wilson as staging posts, for the only roads were narrow tracks linking one village to another. Wilson married a local girl, Gulabi, from the village of Mukhba, and the portraits of the Wilsons (early examples of the photographer's art) still hang in these sturdy little bungalows. At any rate, I found their pictures at Bhatwari. Harsil is now out of bounds to civilians, and I believe part of the old house was destroyed in a fire a few years ago. This sturdy building withstood the earthquake which devastated the area in 1991.

Amongst other things, Wilson introduced the apple into this area, 'Wilson apples'—large, red and juicy—sold to travellers and pilgrims on their way to Gangotri. This fascinating man also acquired an encyclopaedic knowledge of the wildlife of the region, and his articles, which appeared in *Indian Sporting Life* in the 1860s, were later plundered by so-called wildlife writers for their own works.

He acquired properties in Dehra Dun and Mussoorie, and his wife lived there in some style, giving him three sons. Two died young. The third, Charlie Wilson, went through most of his father's fortune. His grave lies next to my grandfather's grave in the old Dehra Dun cemetery. Gulabi is buried in Mussoorie, next to her husband. I wrote this haiku for her:

Her beauty brought her fame,
But only the wild rose growing beside her grave
Is there to hear her whispered name—
Gulabi.

I remember old Mrs Wilson, Charlie's widow, when I was a boy in Dehra. She lived next door in what was the last of the Wilson properties. Her nephew, Geoffrey Davis, went to school with me in Shimla, and later joined the Indian Air Force. But luck never went the way of Wilson's descendants, and Geoffrey died when his plane crashed.

Wilson's life is fit subject for a romance; but even if one were never written, his legend would live on, as it has done for over a hundred years. There has never been any attempt to commemorate him, but people in the valley still speak of him in awe and admiration, as though he had lived only yesterday.

Some men leave a trail of legend behind them because they give their spirit to the place where they have lived, and remain forever a part of the rocks and mountain streams.

Gangotri is situated at just a little over 10,300 feet. On the right bank of the river is the Gangotri temple, a small neat building without too much ornamentation, built by Amar Singh Thapa, a Nepali General, early in the nineteenth century. It was renovated by the Maharaja of Jaipur in the 1920s. The rock on which it stands is called Bhagirath Shila and is said to be the place where Prince Bhagirath did penance in order that Ganga be brought down from her abode of eternal snow. Here the rocks are carved and polished by ice and water, so smooth that in places they look like rolls of silk. The fast flowing waters of this mountain torrent look very different from the huge sluggish river that finally empties its waters into the Bay of Bengal fifteen hundred miles away.

The river emerges from beneath a great glacier, thickly studded with enormous loose rocks and earth. The glacier is about a mile in width and extends upwards for many miles. The chasm in the glacier through which the stream rushed forth into the light of day is named Gaumukh, the cow's mouth, and is held in deepest reverence by Hindus. The regions of eternal frost in the vicinity were the scene of many of their most sacred mysteries.

The Ganga enters the world no puny stream, but bursts from its icy womb a river thirty or forty yards in breadth. At Gauri Kund (below the Gangotri temple) it falls over a rock of considerable height and continues tumbling over a succession of small cascades until it enters the Bhaironghati gorge.

A night spent beside the river, within the sound of the fall, is an eerie experience. After some time it begins to sound, not like one fall but a hundred, and this sound permeates both one's dreams and waking hours. Rising early to greet the dawn proved rather pointless at Gangotri, for the surrounding peaks did not let the sun in till after 9 a.m. Everyone rushed about to keep warm, exclaiming delightedly at what they call 'gulabi thand', literally, 'rosy cold'. Guaranteed to turn the cheeks a rosy pink! A charming expression, but I prefer a rosy sunburn, and remained beneath a heavy quilt until the sun came up to throw its golden shafts across the river.

This is mid-October, and after Diwali the shrine and the small township will close for winter, the pandits retreating to the relative warmth of Mukbha. Soon snow will cover everything, and even the hardy purple-plumaged whistling thrushes, lovers of deep shade, will move further down the valley. And down below the forest-line, the Garhwali farmers go about harvesting their terraced fields which form patterns of yellow, green and gold above the deep green of the river.

Yes, the Bhagirathi is a green river. Although deep and swift, it does not lose its serenity. At no place does it look hurried or confused—unlike the turbulent Alaknanda, fretting and frothing as it goes crashing down its boulder-strewn bed. The Alaknanda gives one a feeling of being trapped, because the river itself is trapped. The Bhagirathi is free-flowing, easy. At all times and places it seems to find its true level.

In the old days, only the staunchest of pilgrims visited the shrines at Gangotri and Jamnotri. The roads were rocky and dangerous, winding along in some places, ascending and descending the faces of deep precipices and ravines, at times leading along banks of loose earth where landslides had swept the original path away.

There are still no large towns above Uttarkashi, and this absence of large centres of population may be reason why the forests are better preserved than those in the Alaknanda valley, or further downstream. Uttarkashi, though a large and growing town, is as yet uncrowded. The seediness of towns like Rishikesh and parts of Dehra Dun is not yet evident here. One can take a leisurely walk through its long (and well-supplied) bazaar, without being jostled by crowds or knocked over by three-wheelers. Here, too, the river is always with you, and you must live in harmony with its sound as it goes rushing and humming along its shingly bed.

Uttarkashi is not without its own religious and historical importance, although all traces of its ancient town of Barahat appear to have vanished. There are four important temples here, and on the occasion of Makar Sankranti, early in January a week-long fair is held when thousands from the surrounding areas throng the roads to the town. To the beating of drums and blowing of trumpets, the gods and goddesses are brought to the fair in gaily decorated palanquins. The surrounding villages wear a deserted look that day as everyone flocks to the temples and bathing ghats and to the entertainments of the fair itself.

We have to move far downstream to reach another large centre of population, the town of Tehri, and this is a very different place from Uttarkashi. Tehri has all the characteristics of a small town in the plains—crowds, noise, traffic congestion, dust and refuse, scruffy dhabas—with this difference that here it is all ephemeral, for Tehri is destined to be submerged by the water of the Bhagirathi when the Tehri dam is finally completed.

The rulers of Garhwal were often changing their capitals, and when, after the Gurkha War (of 1811–15), the former capital of Srinagar became part of British Garhwal, Raja Sudershan Shah established his new capital at Tehri. It is said that when he reached this spot, his horse refused to go any further. This was enough for the king, it seems; or so the story goes.

Perhaps Prince Bhagirath's chariot will come to a halt here too, when the dam is built. The two hundred and forty-six metre high earthen dam, with forty-two square miles of reservoir capacity, will submerge the town and about thirty villages.

But as we leave the town and cross the narrow bridge over the river, a mighty blast from above sends rocks hurtling down the defile, just to remind us that work is indeed in progress.

Unlike the Raja's horse, I have no wish to be stopped in my tracks at Tehri. There are livelier places upstream. And as for Ganga herself, that deceptively gentle river, I wonder if she will take kindly to our efforts to contain her.

4

Falling for Mandakini

A great river at its confluence with another great river is, for me, a special moment in time. And so it was with the Mandakini at Rudraprayag, where its waters joined the waters of the Alaknanda, the one having come from the glacial snows above Kedarnath, the other from the Himalayan heights beyond Badrinath. Both sacred rivers, destined to become the holy Ganga further downstream.

I fell in love with the Mandakini at first sight. Or was it the valley that I fell in love with? I am not sure, and it doesn't really matter. The valley is the river.

While the Alaknanda valley, especially in its higher reaches, is a deep and narrow gorge where precipitous outcrops of rock hang threateningly over the traveller, the Mandakini valley is broader, gentler, the terraced fields wider, the banks of the river a green sward in many places. Somehow, one does not feel that one is at the mercy of the Mandakini whereas one is always at the mercy of the Alaknanda with its sudden floods.

Rudraprayag is hot. It is probably a pleasant spot in winter, but at the end of June, it is decidedly hot. Perhaps its chief claim to fame is that it gave its name to the dreaded man-eating leopard of Rudraprayag, who in the course of seven years (1918–25) accounted for more than 300 victims. It was finally shot by Jim Corbett, who recounted the saga of his long hunt for the killer in his fine book, *The Man-eating Leopard of Rudraprayag.*

The place at which the leopard was shot was the village of Gulabrai, two miles south of Rudraprayag. Under a large mango tree stands a memorial raised to Jim Corbett by officers and Men of the Border Roads Organisation. It is a touching gesture to one who loved Garhwal and India. Unfortunately, several buffaloes are tethered close by, and one has to wade through slush and buffalo dung to get to the memorial stone. A board tacked on to the mango tree attracts the attention of motorists who might pass without noticing the memorial, which is off to one side.

The killer leopard was noted for its direct method of attack on humans; and, in spite of being poisoned, trapped in a cave, and shot at innumerable times, it did not lose its contempt for man. Two English sportsmen covering both ends to the old suspension bridge over the Alaknanda fired several times at the man-eater but to little effect.

It was not long before the leopard acquired a reputation among the hill folk for being an evil spirit. A sadhu was suspected of turning into the leopard by night, and was only saved from being lynched by the ingenuity of Philip Mason, then deputy commissioner of Garhwal. Mason kept the sadhu in custody until the leopard made his next attack, thus proving the man innocent. Years later, when Mason turned novelist and (using the pen name Philip Woodruffe) wrote *The Wild Sweet Witch*, he had one of the characters, a beautiful young woman who apparently turns into a man-eating leopard by night.

Corbett's host at Gulabrai was one of the few who survived an encounter with the leopard. It left him with a hole in his throat. Apart from being a superb storyteller, Corbett displayed great compassion for people from all walks of life and is still a legend in Garhwal and Kumaon amongst people who have never read his books.

In June, one does not linger long in the steamy heat of Rudraprayag. But as one travels up the river, making a gradual ascent of the Mandakini valley, there is a cool breeze coming down from the snows, and the smell of rain is in the air.

The thriving little township of Agastmuni spreads itself along the wide river banks. Further upstream, near a little place called Chandrapuri, we cannot resist breaking our journey to sprawl on the tender green grass that slopes gently down to the swift flowing river. A small rest house is in the making. Around it, banana fronds sway and poplar leaves dance in the breeze.

This is no sluggish river of the plains, but a fast moving current, tumbling over rocks, turning and twisting in its efforts to discover the easiest way for its frothy snow-fed waters to escape the mountains. Escape is the word! For the constant plaint of many a Garhwali is that, while his hills abound in rivers, the water runs down and away, and little if any reaches the fields and villages above it. Cultivation must depend on the rain and not on the river.

The road climbs gradually, still keeping to the river. Just outside Guptakashi, my attention is drawn to a clump of huge trees sheltering a small but ancient temple. We stop here and enter the shade of the trees.

The temple is deserted. It is a temple dedicated to Shiva, and in the courtyard are several river-rounded stone lingams on which leaves and blossoms have fallen. No one seems to come here, which is strange, since it is on the pilgrim route. Two boys from a neighbouring field leave their yoked bullock to come and talk to me, but they cannot tell me much about the temple except to confirm that it is seldom visited. 'The buses do not stop here.' That seems explanation enough. For where the buses go, the pilgrims go; and where the pilgrims go, other pilgrims will follow. Thus far and no further.

The trees seem to be magnolias. But I have never seen magnolia trees grow to such huge proportions. Perhaps they are something else. Never mind; let them remain a mystery.

Guptakashi in the evening is all a bustle. A coachload of pilgrims (headed for Kedarnath) has just arrived, and the tea shops near the bus-stand are doing brisk business. Then the 'local' bus from Ukhimath, across the river arrives, and many of the passengers head for a tea shop famed for its samosas. The local bus is called the *Bhook Hartal,* the 'Hunger Strike' bus.

'How did it get that name?' I asked one of the samosa-eaters.

'Well, it's an interesting story. For a long time we had been asking the authorities to provide a bus service for the local people and for the villagers who live off the roads. All the buses came from Srinagar or Rishikesh, and were taken up by pilgrims. The locals couldn't find room in them. But our pleas went unheard until the whole town, or most of it, decided to go on hunger strike.'

'They nearly put me out of business too,' said the tea shop owner cheerfully. 'Nobody ate any samosas for two days!'

There is no cinema or public place of entertainment at Guptakashi, and the town goes to sleep early. And wakes early.

At six, the hillside, green from recent rain, sparkles in the morning sunshine. Snow-capped Chaukhamba (7,140 metres) is dazzling. The air is clear; no smoke or dust up here. The climate, I am told, is mild all the year round judging by the scent and shape of the flowers, and the boys call them Champs, Hindi for champa blossom. Ukhimath, on the other side of the river, lies in the shadow. It gets the sun at nine. In winter, it must wait till afternoon.

Guptakashi has not yet been rendered ugly by the barrack-type architecture that has come up in some growing hill towns. The old double storeyed houses are built of stone, with gray slate roofs. They blend well with the hillside. Cobbled paths meander through the old bazaar.

One of these takes up to the famed Guptakashi temple, tucked away above the old part of the town. Here, as in Benaras, Shiva is worshipped as Vishwanath, and two underground streams representing the sacred Jamuna and Bhagirathi rivers feed the pool sacred to the God. This temple gives the town its name, Gupta-Kashi, the 'Invisible Benaras', just as Uttarkashi on the Bhagirathi is 'Upper Benaras'.

Guptakashi and its environs have so many lingams that the saying *'Jitne Kankar Utne Shankar'*—'As many stones, so many Shivas'—has become a proverb to describe its holiness.

From Guptakashi, pilgrims proceed north to Kedarnath, and the last stage of their journey—about a day's march—must be covered on foot or horseback. The temple of Kedarnath, situated at a height of 11.753 feet, is encircled by snowcapped peaks, and Atkinson has conjectured that 'the symbol of the linga may have arisen front the pointed peaks around his (God Shiva's) original home.'

The temple is dedicated to Sadashiva, the subterranean form of the God, who, 'fleeing from the Pandavas took refuge here in the form of a he-buffalo and finding himself hard-pressed, dived into the ground leaving the hinder parts on the surface, which continue to be the subject of adoration.' (Atkinson).

The other portions of the God are worshipped as follows: the arms at Tungnath, at a height of 13,000 feet, the face at Rudranath (12,000 feet), the belly at Madmaheshwar, 18 miles northeast of Guptakashi; and the hair and head at Kalpeshwar, near Joshimath. These five sacred shrines form the 'Panch Kedar' (five Kedars).

We leave the Mandakini to visit Tungnath on the Chandrashila range. But I will return to this river. It has captured my mind and heart.

COLD BEER AT CHUTMALPUR

Just outside the small market town of Chutmalpur (on the way back from Delhi) one is greeted by a large signboard with just two words on it: Cold Beer. The signboard is almost as large as the shop from which the cold beer is dispensed; but after a gruelling five-hour drive from Delhi, in the heat and dust of May, a glass of chilled beer is welcome—except, of course, to teetotallers who will find other fizzy ways to satiate their thirst.

Chutmalpur is not the sort of place you'd choose to retire in. But it has its charms, not the least of which is its Sunday Market, when the varied produce of the rural interior finds its way on to the dusty pavements, and the air vibrates with noise, colour and odours. Carpets of red chillies, seasonal fruits, stacks of grain and vegetables, cheap toys for the children, bangles of lac, wooden artifacts, colourful underwear, sweets of every description, churan to go with them...

'*Lakar hajam, pathar hajam!*' cries the churan-seller. Translated: Digest wood, digest stones! That is, if you partake of this particular digestive pill which, when I tried it, appeared to be one part hing (asafoetida) and one part gunpowder. Things are seldom what they seem to be. Passing through the small town of Purkazi, I noticed a sign-board which announced the availability of 'Books'—just that. Intrigued, I stopped to find out more about this bookshop in the wilderness. Perhaps I'd find a rare tome to add to my library. Peeping in, I discovered that the dark interior was stacked from floor to ceiling with exercise books! Apparently the shop-owner was the supplier for the district.

Rare books can be seen in Roorkee, in the University's old library. Here, not many years ago, a First Folio Shakespeare turned up and was celebrated in the Indian Press as a priceless discovery. Perhaps it's still there.

Also in the library is a bust of Sir Proby Cautley, who conceived and built the Ganga Canal, which starts at Haridwar and passes through Roorkee on its way across the Doab. Hardly anyone today has heard of Cautley, and yet surely his achievement outstrips that of many Englishmen in India—soldiers and statesmen who became famous for doing all the wrong things.

Cautley's Canal

Cautley came to India at the age of seventeen and joined the Bengal Artillery. In 1825, he assisted Captain Robert Smith, the engineer in charge of constructing the Eastern Yamuna Canal. By 1836 he was Superintendent-General of Canals. From the start, he worked towards his dream of building a Ganga Canal, and spent six months walking and riding through the jungles and countryside, taking each level and measurement himself, sitting up all night to transfer them to his maps. He was confident that a 500-kilometre canal was feasible. There were many objections and obstacles to his project, most of them financial, but Cautley persevered and eventually persuaded the East India Company to back him.

Digging of the canal began in 1839. Cautley had to make

his own bricks—millions of them—his own brick kiln, and his own mortar. A hundred thousand tonnes of lime went into the mortar, the other main ingredient of which was surkhi, made by grinding over-burnt bricks to a powder. To reinforce the mortar, ghur, ground lentils and jute fibres were added to it.

Initially, opposition came from the priests in Haridwar, who felt that the waters of the holy Ganga would be imprisoned. Cautley pacified them by agreeing to leave a narrow gap in the dam through which the river water could flow unchecked. He won over the priests when he inaugurated his project with aarti, and the worship of Ganesh, god of good beginnings. He also undertook the repair of the sacred bathing ghats along the river. The canal banks were also to have their own ghats with steps leading down to the water.

The headworks of the canal are at Haridwar, where the Ganga enters the plains after completing its majestic journey through the Himalayas. Below Haridwar, Cautley had to dig new courses for some of the mountain torrents that threatened the canal. He collected them into four steams and took them over the canal by means of four passages. Near Roorkee, the land fell away sharply and here Cautley had to build an aqueduct, a masonry bridge that carries the canal for half a kilometre across the Solani torrent—a unique engineering feat. At Roorkee, the canal is twenty-five metres higher than the parent river which flows almost parallel to it.

Most of the excavation work on the canal was done mainly by the Oads, a gypsy tribe who were professional diggers for most of northwest India. They took great pride in their work. Though extremely poor, Cautley found them a happy and carefree lot who worked in a very organized manner.

When the canal was formally opened on the 8 April 1854, its main channel was 348 miles long, its branches 306 and the distributaries over 3,000. Over 7,67,000 acres in 5,000 villages were irrigated. One of its main branches re-entered the Ganga at Kanpur; it also had branches to Fatehgarh, Bulandshahr and Aligarh.

Cautley's achievements did not end there. He was also actively involved in Dr Falconer's fossil expedition in the Siwaliks. He presented to the British Museum an extensive collection of fossil mammalia—including hippopotamus and crocodile fossils, evidence that the region was once swampland or an inland sea. Other animal remains found here included the sabre-toothed tiger; Elephis ganesa, an elephant with a trunk ten-and-a-half feet long; a three-toed ancestor of the horse; the bones of a fossil ostrich; and the remains of giant cranes and tortoises. Exciting times, exciting finds.

Nor did Cautley's interests and activities end in fossil excavation. My copy of Surgeon General Balfour's Cyclopedia of India (1873) lists a number of fascinating reports and papers by Cautley. He wrote on a submerged city, twenty feet underground, near Behut in the Doab; on the coal and lignite in the Himalayas; on gold washings in the Siwalik Hills, between the Jamuna and Sutlej rivers; on a new species of snake; on the mastodons of the Siwaliks; on the manufacture of tar; and on Panchukkis or corn mills.

How did he find time for all this, I wonder. Most of his life was spent in tents, overseeing the canal work or digging up fossils. He had a house in Mussoorie (one of the first), but he could not have spent much time in it. It is today part of the Manav Bharti School, and there is still a plaque in the office stating that Cautley lived there. Perhaps he wrote some of his reports and expositions during brief sojourns in the hills. It is said that his wife left him, unable to compete against the rival attractions of canals and fossils remains.

I wonder, too, if there was any follow up on his reports of the submerged city—is it still there, waiting to be re-discovered—or his findings on gold washings in the Siwaliks. Should my royalties ever dry up, I might just wonder off into the Siwaliks, looking for 'gold in them that hills'. Meanwhile, whenever I travel by road from Delhi to Haridwar, and pass over that placid canal at various places en-route, I think of the man who spent more than twenty years of his life in executing this magnificent project, and others equally demanding. And then, his work done, walking away from it all without thought of fame or fortune.

A Jungle Princess

From Roorkee separate roads lead to Haridwar, Saharanpur, Dehradun. And from the Saharanpur road you can branch off to Paonta Sahib, with its famous gurudwara glistening above the blue waters of the Yamuna. Still blue up here, but not so blue by the time it enters Delhi. Industrial affluents and human waste soon muddy the purest of rivers.

From Paonta you can turn right to Herbertpur, a small township originally settled by an Anglo-Indian family early in the nineteenth century. As may be inferred by its name, Herbert was the scion of the family, but I have been unable to discover much about him. When I was a boy, the Carberry family owned much of the land around here, but by the time Independence came, only one of the family remained—Doreen, a sultry, dusky beauty who become known in Dehra as the 'Jungle Princess'. Her husband had deserted her, but she had a small daughter who grew up on the land. Doreen's income came from her mango and guava orchards, and she seemed quite happy living in this isolated rural area near the river. Occasionally she came into Dehra Dun, a bus ride of a couple of hours, and she would visit my mother, a childhood friend, and occasionally stay overnight.

On one occasion we went to Doreen's jungle home for a couple of days. I was just seven or eight years old. I remember Doreen's daughter (about my age) teaching me to climb trees. I managed the guava tree quite well, but some of the others were too difficult for me.

How did this jungle queen manage to live by herself in this remote area, where her house, orchard and fields were bordered by forest on one side and the river on the other?

Well, she had her servants of course, and they were loyal to her. And she also possessed several guns, and could handle them very well. I saw her bring down a couple of pheasants with her twelve-bore spread shot. She had also killed a cattle-lifting tiger which had been troubling a nearby village, and a marauding leopard that had taken one of her dogs. So she was quite capable of taking care of herself. When I last saw her, some twenty-five years ago, she was in her seventies. I believe she sold her land and went to live elsewhere with her daughter, who by then had a family of her own.

TIME STOPS AT SHAMLI

The Dehra Express usually drew into Shamli at about five o'clock in the morning, at which time the station would be dimly lit and the jungle across the tracks would just be visible in the faint light of dawn. Shamli is a small station at the foot of the Siwalik hills, and the Siwaliks lie at the foot of the Himalayas, which in turn lie at the feet of God.

The station, I remember, had only one platform, an office for the stationsmaster, and a waiting-room. The platform boasted a tea-stall, a fruit vendor, and a few stray dogs; not much else was required, because the train stopped at Shamli for only five minutes before rushing on into the forests.

Why it stopped at Shamli, I never could tell. Nobody got off the train and nobody got in. There were never any coolies on the platform. But the train would stand there a full five minutes, and the guard would blow his whistle, and presently Shamli would be left behind and forgotten....until I passed that way again....

I was paying my relations in Saharanpur an annual visit, when the night train stopped at Shamli. I was thirty-six at the time, and still single.

On this particular journey, the train came into Shamli just as I awoke from a restless sleep. The third class compartment was crowded beyond capacity, and I had been sleeping in an upright position, with my back to the lavatory door. Now someone was trying to get into the lavatory. He was obviously hardpressed for time.

'I'm sorry, brother,' I said, moving as much as I could do to one side.

He stumbled into the closet without bothering to close the door.

'Where are we now?' I asked the man sitting beside me. He was smoking a strong aromatic bidi.

'Shamli station,' he said, rubbing the palm of a large calloused hand over the frosted glass of the window.

I let the window down and stuck my head out. There was a cool breeze blowing down the platform, a breeze that whispered of autumn in the hills. As usual there was no activity, except for the fruit-vendor walking up and down the length of the train with his basket of mangoes balanced on his head. At the tea-stall, a kettle was steaming, but there was no one to mind it. I rested my forehead on the window-ledge, and let the breeze play on my temples. I had been feeling sick and giddy but there was a wild sweetness in the wind that I found soothing.

'Yes,' I said to myself, 'I wonder what happens in Shamli, behind the station walls.'

My fellow passenger offered me a bidi. He was a farmer, I think, on his way to Dehra. He had a long, untidy, sad moustache.

We had been more than five minutes at the station, I looked up and down the platform, but nobody was getting on or off the train. Presently, the guard came walking past our compartment.

'What's the delay?' I asked him.

'Some obstruction further down the line,' he said.

'Will we be here long?'

'I don't know what the trouble is. About half an hour, at the least.'

My neighbour shrugged, and, throwing the remains of his bidi out of the window, closed his eyes and immediately fell asleep. I moved restlessly in my seat, and then the man came out of the lavatory, not so urgently now, and with obvious peace of mind. I closed the door for him.

I stood up and stretched; and this stretching of my limbs seemed to set in motion a stretching of the mind, and I found myself thinking: 'I am in no hurry to get to Saharanpur, and I have always wanted to see Shamli, behind the station walls. If I get down now, I can spend the day here, it will be better than sitting in this train for another hour. Then in the evening I can catch the next train home.'

In those days I never had the patience to wait for second thoughts, and so I began pulling my small suitcase out from under the seat.

The farmer woke up and asked, 'What are you doing, brother?'

'I'm getting out,' I said.

He went to sleep again.

It would have taken at least fifteen minutes to reach the door, as people and their belongings cluttered up the passage; so I let my suitcase down from the window and followed it on to the platform.

There was no one to collect my ticket at the barrier, because there was obviously no point in keeping a man there to collect tickets from passengers who never came; and anyway, I had a through-ticket to my destination, which I would need in the evening.

I went out of the station and came to Shamli.

Outside the station there was a neem tree, and under it stood a tonga. The tonga-pony was nibbling at the grass at the foot of the tree. The youth in the front seat was the only human in sight; there were no signs of inhabitants or habitation. I approached the tonga, and the youth stared at me as though he couldn't believe his eyes.

'Where is Shamli?' I asked.

'Why, friend, this is Shamli,' he said.

I looked around again, but couldn't see any signs of life. A dusty road led past the station and disappeared in the forest.

'Does anyone live here?' I asked.

'I live here,' he said, with an engaging smile. He looked an amiable, happy-go-lucky fellow. He wore a cotton tunic and dirty white pyjamas.

'Where?' I asked.

'In my tonga, of course,' he said. 'I have had this pony five years now. I carry supplies to the hotel. But today the manager has not come to collect them. You are going to the hotel? I will take you.'

'Oh, so there's a hotel?'

'Well, friend, it is called that. And there are a few houses too, and some shops, but they are all about a mile from the station. If they were not a mile from here, I would be out of business.'

I felt relieved, but I still had the feeling of having walked into a town consisting of one station, one pony and one man.

'You can take me,' I said. 'I'm staying till this evening.'

He heaved my suitcase into the seat beside him, and I climbed in at the back. He flicked the reins and slapped his pony on the buttocks; and, with a roll and a lurch, the buggy moved off down the dusty forest road.

'What brings you here?' asked the youth.

'Nothing,' I said. 'The train was delayed, I was feeling bored, and so I got off.'

He did not believe that; but he didn't question me further. The sun was reaching up over the forest, but the road lay in the shadow of tall trees, eucalyptus, mango and neem.

'Not many people stay in the hotel,' he said. 'So it is cheap, you will get a room for five rupees.'

'Who is the manager?'

'Mr Satish Dayal. It is his father's property. Satish Dayal could not pass his exams or get a job, so his father sent him here to look after the hotel.'

The jungle thinned out, and we passed a temple, a mosque, a few small shops. There was a strong smell of burnt sugar in the air, and in the distance I saw a factory chimney: that, then, was the reason for Shamli's existence. We passed a bullock-cart laden with sugarcane. The road went through fields of cane and maize, and then, just as we were about to re-enter the jungle, the youth pulled his horse to a side road and the hotel came in sight.

It was a small white bungalow, with a garden in the front, banana trees at the sides, and an orchard of guava trees at the back. We came jingling up to the front verandah. Nobody appeared, nor was there any sign of life on the premises.

'They are all asleep,' said the youth.

I said, 'I'll sit in the verandah and wait.' I got down from the tonga, and the youth dropped my case on the verandah steps. Then he stood in front of me, smiling amiably, waiting to be paid.

'Well, how much?' I asked.

'As a friend, only one rupee.'

'That's too much,' I complained. 'This is not Delhi.'

'This is Shamli,' he said. 'I am the only tonga-driver in Shamli. You may not pay me anything, if that is your wish. But then, I will not take you back to the station this evening, you will have to walk.'

I gave him the rupee. He had both charm and cunning, an effective combination.

'Come in the evening at about six,' I said.

'I will come,' he said, with an infectious smile, 'Don't worry.'

I waited till the tonga had gone round the bend in the road before walking up the verandah steps.

The doors of the house were closed, and there were no bells to ring. I didn't have a watch, but I judged the time to be a little past six o'clock. The hotel didn't look very impressive; the whitewash was coming off the walls, and the cane-chairs on the verandah were old and crooked. A stag's head was mounted over the front door, but one of its glass eyes had fallen out; I had often heard hunters speak of how beautiful an animal looked before it died, but how could anyone with a true love of the beautiful care for the stuffed head of an animal, grotesquely mounted, with no resemblance to its living aspect?

I felt too restless to take any of the chairs. I began pacing up and down the verandah, wondering if I should start banging on the doors. Perhaps the hotel was deserted; perhaps the tonga-driver had played a trick on me. I began to regret my impulsiveness in leaving the train. When I saw the manager I would have to invent a reason for coming to his hotel. I was good at inventing reasons. I would tell him that a friend of mine had stayed here some years ago, and that I was trying to trace him. I decided that my friend would have to be a little eccentric (having chosen Shamli to live in), that he had become a recluse, shutting himself off from the world; his parents—no, his sister—for his parents would be dead—had asked me to find him if I could; and, as he had last been heard of in Shamli, I had taken the opportunity to enquire after him. His name would be Major Roberts, retired.

I heard a tap running at the side of the building, and walking around, found a young man bathing at the tap. He was strong and well-built, and slapped himself on the body with great enthusiasm. He had not seen me approaching, and I waited until he had finished bathing and had began to dry himself.

'Hullo,' I said.

He turned at the sound of my voice, and looked at me for a few moments with a puzzled expression, he had a round, cheerful face and crisp black hair. He smiled slowly, but it was a more genuine smile than the tonga-driver's. So far I had met two people in Shamli, and they were both smilers; that should have cheered me, but it didn't. 'You have come to stay?' he asked, in a slow easy going voice.

'Just for the day,' I said. 'You work here?'

'Yes, my name is Daya Ram. The manager is asleep just now, but I will find a room for you.'

He pulled on his vest and pyjamas, and accompanied me back to the verandah. Here he picked up my suitcase and, unlocking a side door, led me into the house. We went down a passage way; then Daya Ram stopped at the door on the right, pushed it open, and took me into a small, sunny room that had a window looking out on the orchard. There was a bed, a desk, a couple of cane-chairs, and a frayed and faded red carpet.

'Is it alright?' said Daya Ram

'Perfectly alright.'

'They have breakfast at eight o'clock. But if you are hungry, I will make something for you now.'

'No, it's alright. Are you the cook too?'

'I do everything here.'

'Do you like it?'

'No,' he said, and then added, in a sudden burst of confidence, 'There are no women for a man like me.'

'Why don't you leave, then?'

'I will,' he said, with a doubtful look on his face. 'I will leave...'

After he had gone I shut the door and went into the bathroom to bathe. The cold water refreshed me and made me feel one with the world. After I had dried myself, I sat on the bed, in front of the open window. A cool breeze, smelling of rain, came through the window and played over my body. I thought I saw a movement among the trees.

And getting closer to the window, I saw a girl on a swing. She was a small girl, all by herself, and she was swinging to and fro, and singing, and her song carried faintly on the breeze.

I dressed quickly, and left my room. The girl's dress was billowing in the breeze, her pigtails flying about. When she saw me approaching, she stopped swinging, and stared at me. I stopped a little distance away.

'Who are you?' she asked.

'A ghost.' I replied.

'You look like one,' she said.

I decided to take this as a compliment, as I was determined to make friends. I did not smile at her, because some children dislike adults who smile at them all the time.

'What's your name?' I asked.

'Kiran,' she said, 'I'm ten.'

'You are getting old.'

'Well, we all have to grow old one day. Aren't you coming any closer?'

'May I?' I asked.

'You may. You can push the swing.'

One pigtail lay across the girl's chest, the other behind her shoulder. She had a serious face, and obviously felt she had responsibilities; she seemed to be in a hurry to grow up, and I suppose she had no time for anyone who treated her as a child. I pushed the swing, until it went higher and higher, and then I stopped pushing, so that she came lower each time and we could talk.

'Tell me about the people who live here,' I said.

'There is Heera,' she said. 'He's the gardener. He's nearly a hundred. You can see him behind the hedges in the garden. You can't see him unless you look hard. He tells me stories, a new story every day. He's much better than the people in the hotel, and so is Daya Ram.'

'Yes, I met Daya Ram'

'He's my bodyguard. He brings me nice things from the kitchen when no one is looking.'

'You don't stay here?'

'No, I live in another house, you can't see it from here. My father is the manager of the factory.'

'Aren't there any other children to play with?' I asked.

'I don't know any,' she said.

'And the people staying here?'

'Oh, they.' Apparently Kiran didn't think much of the hotel guests. 'Miss Deeds is funny when she's drunk. And Mr Lin is the strangest.'

'And what about the manager, Mr Dayal?'

'He's mean. And he gets frightened of slightest things. But Mrs Dayal is nice, she lets me take flowers home. But she doesn't talk much.'

I was fascinated by Kiran's ruthless summing up of the guests. I brought the swing to a standstill and asked, 'And what do you think of me?'

'I don't know as yet,' said Kiran quite seriously. 'I'll think about you.'

◆

As I came back to the hotel, I heard the sound of a piano in one of the front rooms. I didn't know enough about music to be able to recognize the piece, but it had sweetness and melody, though it was played with some hesitancy. As I came nearer, the sweetness deserted the music, probably because the piano was out of tune.

The person at the piano had distinctive Mongolian features, and so I presumed he was Mr Lin. He hadn't seen me enter the room, and I stood beside the curtains of the door, watching him play. He had full round lips, and high slanting cheekbones. His eyes were large and round and full of melancholy. His long, slender fingers hardly touched the keys.

I came nearer; and then he looked up at me, without any show of surprise or displeasure, and kept on playing.

'What are you playing?' I asked.

'Chopin,' he said.

'Oh, yes. It's nice, but the piano is fighting it.'

'I know. This piano belonged to one of Kipling's aunts. It hasn't been tuned since the last century.'

'Do you live here?'

'No, I come from Calcutta,' he answered readily. 'I have some business here with the sugarcane people, actually, though, I am not a businessman.' He was playing softly all the time, so that our conversation was not lost in the music. 'I don't know anything about business. But I have to do something.'

'Where did you learn to play the piano?'

'In Singapore. A French lady taught me. She had great hopes of my becoming a concert pianist when I grew up. I would have toured Europe and America.'

'Why didn't you?'

'We left during the War, and I had to give up my lessons.'

'And why did you go to Calcutta?'

'My father is a Calcutta businessman. What do you do, and why do you come here?' he asked. 'If I am not being too inquisitive.'

Before I could answer, a bell rang, loud and continuously, drowning the music and conversation.

'Breakfast,' said Mr Lin.

A thin dark man, wearing glasses, stepped nervously into the room and peered at me in an anxious manner.

'You arrived last night?'

'That's right,' I said, 'I just want to stay the day. I think you're the manager?'

'Yes. Would you like to sign the register?'

I went with him past the bar and into the office. I wrote my name and Mussoorie address in the register, and the duration of my stay. I paused at the column marked 'Profession', thought it would be best to fill it with something and wrote 'Author'.

'You are here on business?' asked Mr Dayal.

'No, not exactly. You see, I'm looking for friend of mine who was heard of in Shamli, about three years ago. I thought I'd make a few enquiries in case he's still here.'

'What was his name? Perhaps he stayed here.'

'Major Roberts,' I said. 'An Anglo-Indian.'

'Well, you can look through the old registers after breakfast.'

He accompanied me into the dining-room. The establishment was really more of a boarding-house than a hotel, because Mr Dayal ate with his guests. There was a round mahogany dining-table in the centre of the room, and Mr Lin was the only one seated at it. Daya Ram hovered about with plates and trays. I took my seat next to Lin, and, as I did so, a door opened from the passage, and a woman of about thirty-five came in.

She had on a skirt and blouse, which accentuated a firm, well-rounded figure, and she walked on high-heels, with a rhythmical swaying of the hips. She had an uninteresting face, camouflaged with lipstick, rouge and powder—the powder so thick that is had become embedded in the natural lines of her face—but her figure compelled admiration.

'Miss Deeds,' whispered Lin.

There was a false note to her greeting.

'Hallo, everyone,' she said heartily, straining for effect. 'Why are you all so quiet? Has Mr Lin been playing the Funeral March again? She sat down and continued talking. 'Really, we must have a dance or something to liven things up. You must know some good numbers Lin, after your experience in Singapore nightclubs. What's for breakfast? Boiled eggs. Daya Ram, can't you make an omelette for a change? I know you're not a professional cook, but you don't have to give us the same thing every day, and there's absolutely no reason why you should burn the toast. You'll have to do something about a cook, Mr Dayal.' Then she noticed me sitting opposite her. 'Oh, hallo,' she said, genuinely surprised. She gave me a long appraising look.

'This gentleman,' said Mr Dayal introducing me, 'is an author.'

'That's nice,' said Miss Deeds. 'Are you married?'

'No,' I said. 'Are you?'

'Funny, isn't it,' she said, without taking offence, 'No one in this house seems to be married.'

'I'm married,' said Mr Dayal.

'Oh, yes, of course,' said Miss Deeds. 'And what brings you

to Shamli?' she asked, turning to me.

'I'm looking for a friend called Major Roberts.'

Lin gave an exclamation of surprise. I thought he had seen through my deception.

But another game had begun.

'I knew him,' said Lin. 'A great friend of mine.'

◆

'Yes,' continued Lin. 'I knew him. A good chap, Major Roberts.'

Well, there I was, inventing people to suit my convenience, and people like Mr Lin started inventing relationships with them. I was too intrigued to try and discourage him. I wanted to see how far he would go.

'When did you meet him?' asked Lin, taking the initiative.

'Oh, only about three years back. Just before he disappeared. He was last heard of in Shamli.'

'Yes, I heard he was here,' said Lin. 'But he went away, when he thought his relatives had traced him. He went into the mountains near Tibet.'

'Did he?' I said, unwilling to be instructed further. 'What part of the country? I come from the hills myself. I know the Mana and Niti passes quite well. If you have any idea of exactly where he went, I think I could find him.' I had the advantage in this exchange, because I was the one who had originally invented Roberts. Yet I couldn't bring myself to end his deception, probably because I felt sorry for him. A happy man wouldn't take the trouble of inventing friendships with people who didn't exist, he'd be too busy with friends who did.

'You've had a lonely life, Mr Lin?' I asked.

'Lonely?' said Mr Lin, with forced incredulousness. 'I'd never been lonely till I came here a month ago. When I was in Singapore…'

'You never get any letters though, do you?' asked Miss Deeds suddenly.

Lin was silent for a moment. Then he said, 'Do you?'

Miss Deeds lifted her head a little, as a horse does when it is annoyed, and I thought her pride had been hurt; but then she laughed unobstrusively and tossed her head.

'I never write letters,' she said. 'My friends gave me up as hopeless years ago. They know it's no use writing to me, because they rarely get a reply. They call me the Jungle Princess.'

Mr Dayal tittered, and I found it hard to suppress a smile. To cover up my smile I asked, 'You teach here?'

'Yes, I teach at the girl's school,' she said with a frown. 'But don't talk to me about teaching. I have enough of it all day.'

'You don't like teaching?'

She gave an aggressive look. 'Should I?' she asked.

'Shouldn't you?' I said.

She paused, and then said, 'Who are you, anyway, the Inspector of Schools?'

'No,' said Mr Dayal who wasn't following very well, 'He's a journalist.'

'I've heard they are nosey,' said Miss Deeds.

Once again Lin interrupted to steer the conversation away from a delicate issue.

'Where's Mrs Dayal this morning?' asked Lin.

'She spent the night with our neighbours,' said Mr Dayal. 'She should be here after lunch.'

It was the first time Mrs Dayal had been mentioned. Nobody spoke either well or ill of her; I suspected that she kept her distance from the others, avoiding familiarity. I began to wonder about Mrs Dayal.

◆

Daya Ram came in from the verandah, looking worried.

'Heera's dog has disappeared,' he said. 'He thinks a leopard took it.'

Heera, the gardener was standing respectfully outside on the verandah steps. We all hurried out to him, firing questions which he didn't try to answer.

'Yes. It's a leopard' said Kiran, appearing from behind Heera. 'It's going to come into the hotel,' she added cheerfully.

'Be quiet,' said Satish Dayal crossly.

'There are pug marks under the trees,' said Daya Ram

Mr Dayal, who seemed to know little about leopards or pug marks, said 'I will take a look', and led the way to the orchard, the rest of us trailing behind in an ill-assorted procession.

There were marks on the soft earth in the orchard (they could have been a leopard's) which went in the direction of the riverbed. Mr Dayal paled a little and went hurrying back to the hotel. Heera returned to the front garden, the least excited, the most sorrowful. Everyone else was thinking of a leopard, but he was thinking of the dog.

I followed him, and watched him weeding the sunflower beds. His face wrinkled like a walnut, but his eyes were clear and bright. His hands were thin, and bony, but there was a deftness and power in the wrist and fingers, and the weeds flew fast from his spade. He had cracked, parchment-like skin. I could not help thinking of the gloss and glow of Daya Ram's limbs, as I had seen them when he was bathing, and wondered if Heera's had once been like that and if Daya Ram's would ever be like this, and both possibilities—or were they probabilities—saddened me. Our skin, I thought, is like the leaf of a tree, young and green and shiny; then it gets darker and heavier, sometimes spotted with disease, sometimes eaten away; then fading, yellow and red, then falling, crumbling into dust or feeding the flames of fire. I looked at my own skin, still smooth, not coarsened by labour; I thought of Kiran's fresh rose-tinted complexion; Miss Deed's skin, hard and dry; Lin's pale taut skin, stretched tightly across his prominent cheeks and forehead; and Mr Dayal's grey skin, growing thick hair. And I wondered about Mrs Dayal and the kind of skin she would have.

'Did you have the dog for long?' I asked Heera.

He looked up with surprise, for he had been unaware of my presence.

'Six years, sahib,' he said. 'He was not a clever dog, but he was very friendly. He followed me home one day, when I was coming back from the bazaar. I kept telling him to go away, but he wouldn't. It was a long walk and so I began talking to him. I liked talking to him, and I have always talked with him, and we have understood each other. That first night, when I came home, I shut the gate between us. But he stood on the other side, looking at me with trusting eyes. Why did he have to look at me like that?'

'So, you kept him?'

'Yes, I could never forget the way he looked at me. I shall feel lonely now, because he was my only companion. My wife and son died long ago. It seems I am to stay here forever, until everyone has gone, until there are only ghosts in Shamli. Already the ghosts are here...'

I heard a light footfall behind me and turned to find Kiran. The bare-footed girl stood beside the gardener, and with her toes began to pull at the weeds.

'You are a lazy one,' said the old man. 'If you want to help me, sit down and use your hands.'

I looked at the girl's fair round face, and in her bright eyes I saw something old and wise; and I looked into the old man's wise eyes, and saw something forever bright and young. The skin cannot change the eyes; the eyes are the true reflection of a man's age and sensibilities; even a blind man has hidden eyes.

'I hope we shall find the dog,' said Kiran. 'But I would like a leopard. Nothing ever happens here.'

'Not now,' sighed Heera. 'Not now... Why, once there was a band and people danced till morning, but now...'

'I have always been here,' said Heera. 'I was here before Shamli.'

'Before the station?'

'Before there was a station, or a factory, or a bazaar. It was a village then, and the only way to get here was by bullock-cart. Then a bus service was started, then the railway lines were laid and a station built, then they started the sugar factory, and for a few years Shamli was a town. But the jungle was bigger than the town. The rains were heavy and malaria was everywhere. People didn't stay long in Shamli. Gradually, they went back into the hills. Sometimes I too want to go back to the hills, but what is the use when you are old and have no one left in the world except a few flowers in a troublesome garden. I had to choose between the flowers and the hills, and I chose the flowers. I am tired now, and old, but I am not tired of flowers.'

I could see that his real world was the garden; there was more variety in his flower-beds than there was in the town of Shamli. Every month, every day, there were new flowers in the garden, but there were always the same people in Shamli.

I left Kiran with the old man, and returned to my room. It must have been about eleven o'clock.

◆

I was facing the window when I heard my door being opened. Turning, I perceived the barrel of a gun moving slowly round the edge of the door. Behind the gun was Satish Dayal, looking hot and sweaty. I didn't know what his intentions were; so, deciding it would be better to act first and reason later, I grabbed a pillow from the bed and flung it in his face. I then threw myself at his legs and brought him crashing down to the ground.

When we got up, I was holding the gun. It was an old Enfield rifle, probably dating back to the Afghan wars, the kind that goes off at the least encouragment.

'But—but—why?' stammered the dishevelled and alarmed Mr Dayal.

'I don't know,' I said menacingly. 'Why did you come in here pointing this at me?'

'I wasn't pointing it at you. It's for the leopard.'

'Oh, so you came into my room looking for a leopard? You have, I presume been stalking one about the hotel?' (By now I was convinced that Mr Dayal had taken leave of his senses and was hunting imaginary leopards.)

'No, no,' cried the distraught man, becoming more confused, 'I was looking for you. I wanted to ask you if you could use a gun. I was thinking we should go looking for the leopard that took Heera's dog. Neither Mr Lin nor I can shoot.'

'Your gun is not up-to-date.' I said. 'It's not at all suitable for hunting leopards. A stout stick would be more effective. Why don't we arm ourselves with lathis and make a general assault?'

I said this banteringly, but Mr Dayal took the idea quite seriously, 'Yes, yes,' he said with alacrity, 'Daya Ram has got one or two lathis in the godown. The three of us could make an expedition. I have asked Mr Lin but he says he doesn't want to have anything to do with leopards.'

'What about our Jungle Princess?' I said. 'Miss Deeds should be pretty good with a lathi.'

'Yes, yes,' said Mr Dayal humourlessly, 'but we'd better not ask her.'

Collecting Daya Ram and two lathis, we set off for the orchard and began following the pug marks through the trees. It took us ten minutes to reach the riverbed, a dry hot rocky place; then we went into the jungle, Mr Dayal keeping well to the rear. The atmosphere was heavy and humid, and there was not a breath of air amongst the trees. When a parrot squawked suddenly, shattering the silence, Mr Dayal let out a startled exclamation and started for home.

'What was that?' he asked nervously.

'A bird,' I explained.

'I think we should go back now,' he said, 'I don't think the leopard's here.'

'You never know with leopards,' I said, 'They could be anywhere.'

Mr Dayal stepped away from the bushes. 'I'll have to go,' he said. 'I have a lot of work. You keep a lathi with you, and I'll send Daya Ram back later.'

'That's very thoughtful of you,' I said.

Daya Ram scratched his head and reluctantly followed his employer back through the trees. I moved on slowly down the little-used path, wondering if I should also return. I saw two monkeys playing on the branch of a tree, and decided that there could be no danger in the immediate vicinity.

Presently I came to a clearing where there was a pool of fresh clear water. It was fed by a small stream that came suddenly, like a snake, out of the long grass. The water looked cool and inviting; laying down the lathi and taking off my clothes, I ran down the bank until I was waist-deep in the middle of the pool. I splashed about for some time, before emerging; then I lay on the soft grass and allowed the sun to dry my body. I closed my eyes and gave myself up to beautiful thoughts. I had forgotten all about leopards.

I must have slept for about half an hour because when I awoke, I found that Daya Ram had come back and was vigorously threshing about in the narrow confines of the pool. I sat up and asked him the time.

'Twelve o'clock,' he shouted, coming out of water, his dripping body all gold and silver in sunlight. 'They will be waiting for dinner.'

'Let them wait,' I said.

It was a relief to talk to Daya Ram, after the uneasy conversations in the lounge and dining-room.

'Dayal sahib will be angry with me.'

'I'll tell him we found the trail of the leopard, and that we went so far into the jungle that we lost our way. As Miss Deeds is so critical of the food, let her cook the meal.'

'Oh, she only talks like that,' said Daya Ram. 'Inside she is very soft. She is too soft in some ways.'

'She should be married.'

'Well, she would like to be. Only there is no one to marry her. When she came here she was engaged to be married to an English army captain; I think she loved him, but she is the sort of person who cannot help loving many men all at once, and the captain could not understand that—it is just the way she is made, I suppose. She is always ready to fall in love.'

'You seem to know,' I said.

'Oh, yes.'

We dressed and walked back to the hotel. In a few hours, I thought, the tonga will come for me and I will be back at the station; the mysterious charm of Shamli will be no more, but whenever I pass this way I will wonder about these people, about Miss Deeds and Lin and Mrs Dayal.

Mrs Dayal... She was the one person I was yet to meet; it was with some excitement and curiosity that I looked forward to meeting her; she was about the only mystery left to Shamli, now, and perhaps she would be no mystery when I met her. And yet... I felt that perhaps she would justify the impulse that made me get down from the train.

I could have asked Daya Ram about Mrs Dayal, and so satisfied my curiosity; but I wanted to discover her for myself. Half the day was left to me, and I didn't want my game to finish too early.

I walked towards the verandah, and the sound of the piano came through the open door.

'I wish Mr Lin would play something cheerful,' said Miss Deeds. 'He's obsessed with the Funeral March. Do you dance?'

'Oh no,' I said.

She looked disappointed. But when Lin left the piano, she went into the lounge and sat down on the stool. I stood at the door watching her, wondering what she would do.

Lin left the room, somewhat resentfully.

She began to play an old song, which I remembered having heard in a film or on a gramophone record. She sang while she played, in a slightly harsh but pleasant voice:

Rolling round the world
Looking for the sunshine
I know I'm going to find some day...

Then she played 'Am I blue?' and 'Darling, Je Vous Aime Beaucoup'. She sat there singing in a deep husky voice, her eyes a little misty, her hard face suddenly kind and sloppy. When the gong rang, she broke off playing, and shook off her sentimental mood, and laughed derisively at herself.

I don't remember that lunch. I hadn't slept much since the

previous night and I was beginning to feel the strain of my journey. The swim had refreshed me, but it had also made me drowsy. I ate quite well, though, of rice and kofta curry, and then, feeling sleepy, made for the garden to find a shady tree.

There were some books on the shelf in the lounge, and I ran my eye over them in search of one that might condition sleep. But they were too dull to do even that. So I went into the garden, and there was Kiran on the swing, and I went to her tree and sat down on the grass.

'Did you find the leopard?' she asked.

'No,' I said, with a yawn.

'Tell me a story.'

'You tell me one,' I said.

'Alright. Once there was a lazy man with long legs, who was always yawning and wanting to fall asleep...'

I watched the swaying motions of the swing and the movements of the girl's bare legs, and a tiny insect kept buzzing about in front of my nose... 'and fall asleep, and the reason for this was that he liked to dream.' I blew the insect away, and the swing became hazy and distant, and Kiran was a blurred figure in the trees...

'...liked to dream, and what do you think he dreamt about...?' Dreamt about, dreamt about...

◆

When I awoke there was that cool rain-scented breeze blowing across the garden. I remember lying on the grass with my eyes closed, listening to the swishing of the swing. Either I had not slept long, or Kiran had been a long time on the swing; it was moving slowly now, in a more leisurely fashion, without much sound. I opened my eyes and saw that my arm was stained with the juice of the grass beneath me. Looking up, I expected to see

Kiran's legs waving above me. But instead I saw dark slim feet, and above them the folds of a sari. I straightened up against the trunk of the tree to look closer at Kiran, but Kiran wasn't there, it was someone else on the swing, a young woman in a pink sari and with a red rose in her hair.

She had stopped the swing with her foot on the ground, and she was smiling at me.

It wasn't a smile you could see, it was a tender fleeting movement that came suddenly and was gone at the same time, and its going was sad. I thought of the other's smiles, just as I had thought of their skins: the tonga-driver's friendly, deceptive grin: Daya Ram's wide sincere smile; Miss Deed's cynical, derisive smile. And looking at Sushila, I knew a smile could never change. She had always smiled that way.

'You haven't changed,' she said.

I was standing up now, though still leaning against the tree for support. Though I had never thought much about the *sound* of her voice, it seemed as familiar as the sounds of yesterday.

'You haven't changed either,' I said. 'But where did you come from?' I wasn't sure yet if I was awake or dreaming.

She laughed, as she had always laughed at me.

'I came from behind the tree. The little girl has gone.'

'Yes, I'm dreaming,' I said helplessly.

'But what brings you here?'

'I don't know. At least I didn't know when I came. But it must have been you. The train stopped at Shamli, and I don't know why, but I decided I would spend the day here, behind the station walls. You must be married now, Sushila.'

'Yes, I am married to Mr Dayal, the manager of the hotel. And what has been happening with you?'

'I am still a writer, still poor, and still living in Mussoorie.'

'When were you last in Delhi?' she asked. 'I don't mean

Delhi, I mean at home.'

'I have not been to your home since you were there.'

'Oh, my friend,' she said, getting up suddenly and coming to me, 'I want to talk to you. I want to talk about our home and Sunil and our friends and all those things that are so far away now. I have been here two years, and I am already feeling old. I keep remembering our home, how young I was, how happy, and I am all alone with memories. But now *you* are here! It was a bit of magic, I came through the trees after Kiran had gone, and there you were, fast asleep under the tree. I didn't wake you then, because I wanted to see you wake up.'

'As I used to watch you wake up...'

She was near me and I could look at her more closely. Her cheeks did not have the same freshness; they were a little pale, and she was thinned now, but her eyes were the same, smiling the same way. Her voice was the same. Her fingers, when she took my hand, were the same warm delicate fingers.

'Talk to me,' she said. 'Tell me about yourself.'

'You tell me,' I said.

'I am here,' she said. 'That is all there is about myself.'

'Then let us sit down and I'll talk.'

'Not here,' she took my hand and led me through the trees. 'Come with me.'

I heard the jingle of a tonga-bell and a faint shout, I stopped and laughed.

'My tonga,' I said. 'It has come to take me back to the station.'

'But you are not going,' said Sushila, immediately downcast.

'I will tell him to come in the morning,' I said. 'I will spend the night in your Shamli.'

I walked to the front of the hotel where the tonga was waiting. I was glad no one else was in sight. The youth was smiling at me in his most appealing manner.

'I'm not going today,' I said. 'Will you come tomorrow morning?'

'I can come whenever you like, friend. But you will have to pay for every trip, because it is a long way from the station even if my tonga is empty.'

'Alright, how much?'

'Usual fare, friend, one rupee.'

I didn't try to argue but resignedly gave him the rupee. He cracked his whip and pulled on the reins, and the carriage moved off.

'If you don't leave tomorrow,' the youth called out after me, 'you'll never leave Shamli!'

I walked back to trees, but I couldn't find Sushila.

'Sushila, where are you?' I called, but I might have been speaking to the trees, for I had no reply. There was a small path going through the orchard, and on the path I saw a rose petal. I walked a little further and saw another petal. They were from Sushila's red rose. I walked on down the path until I had skirted the orchard, and then the path went along the fringe of the jungle, past a clump of bamboos, and here the grass was a lush green as though it had been constantly watered. I was still finding rose petals. I heard the chatter of seven sisters, and the call of hoopoe. The path bent to meet a stream, there was a willow coming down to the water's edge, and Sushila was waiting there.

'Why didn't you wait?' I said.

'I wanted to see if you were as good at following me as you used to be.'

'Well, I am,' I said, sitting down beside her on the grassy bank of the stream. 'Even if I'm out of practice.'

'Yes, I remember the time you climbed onto an apple tree to pick some fruit for me. You got up alright but then you couldn't come down again. I had to climb up myself and help you.'

'I don't remember that,' I said.

'Of course you do.'

'It must have been your other friend, Pramod.'

'I never climbed trees with Pramod.'

'Well, I don't remember.'

I looked at the little stream that ran past us. The water was no more than ankle-deep, cold and clear and sparkling, like the mountain-stream near my home. I took off my shoes, rolled up my trousers, and put my feet in water. Sushila's feet joined mine.

At first I had wanted to ask her about her marriage, whether she was happy or not, what she thought of her husband; but now I couldn't ask her these things, they seemed far away and of little importance. I could think of nothing she had in common with Mr Dayal; I felt that her charm and attractiveness and warmth could not have been appreciated, or even noticed, by that curiously distracted man. He was much older than her, of course; probably older than me; he was obviously not her choice but her parents'; and so far they were childless. Had there been children, I don't think Sushila would have minded Mr Dayal as her husband. Children would have made up for the absence of passion—or was there passion in Satish Dayal? I remembered having heard that Sushila had been married to a man she didn't like; I remembered having shrugged off the news, because it meant she would never come my way again, and I have never yearned after something that has been irredeemably lost. But she had come my way again. And was she still lost? That was what I wanted to know...

'What do you do with yourself all day?' I asked.

'Oh, I visit the school and help with the classes. It is the only interest I have in this place. The hotel is terrible. I try to keep away from it as much as I can.'

'And what about the guests?'

'Oh, don't let us talk about them. Let us talk about ourselves. Do you have to go tomorrow?'

'Yes, I suppose so. Will you always be in this place?'

'I suppose so.'

That made me silent. I took her hand, and my feet churned up the mud at the bottom of the stream. As the mud subsided, I saw Sushila's face reflected in the water; and looking up at her again, into her dark eyes, the old yearning returned and I wanted to care for her and protect her, I wanted to take her away from that place, from sorrowful Shamli; I wanted her to live again. Of course, I had forgotten all about my poor finances, Sushila's family, and the shoes I wore, which were my last pair. The uplift I was experiencing in this meeting with Sushila, who had always, throughout her childhood and youth, bewitched me as no other had ever bewitched me, made me reckless and impulsive.

I lifted her hand to my lips and kissed her in the soft of the palm.

'Can I kiss you?' I said.

'You have just done so.'

'Can I kiss you?' I repeated.

'It is not necessary.'

I leaned over and kissed her slender neck. I knew she would like this, because that was where I had kissed her often before. I kissed her in the soft of the throat, where it tickled.

'It is not necessary,' she said, but she ran her fingers through my hair and let them rest there. I kissed her behind the ear then, and kept my mouth to her ear and whispered, 'Can I kiss you?'

She turned her face to me so that we were deep in each other's eyes, and I kissed her again, and we put our arms around each other and lay together on the grass, with the water running over our feet; and we said nothing at all, simply lay there for what seemed like several years, or until the first drop of rain.

It was a big wet drop, and it splashed on Sushila's cheek, just next to mine, and ran down to her lips, so that I had to kiss her again. The next big drop splattered on the tip of my nose, and Sushila laughed and sat up. Little ringlets were forming on the stream where the raindrops hit the water, and above us there was a pattering on the banana leaves.

'We must go,' said Sushila.

We started homewards, but had not gone far before it was raining steadily, and Sushila's hair came loose and streamed down her body. The rain fell harder, and we had to hop over pools and avoid the soft mud. Sushila's sari was plastered to her body, accentuating her ripe, thrusting breasts, and I was excited to passion, and pulled her beneath a big tree and crushed her in my arms and kissed her rain-kissed mouth. And then I thought she was crying, but I wasn't sure, because it might have been the raindrops on her cheeks.

'Come away with me,' I said. 'Leave this place. Come away with me tomorrow morning. We will go somewhere where nobody will know us or come between us.'

She smiled at me and said, 'You are still a dreamer, aren't you?'

'Why can't you come?'

'I am married, it is as simple as that.'

'If it is that simple, you can come.'

'I have to think of my parents, too. It would break my father's heart if I were to do what you are proposing. And you are proposing it without a thought for the consequences.'

'You are too practical.' I said.

'If women were not practical, most marriages would be failures.'

'So, your marriage is a success?'

'Of course it is, as a marriage. I am not happy and I do not love him, but neither am I so unhappy that I should hate him. Sometimes, for our own sakes, we have to think of the happiness of others. What happiness would we have living in hiding from everyone we once knew and cared for? Don't be a fool. I am always here and you can come to see me, and nobody will be made unhappy by it. But take me away and we will only have regrets.'

'You don't love me,' I said foolishly.

'That sad word love,' she said, and became pensive and silent.

I could say no more. I was angry again, and rebellious, and there was no one and nothing to rebel against. I could not understand someone who was afraid to break away from an unhappy existence lest that existence should become unhappier; I had always considered it an admirable thing to break away from security and respectability. Of course it is easier for a man to do this, a man can look after himself, he can do without neighbours and the approval of the local society. A woman, I reasoned, would do anything for love provided it was not at the price of security; for a woman loves security as much as a man loves independence.

'I must go back now,' said Suhsila. 'You follow a little later.'

'All you wanted to do was talk,' I complained.

She laughed at that, and pulled me playfully by the hair; then she ran out from under the tree, springing across the grass, and the wet mud flew up and flecked her legs. I watched her through the thin curtain of rain, until she reached the verandah. She turned to wave to me, and then skipped into the hotel. She was still young; but I was no younger.

◆

The rain had lessened, but I didn't know what to do with myself. The hotel was uninviting, and it was too late to leave Shamli. If the grass hadn't been wet I would have preferred to sleep under a tree rather than return to the hotel to sit at that alarming dining-table.

I came out from under the trees and crossed the garden. But instead of making for the verandah I went round to the back of the hotel. Smoke issuing from the barred window of a back room told me I had probably found the kitchen. Daya Ram was inside, squatting in front of a stove, stirring a pot of stew. The stew smelt appetizing. Daya Ram looked up and smiled at me.

'I thought you must have gone,' he said.

'I'll go in the morning,' I said pulling myself upon an empty table. Then I had one of my sudden ideas and said, 'Why don't you come with me? I can find you a good job in Mussoorie. How much do you get paid here?'

'Fifty rupees a month. But I haven't been paid for three months.'

'Could you get your pay before tomorrow morning?'

'No, I won't get anything until one of the guests pays a bill. Miss Deeds owes about fifty rupees on whisky alone. She will pay up, she says, when the school pays her salary. And the school can't pay her until they collect the children's fees. That is how bankrupt everyone is in Shamli.'

'I see,' I said, though I didn't see. 'But Mr Dayal can't hold back your pay just because his guests haven't paid their bills.'

'He can, if he hasn't got any money.'

'I see,' I said, 'Anyway, I will give you my address. You can come when you are free.'

'I will take it from the register,' he said.

I edged over to the stove and, leaning over, sniffed at the

stew. 'I'll eat mine now,' I said; and without giving Daya Ram a chance to object, I lifted a plate off the shelf, took hold of the stirring-spoon and helped myself from the pot.

'There's rice too.' said Daya Ram

I filled another plate with rice and then got busy with my fingers. After ten minutes, I had finished. I sat back comfortably in the hotel, in ruminative mood. With my stomach full I could take a more tolerant view of life and people. I could understand Sushila's apprehensions, Lin's delicate lying, and Miss Deed's aggressiveness. Daya Ram went out to sound the dinner-gong, and I trailed back to my room.

From the window of my room I saw Kiran running across the lawn, and I called to her, but she didn't hear me. She ran down the path and out of the gate, her pigtails beating against the wind.

The clouds were breaking and coming together again, twisting and spiralling their way across a violet sky. The sun was going down behind the Siwaliks. The sky there was bloodshot. The tall slim trunks of the eucalyptus tree were tinged with an orange glow; the rain had stopped, and the wind was a soft, sullen puff, drifting sadly through the trees. There was a steady drip of water from the eaves of the roof on to the window-sill. Then the sun went down behind the old, old hills, and I remembered my own hills, far beyond these.

The room was dark but I did not turn on the light. I stood near the window, listening to the garden. There was a frog warbling somewhere, and there was a sudden flap of wings overhead. Tomorrow morning I would go, and perhaps I would come back to Shamli one day, and perhaps not; I could always come here looking for Major Roberts, and, who knows, one day I might find him. What should he be like, this lost man? A romantic, a man with a dream, a man with brown skin and blue eyes, living in a hut on a snowy mountain-top, chopping wood and catching fish and swimming in cold mountain streams; a rough, free man with a kind heart and a shaggy beard, a man who owed allegiance to no one, who gave a damn for money and politics and cities, and civilizations, who was his own master, who lived at one with nature knowing no fear. But that was not Major Roberts—that was the man I wanted to be. He was not a Frenchman or an Englishman, he was me, a dream of myself. If only I could find Major Roberts.

When Daya Ram knocked on the door and told me the others had finished dinner, I left my room and made for the lounge. It was quite lively in the lounge. Satish Dayal was at the bar, Lin at the piano, and Miss Deeds in the centre of the room, executing a tango on her own. It was obvious she had been drinking heavily.

'All on credit,' complained Mr Dayal to me. 'I don't know when I'll be paid, but I don't dare to refuse her anything for fear she starts breaking up the hotel.'

'She could do that, too,' I said. 'It comes down without much encouragement.'

Lin began to play a waltz (I think it was waltz), and then I found Miss Deeds in front of me, saying 'Wouldn't you like to dance, old boy?'

'Thank you,' I said, somewhat alarmed. 'I hardly know how to.'

'Oh, come on, be a sport,' she said, pulling me away from the bar. I was glad Sushila wasn't present; she wouldn't have minded, but she'd have laughed as she always laughed when I made a fool of myself.

We went round the floor in what I suppose was waltz-time, though all I did was mark time to Miss Deeds' motions; we were not very steady—this because I was trying to keep her at arm's length, whilst she was determined to have me crushed to her bosom. At length, Lin finished the waltz. Giving him a grateful look, I pulled myself free. Miss Deeds went over to the piano, leant right across it, and said, 'Play some lively, dear Mr Lin, play some hot stuff.'

To my surprise Mr Lin without so much as an expression of distaste or amusement, began to execute what I suppose was the frug or the jitterbug. I was glad she hadn't asked me to dance that one with her.

It all appeared very incongruous to me: Miss Deeds letting herself go in crazy abandonment, Lin playing the piano with great seriousness, and Mr Dayal watching from the bar with an anxious frown. I wondered what Sushila would have thought of them now.

Eventually, Miss Deeds collapsed on the couch breathing heavily. 'Give me a drink,' she cried.

With the noblest of intentions I took her a glass of water. Miss Deeds took a sip and made a face. 'What's this stuff?' she asked. 'It is different.'

'Water,' I said.

'No,' she said, 'now don't joke, tell me what it is.'

'It's water, I assure you,' I said.

When she saw that I was serious, her face coloured up, and I thought she would throw the water at me; but she was too tired to do this, and contented herself by throwing the glass over her shoulder. Mr Dayal made a dive for the flying glass, but he wasn't in time to rescue it, and it hit the wall and fell to pieces on the floor.

Mr Dayal wrung his hands. 'You'd better take her to her room,' he said, as though I were personally responsible for her behaviour just because I'd danced with her.

'I can't carry her alone,' I said, making an unsuccessful

attempt at helping Miss Deeds up from the couch.

Mr Dayal called for Daya Ram, and the big amiable youth came lumbering into the lounge. We took an arm each and helped Miss Deeds, feet dragging, across the room. We got her to her room and on to her bed. When we were about to withdraw she said, 'Don't go, my dear, stay with me a little while.'

Daya Ram had discreetly slipped outside. With my hand on the doorknob I said, 'Which of us?'

'Oh, are there two of you,' said Miss Deeds, without a trace of disappointment.

'Yes, Daya Ram helped me carry you here.'

'Oh, and who are you?'

'I'm the writer. You danced with me, remember?'

'Of course. You dance divinely, Mr Writer. Do stay with me. Daya Ram can stay too if he likes.'

I hesitated, my hand on the doorknob. She hadn't opened her eyes all the time I'd been in the room, her arms hung loose, and one bare leg hung over the side of the bed. She was fascinating somehow, and desirable, but I was afraid of her. I went out of the room and quietly closed the door.

♦

As I lay awake in bed I heard the jackal's 'pheau', the cry of fear, which it communicates to all the jungle when there is danger about, a leopard or a tiger. It was a weird howl, and between each note there was a kind of low gurgling. I switched off the light and peered through the closed window. I saw the jackal at the edge of the lawn. It sat almost vertically on its haunches, holding its head straight up to the sky, making the neighbourhood vibrate with the eerie violence of its cries. Then suddenly it started up and ran off into the trees.

Before getting back into bed I made sure the window was fast. The bull-frog was singing again, 'ing-ong; ing-ong', in some foreign language. I wondered if Sushila was awake too, thinking about me. It must have been almost eleven o'clock. I thought of Miss Deeds, with her leg hanging over the edge of the bed. I tossed resdessly, and then sat up. I hadn't slept for two nights but I was not sleepy. I got out of bed without turning on the light and, slowly opening my door, crept down the passageway. I stopped at the door of Miss Deed's room. I stood there listening, but I heard only the ticking of the big clock that might have been in the room or somewhere in the passage. I put my hand on the doorknob, but the door was bolted. That settled the matter.

I would definitely leave Shamli the next morning. Another day in the company of these people and I would be behaving like them. Perhaps I was already doing so! I remembered the tonga-driver's words, 'Don't stay too long in Shamli or you will never leave!'

When the rain came, it was not with a preliminary patter or shower, but all at once, sweeping across the forest like a massive wall, and I could hear it in the trees long before it reached the house. Then it came crashing down on the corrugated roofing, and the hailstones hit the window panes with a hard metallic sound, so that I thought the glass would break. The sound of thunder was like the booming of big guns, and the lightning kept playing over the garden, at every flash of lightning I sighted the swing under the tree, rocking and leaping in the air as though some invisible, agitated being was sitting on it. I wondered about Kiran. Was she sleeping through all this, blissfully unconcerned, or was she lying awake in bed, starting at every clash of thunder, as I was; or was she up and about, exulting in the storm? I half expected to see her come running through the trees, through the rain, to stand on the swing with her hair blowing wild in the wind, laughing at the thunder and the angry skies. Perhaps I did see her, perhaps she was there. I wouldn't have been surprised if she were some forest nymph, living in the hole of a tree, coming out sometimes to play in the garden.

A crash, nearer and louder than any thunder so far, made me sit up in the bed with a start. Perhaps lightning had struck the house. I turned on the switch, but the light didn't come on. A tree must have fallen across the line.

I heard voices in the passage, the voices of several people. I stepped outside to find out what had happened, and started at the appearance of a ghostly apparition right in front of me; it was Mr Dayal standing on the threshold in an oversized pyjama suit, a candle in his hand.

'I came to wake you,' he said. 'This storm.'

He had the irritating habit of stating the obvious.

'Yes, the storm,' I said. 'Why is everybody up?'

'The back wall has collapsed and part of the roof has fallen in. We'd better spend the night in the lounge, it is the safest room. This is a very old building,' he added apologetically.

'Alright,' I said. 'I am coming.'

The lounge was lit by two candles; one stood over the piano, the other on a small table near the couch. Miss Deeds was on the couch, Lin was at the piano-stool, looking as though he would start playing Stravinsky any moment, and Mr Dayal was fussing about the room. Sushila was standing at a window, looking out at the stormy night. I went to the window and touched her, She didn't look round or say anything. The lightning flashed and her dark eyes were pools of smouldering fire.

'What time will you be leaving?' she said.

'The tonga will come for me at seven.'

'If I come,' she said. 'If I come with you, I will be at the station before the train leaves.'

'How will you get there?' I asked, and hope and excitement rushed over me again.

'I will get there,' she said. 'I will get there before you. But if I am not there, then do not wait, do not come back for me. Go on your way. It will mean I do not want to come. Or I will be there.'

'But are you sure?'

'Don't stand near me now. Don't speak to me unless you have to.' She squeezed my fingers, then drew her hand away. I sauntered over to the next window, then back into the centre of the room. A gust of wind blew through a cracked window-pane and put out the candle near the couch.

'Damn the wind,' said Miss Deeds.

◆

The window in my room had burst open during the night, and there were leaves and branches strewn about the floor. I sat down on the damp bed, and smelt eucalyptus. The earth was red, as though the storm had bled it all night.

After a little while, I went into the verandah with my suitcase, to wait for the tonga. It was then that I saw Kiran under the trees. Kiran's long black pigtails were tied up in a red ribbon, and she looked fresh and clean like the rain and the red earth. She stood looking seriously at me.

'Did you like the storm?' she asked.

'Some of the time,' I said. 'I'm going soon. Can I do anything for you?'

'Where are you going?'

'I'm going to the end of the world. I'm looking for Major Roberts, have you seen him anywhere?'

'There is no Major Roberts,' she said perceptively. 'Can I

come with you to the end of the world?'

'What about your parents?'

'Oh, we won't take them.'

'They might be annoyed if you go off on your own.'

'I can stay on my own. I can go anywhere.'

'Well, one day I'll come back here and I'll take you everywhere and no one will stop us. Now is there anything else I can do for you?'

'I want some flowers, but I can't reach them,' she pointed to a hibiscus tree that grew against the wall. It meant climbing the wall to reach the flowers. Some of the red flowers had fallen during the night and were floating in a pool of water.

'Alright,' I said and pulled myself up on the wall. I smiled down into Kiran's serious upturned face. 'I'll throw them to you and you can catch them.'

I bent a branch, but the wood was young and green, and I had to twist it several times before it snapped.

'I hope nobody minds,' I said, as I dropped the flowering branch to Kiran.

'It's nobody's tree,' she said.

'Sure?'

She nodded vigorously. 'Sure, don't worry.'

I was working for her and she felt immensely capable of protecting me. Talking and being with Kiran, I felt a nostalgic longing for the childhood: emotions that had been beautiful because they were never completely understood.

'Who is your best friend?' I said.

'Daya Ram,' she replied. 'I told you so before.'

She was certainly faithful to her friends.

'And who is the second best?'

She put her finger in her mouth to consider the question; her head dropped sideways in concentration.

'I'll make you the second best,' she said.

I dropped the flowers over her head. 'That is so kind of you. I'm proud to be your second best.'

I heard the tonga bell, and from my perch on the wall saw the carriage coming down the driveway. 'That's for me,' I said. 'I must go now.'

I jumped down the wall. And the sole of my shoe came off at last.

'I knew that would happen,' I said.

'Who cares for shoes,' said Kiran.

'Who cares,' I said.

I walked back to the verandah, and Kiran walked beside me, and stood in front of the hotel while I put my suitcase in the tonga.

'You nearly stayed one day too late,' said the tonga-driver. 'Half the hotel has come down, and tonight the other half will come down.'

I climbed into the back seat. Kiran stood on the path, gazing intently at me.

'I'll see you again,' I said.

'I'll see you in Iceland or Japan,' she said. 'I'm going everywhere.'

'Maybe,' I said, 'maybe you will.'

We smiled, knowing and understanding each other's importance. In her bright eyes I saw something old and wise. The tonga-driver cracked his whip, the wheels cracked, the carriage rattled down the path. We kept waving to each other. In Kiran's hand was a spring of hibiscus. As she waved, the blossoms fell apart and danced a little in breeze.

◆

Shamli station looked the same as it had the day before. The same train stood at the same platform, and the same dogs prowled beside the fence. I waited on the platform until the bell clanged for the train to leave, but Sushila did not come.

Somehow, I was not disappointed. I had never really expected her to come. Unattainable, Sushila would always be more bewitching and beautiful than if she were mine.

Shamli would always be there. And I could always come back, looking for Major Roberts.

THE STORY OF MADHU

I met little Madhu several years ago, when I lived alone in an obscure town near the Himalayan foothills. I was in my late twenties then, and my outlook on life was still quite romantic; the cynicism that was to come with the thirties had not yet set in.

I preferred the solitude of the small district town to the kind of social life I might have found in the cities; and in my books, my writing and the surrounding hills, there was enough for my pleasure and occupation.

On summer mornings I would often sit beneath an old mango tree, with a notebook or a sketch pad on my knees. The house which I had rented (for a very nominal sum) stood on the outskirts of the town; and a large tank and a few poor houses could be seen from the garden wall. A narrow public pathway passed under the low wall.

One morning, while I sat beneath the mango tree, I saw a young girl of about nine, wearing torn clothes, darting about on the pathway and along the high banks of the tank.

Sometimes she stopped to look at me; and, when I showed that I noticed her, she felt encouraged and gave me a shy, fleeting smile. The next day I discovered her leaning over the garden wall, following my actions as I paced up and down on the grass.

In a few days an acquaintance had been formed. I began to

take the girl's presence for granted, and even to look for her; and she, in turn, would linger about on the pathway until she saw me come out of the house.

One day, as she passed the gate, I called her to me.

'What is your name?' I asked. 'And where do you live?'

'Madhu,' she said, brushing back her long untidy black hair and smiling at me from large black eyes. She pointed across the road: 'I live with my grandmother.'

'Is she very old?' I asked.

Madhu nodded confidingly and whispered, 'A hundred years…'

'We will never be that old,' I said. She was very slight and frail, like a flower growing in a rock, vulnerable to wind and rain.

I discovered later that the old lady was not her grandmother but a childless woman who had found the baby girl on the banks of the tank. Madhu's real parentage was unknown; but the wizened old woman had, out of compassion, brought up the child as her own.

My gate once entered, Madhu included the garden in her circle of activities. She was there every morning, chasing butterflies, stalking squirrels and myna, her voice brimming with laughter, her slight figure flitting about between the trees.

Sometimes, but not often, I gave her a toy or a new dress; and one day she put aside her shyness and brought me a present of a nosegay, made up of marigolds and wild blue-cotton flowers.

'For you,' she said, and put the flowers in my lap.

'They are very beautiful,' I said, picking out the brightest marigold and putting it in her hair. 'But they are not as beautiful as you.'

More than a year passed before I began to take more than a mildly patronizing interest in Madhu.

It occurred to me after some time that she should be taught to read and write, and I asked a local teacher to give her lessons in the garden for an hour every day. She clapped her hands with pleasure at the prospect of what was to be for her a fascinating new game.

In a few weeks Madhu was surprising us with her capacity for absorbing knowledge. She always came to me to repeat the lessons of the day, and pestered me with questions on a variety of subjects. How big was the world? And were the stars really like our world? Or were they the sons and daughters of the sun and the moon?

My interest in Madhu deepened, and my life, so empty till then, became imbued with a new purpose. As she sat on the grass beside me, reading aloud, or listening to me with a look of complete trust and belief, all the love that had been lying dormant in me during my years of self-exile surfaced in a sudden surge of tenderness.

Three years glided away imperceptibly, and at the age of thirteen Madhu was on the verge of blossoming into a woman. I began to feel a certain responsibility towards her.

It was dangerous, I knew, to allow a child so pretty to live almost alone and unprotected, and to run unrestrained about the grounds. And in a censorious society she would be made to suffer if she spent too much time in my company.

She could see no need for any separation but I decided to send her to a mission school in the next district, where I could visit her from time to time.

'But why?' said Madhu. 'I can learn more from you, and from the teacher who comes. I am so happy here.'

'You will meet other girls and make many friends,' I told her. 'I will come to see you. And, when you come home, we will be even happier. It is good that you should go.'

It was the middle of June, a hot and oppressive month in the Siwaliks. Madhu had expressed her readiness to go to school, and when, one evening, I did not see her as usual in the garden, I thought nothing of it; but the next day I was informed that she had fever and could not leave the house.

Illness was something Madhu had not known before, and for this reason I felt afraid. I hurried down the path which led to the old woman's cottage. It seemed strange that I had never once entered it during my long friendship with Madhu.

It was a humble mud hut, the ceiling just high enough to enable me to stand upright, the room dark but clean. Madhu was lying on a string cot, exhausted by fever, her eyes closed, her long hair unkempt, one small hand hanging over the side.

It struck me then how little, during all this time, I had thought of her physical comforts. There was no chair; I knelt down, and took her hand in mine. I knew, from the fierce heat of her body, that she was seriously ill.

She recognized my touch, and a smile passed across her face before she opened her eyes. She held on to my hand, then laid it across her cheek.

I looked round the little room in which she had grown up. It had scarcely an article of furniture apart from two string cots, on one of which the old woman sat and watched us, her white, wizened head nodding like a puppet's.

In a corner lay Madhu's little treasures. I recognized among them the presents which during the past four years I had given her. She had kept everything. On her dark arm she still wore a small piece of ribbon which I had playfully tied there about a year ago. She had given her heart, even before she was conscious of possessing one, to a stranger unworthy of the gift. As the evening drew on, a gust of wind blew open the door of the dark room, and a gleam of sunshine streamed in, lighting up a portion of the wall. It was the time when every evening she would join me under the mango tree. She had been quiet for almost an hour, and now a slight pressure of her hand drew my eyes back to her face.

'What will we do now?' she said. 'When will you send me to school?'

'Not for a long time. First you must get well and strong. That is all that matters.'

She didn't seem to hear me. I think she knew she was dying, but she did not resent it happening.

'Who will read to you under the tree?' she went on. 'Who will look after you?' she asked, with the solicitude of a grown woman.

'You will, Madhu. You are grown up now. There will be no one else to look after me.'

The old woman was standing at my shoulder. A hundred years old—and little Madhu was slipping away. The woman took Madhu's hand from mine, and laid it gently down. I sat by the cot a little longer, and then I rose to go, all the loneliness in the world pressing upon my heart.

TALES OF OLD MUSSOORIE

At one time visitors to Mussoorie frequently found themselves persuaded to climb to the top of a local peak called 'Gun Hill', from which one is able to obtain a view of the greater Himalayas. Today a cable-car takes tourists to the top of the hill, from which, besides the snows, Mussoorie waterworks, too, can be seen, but of a 'gun' there is no sign and they may be pardoned for wondering how the hill acquired its impressive name. We hope to enlighten them on this, and other aspects, of the hill station's distant though not ancient past.

Before 1919, noon-time was indicated by the firing of a cannon from the top of 'Gun Hill', possibly because cannons were cheaper than clocks in those days. At first the gun faced east; then soon after its installation, a complaint came from the Grey Castle Nursing Home that the gun when fired 'often let loose plaster from the ceiling of the wards, which fell on patients' beds and unnerved them'. It could not be pointed north because it would then have blasted away a house called 'Dilkush'; so it was faced northeast, but that again couldn't be made its permanent position, for the Crystal Bank then complained. Turned to the south, it almost succeeded in fulfilling its legitimate duty, but that was before the gunner forgot to remove the ramrod from the barrel; and on booming noon to the populace, the cannon sent the ramrod clean through the roof of the Savoy hotel.

Public opinion consequently was mounting against the gun, and it was turned around once more to face the Mall. The boom was usually produced by ramming down the barrel a mixture of moist grass and cotton waste, after the powder was in place. Due to an accidental overcharge of powder, one of these cannon-balls landed with some force right in the lap of a lady who was being taken along the Mall in a rickshaw. It was the last straw or, to be exact, the last cannon-ball, for the gun was dismantled soon after the incident.

A peep into the life of the hill station before the turn of the century is a fascinating exercise; but before giving the reader further anecdotes, we should fill in the background with a brief historical sketch of the hill station.

In the year 1825, the Superintendent of the Doon was a certain Mr Shore, who occasionally found time from his official duties to scramble up the range, then known as 'Mansuri' because of the prevalence of a shrub known in the vernacular as the Mansur plant. He found that the range had a number of 'flats', some of which accommodated the huts of cowherds who grazed their cattle on them during the summer months. The hills were then well-forested and game plentiful; so the first construction was a shooting-box built jointly by Mr Shore and Captain Young of the Sirmur Rifles. It has long since disappeared, but is said to have been located on the Camel's Back, facing north. The first home—still recognizable—was 'Mullingar' in Landour, built in 1826 by Captain Young. Landour soon became a convalescent depot for British troops; the old convalescent hospital now forms the nucleus of the offices of the Defence Institute of Work Study. Soon civilians were flocking to Mussoorie, building houses as far apart as 'Cloud End' to the west and 'Dahlia Bank' to the east, separated by some 12 miles. In 1832, Colonel Everest (after whom the mountain is named) as Surveyor-General opened his Survey of India office in 'The Park' and made a road to it.

People came to Mussoorie for health, business and pleasure; and amongst the pleasure-seekers we find the Hon'ble Emily Eden, sister of Lord George Eden, Earl of Auckland, Governor General of India. One of our earliest visitors, she records in her famous diaries that:

> ...in the afternoon we took a beautiful ride up to Landour, but the paths are very narrow on that side, and our courage somehow oozed out, and first we came to a place where they said, 'This was where poor Major Blundell and his pony fell over and they were both dashed to atoms,' and then there was a board stuck in a tree, 'From this spot a private in the Cameroons fell and was killed...' We had to get off our ponies and lead them, and altogether I thought much of poor Major Blundell. It is impossible to imagine more beautiful scenery.

Though there were no proper roads in Mussoorie in those early days, some of the cliff-edge accidents were undoubtedly caused by the beer that was then so cheap and plentiful in the hill station.

Mr Bohle, one of the pioneers of brewing in India, started the 'Old Brewery' near Hathipaon in 1830. Two years later he got into trouble for supplying beer to soldiers who were alleged to have presented forged passes. Mr Bohle was called to account by Captain (by now Colonel) Young for distilling spirits without a licence, and had to close his concern. Undaunted, he was back in 1834, building 'Bohle's Brewery', and became a popular figure in Mussoorie society. His tomb in the Camel's Back cemetery is still one of the most impressive.

Scandal again erupted in the brewery business in 1876, when everyone suddenly started talking of a much improved brew. It came from Vat 42 in Whymer and Company's 'Crown Brewery'. The beer was retasted until the diminishing level of the barrel revealed the perfectly brewed remains of a human! Someone had fallen into the vat and been drowned, and, all unknown to himself, had given the beer-trade a real fillip. The author of *A Mussoorie Miscellany* (H.C. Williams) informs us that 'meat was thereafter recognised as the missing component and scrupulosuly added till more modern, and less cannibalistic, means were discovered to satiate the froth-blower'.

A bold, bad place was Mussoorie in those days, according to the correspondent of the *Statesman,* who, in his paper of 22nd October 1884, wrote 'Ladies and gentlemen, after attending church, proceeded to a drinking shop, a restaurant adjoining the library, and there indulged freely in pegs, not one but many; and at a Fancy Bazaar held this season, a lady stood up on her chair and offered her kisses to gentlemen at ₹5 each. What would they think of such a state of society at home?'

Fifty years later, a Mussoorie lady auctioned a single kiss for ₹300. A vivid illustration of the inflationary process throughout history.

But inspite of such goings-on, or perhaps because of them, the inhabitants were conscious of their spiritual needs, and a number of churches were soon dotted about the hill station, the oldest of them being Christ Church (1836).

When, in March 1905, Her Royal Highness the Princess of Wales (later Queen Mary) visited Mussoorie, she planted a deodar tree outside Christ Church. The plaque commemorating this event can still be seen, now almost embedded in the trunk of the tree.

Some thirty years later, the chaplain of Christ Church was the fair-minded Reverend T.W. Chisolm. In his usual Sunday service prayers, in the year 1933, he sought God's help for veteran Indian leader and freedom-fighter, Pandit Motilal Nehru, a regular visitor to Mussoorie, who was then seriously ill. There was an immediate hullaballoo in all official tea sessions, and the chaplain was reprimanded. This caused him to comment, 'that in these years of our Lord, Holy Orders can be interpreted to mean wholly Government orders.'

It is easy enough to get to Mussoorie today, but how did visitors manage it before the advent of the railway and the motorcar? It was surely a difficult exercise. Mr Shore and Captain Young merely scrambled up the goat tracks to get here; and Lady Eden used her pony to canter along paths and 'up precipices'; but before that, one detrained at Ghaziabad (near Delhi), engaged a bullock-cart or tonga, and then proceeded in the direction of the Himalayas as speedily as only a bullock-cart or tonga could go. After that, one either walked, rode a pony, or was carried uphill in a doolie, a crude sort of palanquin.

By the turn of the century, the 'Sind, Punjab and Delhi Railway' had got as far as Saharanpur, and the bullock-cart had given way to the dak-ghari.

The only way to reach Dehra Dun, en route to Mussoorie, was by the dak-ghari or 'night-mail'.

Dak-ghari ponies were different animals, 'always attempting to turn around and get into carriage with the passengers,' as one disgruntled traveller described them. It was only when the coachman used his whip liberally and reviled the ponies' ancestors as far back as three or four generations that the beasts could be persuaded to move. And once they started, there was no stopping them; it was a gallop all the way to the first stage, where the ponies were changed to the accompaniment of a bugle blown by the coachman in true Dickensian fashion.

The journey through the Siwaliks really began—as it still does—at the Mohand Pass. The ascent starts with a gradual gradient, which increases as the road becomes more steep and winding. The hills are abrupt and perpendicular on the southern side, but slope gently away to the north.

At this stage of the journey, drums were beaten (if it was daytime) and torches were lit (if it was night), because frequently wild elephants resented the approach of the dak-ghari and, trumpeting a challenge, would throw the ponies into panic and confusion and send them racing back to the plains.

The railway reached Dehra Dun in 1901. Till then the main overnight stop was at Rajpur, and the well-known hostelries and forwarding agencies at Rajpur were the 'Ellenborough Hotel', the 'Prince of Wales Hotel', and the 'Agency Retiring Rooms' of Messrs Buckle and Company's 'Bullock Train Agency'. They have long since disappeared. As Dehra Dun grew in importance, Rajpur's importance dwindled, and for many years its long winding bazaar resembled a ghost-town.

Soon the Savoy and Charleville Hotels opened. Massive furniture, grand-pianos, billiard-tables, barrels of cider and crates of champagne had all come up the hill in lumbering bullock-carts. In 1909, the hotels were suddenly ablaze with light, for this was the year when electricity came to Mussoorie. Before that, the ballrooms and dining-rooms had been hung with chandeliers, the rooms lit by candlelight, and the kitchens with spirit-lamps.

It was after World War I in the 'gay twenties' that the Charleville and the Savoy entered the most popular era, when they were to be as well-known as Raffles in Singapore or the Imperial in Tokyo. Wealthy Indian princes and their families and staff occupied entire wings of the Savoy Hotel. The Savoy

Orchestra played every night, and the ballroom was full of couples doing the tango or fox-trot, the latest dancing craze of those days.

After India's Independence in 1947, Mussoorie went through a difficult period. The British had gone, and the wealthy princes and landowners were also finding times difficult. Hotels and boarding-houses began to close down. Then, in the early 1960s, the prosperous Indian middle-classes became hill station conscious, and once again crowds thronged the Mall on summer evenings. These days the foreign tourist is discovering the delights of the lower Himalayas.

Those who wish to move further into the mountains, either on foot or by road, have a wealth of flora and fauna to discover and enjoy. One of the remarkable features of the Himalayas is the abruptness with which they rise from the plains, and this gives them a verdure that is totally different from that of the plains.

None of the common trees of the plains are to be found in the hills. At elevations of 4,000 ft, the long-leaved pine appears. From 5,000 ft there are several kinds of evergreen oak, and above 6,000 ft you find rhododendron, deodar, maple, the hill crypress, and the beautiful horse-chestnut. Still higher up, the silver fir is common; but at 12,000 ft the firs become stunted and dwarfed, and the birch and juniper replace them. At this height raspberries grow wild, amongst yellow colt's-foot dandelion, blue gentian, purple columbine, anemone and edelweiss.

Not every hillside is covered with foliage. Many hills are bare and rugged, too precipitous for cultivation. Sometimes they are masses of quartz, limestone or granite.

Just as the trees of the plains differ from those of the hills, so do the animals and birds. The bear, the goral (a goat-like animal), the marten, the civet-cat, the snow leopard, and the musk-deer, all belong to the Himalayas. The caw of the house-crow is replaced by the deeper note of the corby, and the melodious green hill-pigeon takes the place of the small brown dove.

You do not always see the birds, but you can hear them. As you trek in the interior, or wander along a quiet road in the hill station, the sound of birds is very pleasant to hear; just as the sound of water in the valleys, the singing of the hill people, the smell of the pines, and the blue smoke rising from the villages, are always with you in the Himalayas.

DUST ON THE MOUNTAIN

I

Winter came and went, without so much as a drizzle. The hillside was brown all summer and the fields were bare. The old plough that was dragged over the hard ground by Bisnu's lean oxen made hardly any impression. Still, Bisnu kept his seeds ready for sowing. A good monsoon, and there would be plenty of maize and rice to see the family through the next winter.

Summer went its scorching way, and a few clouds gathered on the south-western horizon.

'The monsoon is coming,' announced Bisnu.

His sister Puja was at the small stream, washing clothes. 'If it doesn't come soon, the stream will dry up,' she said. 'See, it's only a trickle this year. Remember when there were so many different flowers growing here on the banks of the stream? This year there isn't one.'

'The winter was dry. It did not even snow,' said Bisnu. 'I cannot remember another winter when there was no snow,' said his mother. 'The year your father died, there was so much snow the villagers could not light his funeral pyre for hours And now there are fires everywhere.' She pointed to the next mountain, half-hidden by the smoke from a forest fire. At night they sat outside their small house, watching the fire spread. A red line stretched right across the mountain. Thousands of Himalayan trees were perishing in the flames. Oaks, deodars, maples, pines; trees that had taken hundreds of years to grow. And now a fire started carelessly by some campers had been carried up the mountain with the help of the dry grass and strong breeze.

There was no one to put it out. It would take days to die down by itself.

'If the monsoon arrives tomorrow, the fire will go out,' said Bisnu, ever the optimist. He was only twelve, but he was the man in the house; he had to see that there was enough food for the family and for the oxen, for the big black dog and the hens.

There were clouds the next day but they brought only a drizzle. 'It's just the beginning,' said Bisnu as he placed a bucket of muddy water on the steps.

'It usually starts with a heavy downpour,' said his mother. But there were to be no downpours that year. Clouds gathered on the horizon but they were white and puffy and soon disappeared.

True monsoon clouds would have been dark and heavy with moisture. There were other signs—or lack of them— that warned of a long dry summer. The birds were silent, or simply absent. The Himalayan barbet, who usually heralded the approach of the monsoon with strident calls from the top of a spruce tree, hadn't been seen or heard. And the cicadas, who played a deafening overture in the oaks at the first hint of rain, seemed to be missing altogether.

Puja's apricot tree usually gave them a basket full of fruit every summer. This year it produced barely a handful of apricots, lacking juice and flavour. The tree looked ready to die, its leaves curled up in despair. Fortunately there was a store of walnuts, and a binful of wheat grain and another of rice stored from the previous year, so they would not be entirely without food; but it looked as though there would be no fresh fruit or vegetables. And there would be nothing to store away for the following winter.

Money would be needed to buy supplies in Tehri, some thirty miles distant. And there was no money to be earned in the village.

'I will go to Mussoorie and find work,' announced Bisnu. 'But Mussoorie is a two-day journey by bus,' said his mother. 'There is no one there who can help you. And you may not get any work.'

'In Mussoorie there is plenty of work during the summer. Rich people come up from the plains for their holidays. It is full of hotels and shops and places where they can spend their money.'

'But they won't spend any money on you.'

'There is money to be made there. And if not, I will come home. I can walk back over the Nag Tibba mountain. It will take only two and a half days and I will save the bus fare!'

'Don't go, Bhai,' pleaded Puja.

'There will be no one to prepare your food—you will only get sick.'

But Bisnu had made up his mind so he put a few belongings in a cloth shoulder bag, while his mother prised several rupee coins out of a cache in the wall of their living room. Puja prepared a special breakfast of parathas and an egg scrambled with onions, the hen having laid just one for the occasion. Bisnu put some of the parathas in his bag. Then, waving goodbye to his mother and sister, he set off down the road from the village. After walking for a mile, he reached the highway where there was a hamlet with a bus stop. A number of villagers were waiting patiently for a bus. It was an hour late but they were used to that. As long as it arrived safely and got them to their destination, they would be content. They were patient people. And although Bisnu wasn't quite so patient, he too had learnt how to wait—for late buses and late monsoons.

II

Along the valley and over the mountains went the little bus with its load of frail humans. A little misjudgement on the part of the driver, and they would all be dashed to pieces on the rocks far below.

'How tiny we are,' thought Bisnu, looking up at the towering peaks and the immensity of the sky. 'Each of us no more than a raindrop... And I wish we had a few raindrops!'

There were still fires burning to the north but the road went south, where there were no forests anyway, just bare brown hillsides. Down near the river there were small paddy fields but unfortunately rivers ran downhill and not uphill, and there was no inexpensive way in which the water could be brought up the steep slopes to the fields that depended on rainfall.

Bisnu stared out of the bus window at the river running far below. On either bank huge boulders lay exposed, for the level of the water had fallen considerably during the past few months. 'Why are there no trees here?' he asked aloud, and received the attention of a fellow passenger, an old man in the next seat who had been keeping up a relentless dry coughing. Even though it was a warm day, he wore a woollen cap and had an old muffler wrapped about his neck.

'There were trees here once,' he said. 'But the contractors took the deodars for furniture and houses. And the pines were tapped to death for resin. And the oaks were stripped of their leaves to feed the cattle—you can still see a few tree skeletons if you look hard—and the bushes that remained were finished off by the goats!'

'When did all this happen?' asked Bisnu.

'A few years ago. And it's still happening in other areas, although it's forbidden now to cut trees. The only forests that remain are in remote places where there are no roads.' A fit of coughing came over him, but he had found a good listener and was eager to continue. 'The road helps you and me to get about but it also makes it easier for others to do mischief. Rich men from the cities come here and buy up what they want—land, trees, people!'

'What takes you to Mussoorie, Uncle?' asked Bisnu politely. He always addressed elderly people as uncle or aunt. 'I have a cough that won't go away. Perhaps they can do something for it at the hospital in Mussoorie. Doctors don't like coming to villages, you know—there's no money to be made in villages. So we must go to the doctors in the towns. I had a brother who could not be cured in Mussoorie. They told him to go to Delhi. He sold his buffaloes and went to Delhi, but there they told him it was too late to do anything. He died on the way back. I won't go to Delhi. I don't wish to die amongst strangers.'

'You'll get well, Uncle,' said Bisnu.

'Bless you for saying so. And you—what takes you to the big town?'

'Looking for work—we need money at home.'

'It is always the same. There are many like you who must go out in search of work. But don't be led astray. Don't let your friends persuade you to go to Bombay to become a film star! It is better to be hungry in your village than to be hungry on the streets of Bombay. I had a nephew who went to Bombay. The smugglers put him to work selling afeem (opium) and now he is in jail. Keep away from the big cities, boy. Earn your money and go home.'

'I'll do that, Uncle. My mother and sister will expect me to return before the summer season is over.'

The old man nodded vigorously and began coughing again. Presently he dozed off. The interior of the bus smelt of tobacco smoke and petrol fumes and as a result Bisnu had a headache. He kept his face near the open window to get as much fresh air as possible, but the dust kept getting into his mouth and eyes.

Several dusty hours later the bus got into Mussoorie, honking its horn furiously at everything in sight. The passengers, looking dazed, got down and went their different ways. The old man trudged off to the hospital.

Bisnu had to start looking for a job straightaway. He needed a lodging for the night and he could not afford even the cheapest of hotels. So he went from one shop to another, and to all the little restaurants and eating places, asking for work—anything in exchange for a bed, a meal, and a minimum wage. A boy at one of the sweet shops told him there was a job at the Picture Palace, one of the town's three cinemas. The hill station's main road was crowded with people, for the season was just starting. Most of them were tourists who had come up from Delhi and other large towns.

The street lights had come on, and the shops were lighting up, when Bisnu presented himself at the Picture Palace.

III

The man who ran the cinema's tea stall had just sacked the previous helper for his general clumsiness. Whenever he engaged a new boy (which was fairly often) he started him off with the warning: 'I will be keeping a record of all the cups and plates you break, and their cost will be deducted from your salary at the end of the month.'

As Bisnu's salary had been fixed at fifty rupees a month,

he would have to be very careful if he was going to receive any of it.

'In my first month,' said Chittru, one of the three tea stall boys, 'I broke six cups and five saucers, and my pay came to three rupees! Better be careful!'

Bisnu's job was to help prepare the tea and samosas, serve these refreshments to the public during intervals in the film, and later wash up the dishes. In addition to his salary, he was allowed to drink as much tea as he wanted or could hold in his stomach. But the sugar supply was kept to a minimum.

Bisnu went to work immediately and it was not long before he was as well-versed in his duties as the other two tea boys, Chittru and Bali. Chittru was an easy-going, lazy boy who always tried to place the brunt of his work on someone else's shoulders. But he was generous and lent Bisnu five rupees during the first week. Bali, besides being a tea boy, had the enviable job of being the poster boy. As the cinema was closed during the mornings, Bali would be busy either pushing the big poster board around Mussoorie, or sticking posters on convenient walls.

'Posters are very useful,' he claimed. 'They prevent old walls from falling down.'

Chittru had relatives in Mussoorie and slept at their house. But both Bisnu and Bali were on their own and had to sleep at the cinema. After the last show the hall was locked up, so they could not settle down in the expensive seats as they would have liked! They had to sleep on a dirty mattress in the foyer, near the ticket office, where they were often at the mercy of icy Himalayan winds.

Bali made things more comfortable by setting his poster board at an angle to the wall, which gave them a little alcove where they could sleep protected from the wind. As they had only one blanket each, they placed their blankets together and rolled themselves into a tight warm ball.

During shows, when Bisnu took the tea around, there was nearly always someone who would be rude and offensive. Once when he spilt some tea on a college student's shoes, he received a hard kick on the shin. He complained to the tea stall owner, but his employer said, 'The customer is always right. You should have got out of the way in time!'

As he began to get used to this life, Bisnu found himself taking an interest in some of the regular customers.

There was, for instance, the large gentleman with the soup-strainer moustache, who drank his tea from the saucer. As he drank, his lips worked like a suction pump, and the tea, after a brief agitation in the saucer, would disappear in a matter of seconds. Bisnu often wondered if there was something lurking in the forests of that gentleman's upper lip, something that would suddenly spring out and fall upon him! The boys took great pleasure in exchanging anecdotes about the peculiarities of some of the customers.

Bisnu had never seen such bright, painted women before. The girls in his village, including his sister Puja, were good-looking and often sturdy; but they did not use perfumes or make-up like these more prosperous women from the towns of the plains. Wearing expensive clothes and jewellery, they never gave Bisnu more than a brief, bored glance. Other women were more inclined to notice him, favouring him with kind words and a small tip when he took away the cups and plates. He found he could make a few rupees a month in tips; and when he received his first month's pay, he was able to send some of it home.

Chittru accompanied him to the post office and helped him to fill in the money order form. Bisnu had been to the village school, but be wasn't used to forms and official paperwork. Chittru, a town boy, knew all about them, even though he could just about read and write.

Walking back to the cinema, Chittru said, 'We can make more money at the limestone quarries.'

'All right, let's try them,' said Bisnu.

'Not now,' said Chittru, who enjoyed the busy season in the hill station. 'After the season—after the monsoon.'

But there was still no monsoon to speak of, just an occasional drizzle which did little to clear the air of the dust that blew up from the plains. Bisnu wondered how his mother and sister were faring at home. A wave of homesickness swept over him. The hill station, with all its glitter, was just a pretty gift box with nothing inside.

One day in the cinema Bisnu saw the old man who had been with him on the bus. He greeted him like a long lost friend. At first the old man did not recognize the boy, but when Bisnu asked him if he had recovered from his illness, the old man remembered and said, 'So you are still in Mussoorie, boy. That is good. I thought you might have gone down to Delhi to make more money.' He added that he was a little better and that he was undergoing a course of treatment at the hospital. Bisnu brought him a cup of tea and refused to take any money for it; it could be included in his own quota of free tea. When the show was over, the old man went his way and Bisnu did not see him again.

In September the town began to get empty. The taps were running dry or giving out just a trickle of muddy water. A thick mist lay over the mountain for days on end, but there was no rain. When the mists cleared, an autumn wind came whispering through the deodars.

At the end of the month the manager of the Picture Palace gave everyone a week's notice, a week's pay, and announced that the cinema would be closing for the winter.

IV

Bali said, 'I'm going to Delhi to find work. I'll come back next summer. What about you, Bisnu, why don't you come with me? It's easier to find work in Delhi.'

'I'm staying with Chittru,' said Bisnu.

'We may work at the quarries.'

'I like the big towns,' said Bali. 'I like shops and people and lots of noise. I will never go back to my village. There is no money there, no fun.'

Bali made a bundle of his things and set out for the bus stand. Bisnu bought himself a pair of cheap shoes, for his old ones had fallen to pieces. With what was left of his money, he sent another money order home. Then he and Chittru set out for the limestone quarries, an eight-mile walk from Mussoorie.

They knew they were nearing the quarries when they saw clouds of limestone dust hanging in the air. The dust hid the next mountain from view. When they did see the mountain, they found that the top of it was missing—blasted away by dynamite to enable the quarries to get at the rich strata of limestone rock below the surface.

The skeletons of a few trees remained on the lower slopes. Almost everything else had gone—grass, flowers, shrubs, birds, butterflies, grasshoppers, ladybirds. A rock lizard popped its head out of a crevice to look at the intruders. Then, like some prehistoric survivor, it scuttled back into its underground shelter. 'I used to come here when I was small,' announced Chittru cheerfully.

'Were the quarries here then?'

'Oh, no. My friends and I—we used to come for the strawberries. They grew all over this mountain. Wild strawberries, but very tasty.'

'Where are they now?' asked Bisnu, looking around at the devastated hillside.

'All gone,' said Chittru. 'Maybe there are some on the next mountain.'

Even as they approached the quarries, a blast shook the hillside. Chittru pulled Bisnu under an overhanging rock to avoid the shower of stones that pelted down on the road. As the dust enveloped them, Bisnu had a fit of coughing. When the air cleared a little, they saw the limestone dump ahead of them.

Chittru, who was older and bigger than Bisnu, was immediately taken on as a labourer; but the quarry foreman took one look at Bisnu and said, 'You're too small. You won't be able to break stones or lift those heavy rocks and load them into the trucks. Be off, boy. Find something else to do.'

He was offered a job in the labourers' canteen, but he'd had enough of making tea and washing dishes. He was about to turn round and walk back to Mussoorie when he felt a heavy hand descend on his shoulder. He looked up to find a grey-bearded, turbanned Sikh looking down at him in some amusement.

'I need a cleaner for my truck,' he said. 'The work is easy, but the hours are long!'

Bisnu responded immediately to the man's gruff but jovial manner.

'What will you pay?' he asked.

'Fifteen rupees a day, and you'll get food and a bed at the depot.'

'As long as I don't have to cook the food,' said Bisnu. The truck driver laughed. 'You might prefer to do so, once you've tasted the depot food. Are you coming on my truck? Make up your mind.'

'I'm your man,' said Bisnu; and waving goodbye to Chittru, he followed the Sikh to his truck.

V

A horn blared, shattering the silence of the mountains, and the truck came round a bend in the road. A herd of goats scattered to left and right.

The goatherds cursed as a cloud of dust enveloped them, and then the truck had left them behind and was rattling along the bumpy, unmetalled road to the quarries.

At the wheel of the truck, stroking his grey moustache with one hand, sat Pritam Singh. It was his own truck. He had never allowed anyone else to drive it. Every day he made two trips to the quarries, carrying truckloads of limestone back to the depot at the bottom of the hill. He was paid by the trip and he was always anxious to get in two trips every day. Sitting beside him was Bisnu, his new cleaner. In less than a month Bisnu had become an experienced hand at looking after trucks, riding in them, and even sleeping in them. He got on well with Pritam, the grizzled, fifty-year-old Sikh, who boasted of two well-off sons—one a farmer in Punjab, the other a wine merchant in far-off London. He could have gone to live with either of them, but his sturdy independence kept him on the road in his battered old truck.

Pritam pressed hard on his horn. Now there was no one on the road—neither beast nor man—but Pritam was fond of the sound of his horn and liked blowing it. He boasted that it was the loudest horn in northern India. Although it struck terror into the hearts of all who heard it—for it was louder than the trumpeting of an elephant—it was music to Pritam's ears.

Pritam treated Bisnu as an equal and a friendly banter had grown between them during their many trips together.

'One more year on this bone-breaking road,' said Pritam, 'and then I'll sell my truck and retire.'

'But who will buy such a shaky old truck?' asked Bisnu. 'It

will retire before you do!'

'Now don't be insulting, boy. She's only twenty years old—there are still a few years left in her!' And as though to prove it he blew the horn again. Its strident sound echoed and re-echoed down the mountain gorge. A pair of wildfowl burst from the bushes and fled to more silent regions.

Pritam's thoughts went to his dinner. 'Haven't had a good meal for days.'

'Haven't had a good meal for weeks,' said Bisnu, although in fact he looked much healthier than when he had worked at the cinema's tea stall.

'Tonight I'll give you a dinner in a good hotel. Tandoori chicken and rice pilaf.'

He sounded his horn again as though to put a seal on his promise. Then he slowed down, because the road had become narrow and precipitous, and trotting ahead of them was a train of mules.

As the horn blared, one mule ran forward, another ran backward. One went uphill, another went downhill. Soon there were mules all over the place. Pritam cursed the mules and the mule drivers cursed Pritam; but he had soon left them far behind.

Along this range, all the hills were bare and dry. Most of the forest had long since disappeared.

'Are your hills as bare as these?' asked Pritam. 'No, we still have some trees,' said Bisnu. 'Nobody has started blasting the hills as yet. In front of our house there is a walnut tree which gives us two baskets of walnuts every year. And there is an apricot tree. But it was a bad year for fruit. There was no rain. And the stream is too far away.'

'It will rain soon,' said Pritam. 'I can smell rain. It is coming from the north. The winter will be early.'

'It will settle the dust.'

Dust was everywhere. The truck was full of it. The leaves of the shrubs and the few trees were thick with it. Bisnu could feel the dust under his eyelids and in his mouth. And as they approached the quarries, the dust increased. But it was a different kind of dust now—whiter, stinging the eyes, irritating the nostrils.

They had been blasting all morning.

'Let's wait here,' said Pritam, bringing the truck to a halt. They sat in silence, staring through the windscreen at the scarred cliffs a little distance down the road. There was a sharp crack of explosives and the hillside blossomed outwards. Earth and rocks hurtled down the mountain.

Bisnu watched in awe as shrubs and small trees were flung into the air. It always frightened him—not so much the sight of—the rocks bursting asunder, as the trees being flung aside and destroyed. He thought of the trees at home—the walnut, the chestnuts, the pines—and wondered if one day they would suffer the same fate, and whether the mountains would all become a desert like this particular range. No trees, no grass, no water—only the choking dust of mines and quarries.

VI

Pritam pressed hard on his horn again, to let the people at the site know that he was approaching. He parked outside a small shed where the contractor and the foreman were sipping cups of tea. A short distance away, some labourers, Chittru among then, were hammering at chunks of rock, breaking them up into manageable pieces. A pile of stones stood ready for loading; while the rock that had just been blasted lay scattered about the hillside.

'Come and have a cup of tea,' called out the contractor. 'I can't hang about all day,' said Pritam. 'There's another trip to make—and the days are getting shorter. I don't want to be driving by night.'

But he sat down on a bench and ordered two cups of tea from the stall. The foreman strolled over to the group of labourers and told them to start loading. Bisnu let down the grid at the back of the truck. Then, to keep himself warm, he began helping Chittru and the men with the loading.

'Don't expect to be paid for helping,' said Sharma, the contractor, for whom every rupee spent was a rupee off his profits.

'Don't worry,' said Bisnu. 'I don't work for contractors, I work for friends.'

'That's right,' called out Pritam.

'Mind what you say to Bisnu—he's no one's servant!'

Sharma wasn't happy until there was no space left for a single stone. Then Bisnu had his cup of tea and three of the men climbed on the pile of stones in the open truck.

'All right, let's go!' said Pritam. 'I want to finish early today Bisnu and I are having a big dinner!'

Bisnu jumped in beside Pritam, banging the door shut. It never closed properly unless it was slammed really hard. But it opened at a touch.

'This truck is held together with sticking plaster,' joked Pritam.

He was in good spirits. He started the engine, and blew his horn just as he passed the foreman and the contractor.

'They are deaf in one ear from the blasting,' said Pritam. 'I'll make them deaf in the other ear!'

The labourers were singing as the truck swung round the sharp bends of the winding road. The door beside Bisnu rattled on its hinges. He was feeling quite dizzy.

'Not too fast,' he said.

'Oh,' said Pritam. 'About my driving?'

'It's just today,' said Bisnu uneasily.

'You're getting old,' said Pritam. 'And since when did you become nervous?'

'It's a feeling, that's all.'

'That's your trouble.'

'I suppose so,' said Bisnu.

Pritam was feeling young, exhilarated. He drove faster. As they swung round a bend, Bisnu looked out of his window.

All he saw was the sky above and the valley below. They were very near the edge; but it was usually like that on this narrow mountain road.

After a few more hairpin bends, the road descended steeply to the valley. Just then a stray mule ran into the middle of the road. Pritam swung the steering wheel over to the right to avoid the mule, but here the road turned sharply to the left. The truck went over the edge.

As it tipped over, hanging for a few seconds on the edge of the cliff, the labourers leapt from the back of the truck. It pitched forward, and as it struck a rock outcrop, the loose door burst open. Bisnu was thrown out.

The truck hurtled forward, bouncing over the rocks, turning over on its side and rolling over twice before coming to rest against the trunk of a scraggly old oak tree. But for the tree, the truck would have plunged several hundred feet down to the bottom of the gorge.

Two of the labourers sat on the hillside, stunned and badly shaken. The third man had picked himself up and was running back to the quarry for help.

Bisnu had landed in a bed of nettles. He was smarting all over, but he wasn't really hurt; the nettles had broken his fall. His first impulse was to get up and run back to the road. Then he realized that Pritam was still in the truck.

Bisnu skidded down the steep slope, calling out, 'Pritam Uncle, are you all right?'

There was no answer.

VII

When Bisnu saw Pritam's arm and half his body jutting out of the open door of the truck, he feared the worst. It was a strange position, half in and half out. Bisnu was about to turn away and climb back up the hill, when he noticed that Pritam had opened a bloodied and swollen eye. It looked straight up at Bisnu.

'Are you alive?' whispered Bisnu, terrified.

'What do you think?' muttered Pritam. He closed his eye again. When the contractor and his men arrived, it took them almost an hour to get Pritam Singh out of the wreckage of the truck, and another hour to get him to the hospital in the next big town. He had broken bones, fractured ribs and a dislocated shoulder. But the doctors said he was repairable—which was more than could be said for the truck.

'So the truck's finished,' said Pritam, between groans when Bisnu came to see him after a couple of days. 'Now I'll have to go home and live with my son. And what about you, boy? I can get you a job on a friend's truck.'

'No,' said Bisnu, 'I'll be going home soon.'

'And what will you do at home?'

'I'll work on my land. It's better to grow things on the land, than to blast things out of it.'

They were silent for some time.

'There is something to be said for growing things,' said Pritam. 'But for that tree, the truck would have finished up at the foot of the mountain, and I wouldn't he here, all bandaged up and talking to you. It was the tree that saved me. Remember that, boy.'

'I'll remember, and I won't forget the dinner you promised me, either.'

It snowed during Bisnu's last night at the quarries. He slept on the floor with Chittru, in a large shed meant for the labourers. The wind blew the snowflakes in at the entrance; it whistled down the deserted mountain pass. In the morning Bisnu opened his eyes to a world of dazzling whiteness. The snow was piled high against the walls of the shed, and they had some difficulty getting out. Bisnu joined Chittru at the tea stall, drank a glass of hot sweet tea, and ate two stale buns. He said goodbye to Chittru and set out on the long march home. The road would be closed to traffic because of the heavy snow, and he would have to walk all the way.

He trudged over the hills all day, stopping only at small villages to take refreshment. By nightfall he was still ten miles from home.

But he had fallen in with other travellers, and with them he took shelter at a small inn. They built a fire and crowded round it, and each man spoke of his home and fields and all were of the opinion that the snow and rain had come just in time to save the winter crops. Someone sang, and another told a ghost story. Feeling at home already, Bisnu fell asleep listening to their tales. In the morning they parted and went their different ways. It was almost noon when Bisnu reached his village. The fields were covered with snow and the mountain stream was in spate. As he climbed the terraced fields to his house, he heard the sound of barking, and his mother's big black mastiff came bounding towards him over the snow. The dog jumped on him and licked his arms and then went bounding back to the house to tell the others.

Puja saw him from the courtyard and ran indoors shouting, 'Bisnu has come, my brother has come!'

His mother ran out of the house, calling, 'Bisnu, Bisnu!'

Bisnu came walking through the fields, and he did not hurry, he did not run; he wanted to savour the moment of his return, with his mother and sister smiling, waiting for him in front of the house.

There was no need to hurry now. He would be with them for a long time, and the manager of the Picture Palace would have to find someone else for the summer season... It was his home, and these were his fields! Even the snow was his. When the snow melted he would clear the fields, and nourish them, and make them rich.

He felt very big and very strong as he came striding over the land he loved.

A WALK THROUGH GARHWAL

I wake to what sounds like the din of a factory buzzer, but is in fact the music of a single vociferous cicada in the lime tree near my window.

Through the open window, I focus on a pattern of small, glossy lime leaves; then through them I see the mountains, the Himalayas, striding away into an immensity of sky.

'In a thousand ages of the gods I could not tell thee of the glories of Himachal.' So confessed a Sanskrit poet at the dawn of Indian history and he came closer than anyone else to capturing the spell of the Himalayas. The sea has had Conrad and Stevenson and Masefield, but the mountains continue to defy the written word. We have climbed their highest peaks and crossed their most difficult passes, but still they keep their secrets and their reserve; they remain remote, mysterious, spirit-haunted.

No wonder then, that the people who live on the mountain slopes in the mist-filled valleys of Garhwal, have long since learned humility, patience and a quiet resignation. Deep in the crouching mist lie their villages, while climbing the mountain slopes are forests of rhododendron, spruce and deodar, soughing in the wind from the ice-bound passes. Pale women plough, they laugh at the thunder as their men go down to the plains for work; for little grows on the beautiful mountains in the north wind.

When I think of Manjari village in Garhwal I see a small river, a tributary of the Ganga, rushing along the bottom of a steep, rocky valley. On the banks of the river and on the terraced hills above, there are small fields of corn, barley, mustard, potatoes and onions. A few fruit trees grow near the village. Some hillsides are rugged and bare, just masses of quartz or granite. On hills exposed to wind, only grass and small shrubs are able to obtain a foothold.

This landscape is typical of Garhwal, one of India's most northerly regions with its massive snow ranges bordering on Tibet. Although thinly populated, it does not provide much of a living for its people. Most Garhwali cultivators are poor, some are very poor. 'You have beautiful scenery,' I observed after crossing the first range of hills.

'Yes,' said my friend, 'but we cannot eat the scenery.'

And yet these are cheerful people, sturdy and with wonderful powers of endurance. Somehow they manage to wrest a precarious living from the unhelpful, calcinated soil. I am their guest for a few days.

My friend Gajadhar has brought me to his home, to his village above the little Nayar river. We took a train into the foothills and then we took a bus and finally, made dizzy by the hairpin bends devised in the last century by a brilliantly diabolical road-engineer, we alighted at the small hill station of Lansdowne, chief recruiting centre for the Garhwal Regiment.

Lansdowne is just over six thousand feet high. From there we walked, covering twenty-five miles between sunrise and sunset, until we came to Manjari village, clinging to the terraced slopes of a very proud, very permanent mountain.

And this is my fourth morning in the village.

Other mornings I was woken by the throaty chuckles of the red-billed blue magpies, as they glided between oak trees and medlars; but today the cicada has drowned all bird song. It is a little out of season for cicadas but perhaps this sudden warm spell in late September has deceived him into thinking it is mating season again.

Early though it is, I am the last to get up. Gajadhar is exercising in the courtyard, going through an odd combination of Swedish exercises and yoga. He has a fine physique with the sturdy legs that most Garhwalis possess. I am sure he will realize his ambition of joining the Indian Army as a cadet. His younger brother Chakradhar, who is slim and fair with high cheek-bones, is milking the family's buffalo. Normally, he would be on his long walk to school, five miles distant; but this is a holiday, so he can stay at home and help with the household chores.

His mother is lighting a fire. She is a handsome woman even though her ears, weighed down by heavy silver earrings have lost their natural shape. Garhwali women usually invest their savings in silver ornaments. And at the time of marriage it is the boy's parents who make a gift of land to the parents of an attractive girl; a dowry system in reverse. There are fewer women than men in the hills and their good looks and sturdy physique give them considerable status among the men-folk.

Chakradhar's father is a corporal in the Indian Army and is away for most of the year.

When Gajadhar marries, his wife will stay in the village to help his mother and younger brother look after the fields, house, goats and buffalo. Gajadhar will see her only when he comes home on leave. He prefers it that way; he does not think a simple hill girl should be exposed to the sophisticated temptations of the plains.

The village is far above the river and most of the fields depend on rainfall. But water must be fetched for cooking, washing and drinking. And so, after a breakfast of hot sweet milk and thick chapattis stuffed with minced radish, the brothers and I set off down the rough track to the river.

The still has climbed the mountains but it has yet to reach the narrow valley. We bathe in the river, Gjadhar and Chakradhar dive off a massive rock; but I wade in circumspectly, unfamiliar with the river's depths and currents. The water, a milky blue has come from the melting snows; it is very cold. I bathe quickly and then dash for a strip of sand where a little sunshine has split down the mountainside in warm, golden pools of light. At the same time the song of the whistling-thrush emerges like a dark secret from the wooded shadows. A little later, buckets filled we toil up the steep mountain. We must go by a better path this time if we are not to come tumbling down with our buckets of water. As we climb we are mocked by it barbet which sits high up in a spruce calling feverishly in its monotonous mournful way.

'We call it the mewli bird,' says Gajadhar, 'there is a story about it. People say that the souls of men who have suffered injuries in the law courts of the plains and who have died of their disappointments, transmigrate into the mewli birds. That is why the birds are always crying *un, raee-oru, un nee ow,* which means "injustice, injustice!"'

The path leads us past a primary school, a small temple, and a single shop in which it is possible to buy salt, soap and a few other necessities. It is also the post office. And today it is serving as a lock-up.

The villagers have apprehended a local thief, who specializes in stealing jewellery from women while they are working in the fields. He is awaiting escort to the Lansdowne police station, and the shop-keeper-cum-postmaster-cum-constable brings him out for us to inspect. He is a mild-looking fellow, clearly shy of the small crowd that has gathered round him. I wonder how he manages to deprive the strong hill-women of their jewellery; it could not be by force! Any cases of crimes and violence are rare in Garhwal; and robbery too, is uncommon for the simple reason that there is very little to rob.

The thief is rather glad of my presence, as it distracts attention from him. Strangers seldom come to Manjari. The crowd leaves him, turns to me, eager to catch a glimpse of the stranger in its midst. The children exclaim, point at me with delight, chatter among themselves. I might be a visitor from another planet instead of just an itinerant writer from the plains.

The postman has yet to arrive. The mail is brought in relays from Lansdowne. The Manjari postman who has to cover eight miles and delivers letters at several small villages on his route, should arrive around noon. He also serves as a newspaper, bringing the villagers news of the outside world. Over the years he has acquired a reputation for being highly inventive, sometimes creating his own news; so much so that when he told the villagers that men had landed on the moon, no one believed him. There are still a few sceptics.

Gajadhar has been walking out of the village every day, anxious to meet the postman. He is expecting a letter giving the results of his army entrance examination. If he is successful he will be called for an interview. And then, if he is accepted, he will be trained as an officer-cadet. After two years he will become a second lieutenant. His father, after twelve years in the army is still only a corporal. But his father never went to school. There were no schools in the hills during his father's youth.

The Manjari school is only up to class five and it has about forty pupils. If these children (most of them boys) want to study any further, then, like Chakradhar, they must walk the five miles to the high school at the next big village.

'Don't you get tired walking ten miles every day?' I ask Chakradhar.

'I am used to it,' he says. 'I like walking.'

I know that he only has two meals a day—one at seven in the morning when he leaves home and the other at six or seven in the evening when he returns from school—and I ask him if he does not get hungry on the way.

'There is always the wild fruit,' he replies.

It appears that he is an expert on wild fruit: the purple berries of the thorny bilberry bushes ripening in May and June; wild strawberries like drops of blood on the dark green monsoon grass; small sour cherries and tough medlars in the winter months. Chakradhar's strong teeth and probing tongue extract whatever tang or sweetness lies hidden in them. And in March there are the rhododendron flowers. His mother makes them into jam. But Chakradhar likes them as they are: he places the petals on his tongue and chews till the sweet juice trickles down his throat.

He has never been ill.

'But what happens when someone is ill?' I ask knowing that in Manjari there are no medicines, no dispensary or hospital.

'He goes to bed until he is better,' says Gajadhar. 'We have a few home remedies. But if someone is very sick, we carry the person to the hospital at Lansdowne.' He pauses as though wondering how much he should say, then shrugs and says: 'Last year my uncle was very ill. He had a terrible pain in his stomach. For two days he cried out with the pain. So we made a litter and started out for Lansdowne. We had already carried him fifteen miles when he died. And then we had to carry him back again.'

Some of the villages have dispensaries managed by compounders but the remoter areas of Garhwal are completely without medical aid. To the outsider, life in the Garhwal hills may seem idyllic and the people simple. But the Garhwali is far from being simple and his life is one long struggle, especially if he happens to be living in a high altitude village snowbound for four months in the year, with cultivation coming to a standstill and people having to manage with the food gathered and stored during the summer months.

Fortunately, the clear mountain air and the simple diet keep the Garhwalis free from most diseases, and help them recover from the more common ailments. The greatest dangers come from unexpected disasters, such as an accident with an axe or scythe, or an attack by a wild animal. A few years back, several Manjari children and old women were killed by a maneating leopard. The leopard was finally killed by the villagers who hunted it down with spears and axes. But the leopard that sometimes prowls round the village at night looking for a stray dog or goat, slinks away at the approach of a human.

I do not see the leopard but at night I am woken by a rumbling and thumping on the roof. I wake Gajadhar and ask him what is happening.

'It is only a bear,' he says.

'Is it trying to get in?'

'No, it's been in the cornfield and now it's after the pumpkins on the roof.'

A little later, when we look out of the small window, we see a black bear making off like a thief in the night, a large pumpkin held securely to his chest.

At the approach of winter when snow covers the higher mountains, the brown and black Himalayan bears descend to lower altitudes in search of food. Because they are short-sighted and suspicious of anything that moves, they can be dangerous; but, like most wild animals, they will avoid men if they can and are aggressive only when accompanied by their cubs.

Gajadhar advises me to run downhill if chased by a bear. He says that bears find it easier to run uphill than downhill.

I am not interested in being chased by a bear, but the following night Gajadhar and I stay up to try and prevent the bear from depleting his cornfield. We take up our position on a highway promontory of rock, which gives us a clear view of the moonlit field.

A little after midnight, the bear comes down to the edge of the field but he is suspicious and has probably smelt us. He is, however, hungry; and so, after standing up as high as possible on his hind legs and peering about to see if the field is empty, he comes cautiously out of the forest and makes his way towards the corn.

When about half-way, his attention is suddenly attracted by some Buddhist prayer-flags which have been strung up recently between two small trees by a band of wandering Tibetans. On spotting the flags the bear gives a little grunt of disapproval and begins to move back into the forest; but the fluttering of the little flags is a puzzle that he feels he must make out (for a bear is one of the most inquisitive animals); so after a few backward steps, he again stops and watches them.

Not satisfied with this, he stands on his hind legs looking at the flags, first at one side and then at the other. Then seeing that they do not attack him and so not appear dangerous, he makes his way right up to the flags taking only two or three steps at a time and having a good look before each advance. Eventually, he moves confidently up to the flags and pulls them all down. Then, after careful examination of the flags, he moves into the field of corn.

But Gajadhar has decided that he is not going to lose any more corn, so he starts shouting, and the rest of the village wakes up and people come out of their houses beating drums and empty kerosene tins.

Deprived of his dinner, the bear makes off in a bad temper. He runs downhill and at a good speed too; and I am glad that I am not in his path just then. Uphill or downhill, an angry bear is best given a very wide berth.

For Gajadhar, impatient to know the result of his array entrance examination, the following day is a trial of his patience.

First, we hear that there has been a landslide and that the postman cannot reach us. Then, we hear that although there has been a landslide, the postman has already passed the spot in safety. Another alarming rumour has it that the postman disappeared with the landslide. This is soon denied. The postman is safe. It was only the mail-bag that disappeared.

And then, at two in the afternoon, the postman turns up. He tells us that there was indeed a landslide but that it took place on someone else's route. Apparently, a mischievous urchin who passed him on the way was responsible for all the rumours. But we suspect the postman of having something to do with them...

Gajadhar had passed his examination and will leave with me in the morning. We have to be up early in order to reach Lansdowne before dark. But Gajadhar's mother insists on celebrating her son's success by feasting with her friends and neighbours. There is a partridge (a present from a neighbour who had decided that Gajadhar will make a fine husband for his daughter), and two chickens: rich fare for folk whose normal diet consists mostly of lentils, potatoes and onions.

After dinner, there are songs, and Gajadhar's mother sings of the homesickness of those who are separated from their loved ones and their home in the hills. It is an old Garhwali folk-song:

Oh, mountain-swift, you are from my father's home;

Speak, oh speak, in the courtyard of my parents,
My mother will hear you; She will send my brother to fetch me.
A grain of rice alone in the cooking pot
Cries, 'I wish I could get out!'
Likewise I wonder:
'Will I ever reach my father's house?'

The hookah is passed round and stories are told. Tales of ghosts and demons mingle with legends of ancient kings and heroes. It is almost midnight by the time the last guest has gone. Chakradhar approaches me as I am about to retire for the night.

'Will you come again?' he asks.

'Yes, I'll come again,' I reply. 'If not next year, then the year after. How many years are left before you finish school?'

'Four'.

'Four years. If you walk ten miles a day for four years, how many miles will that make?'

'Four thousand and six hundred miles,' says Chakradhar after a moment's thought, 'but we have two months' holiday each year. That means I'll walk about twelve thousand miles in four years.'

The moon has not yet risen. Lanterns swing in the dark.

The lanterns flit silently over the hillside and go out one by one. This Garhwali day, which is just like any other day in the hills, slips quietly into the silence of the mountains.

I stretch myself out on my cot. Outside the small window the sky is brilliant with stars. As I close my eyes, someone brushes against the lime tree, brushing its leaves; and the fresh fragrance of lines comes to me on the night air, making the moment memorable for all time.

BUS STOP, PIPALNAGAR

I

My balcony was my window on the world.
The room itself had only one window, a square hole in the wall crossed by two iron bars. The view from it was rather restricted. If I craned my neck sideways, and put my nose to the bars, I could see the end of the building. Below was a narrow courtyard where children played. Across the courtyard, on a level with my room, were three separate windows belonging to three separate rooms, each window barred in the same way, with iron bars. During the day it was difficult to see into these rooms. The harsh, cruel sunlight filled the courtyard, making the windows patches of darkness.

My room was very small. I had paced about in it so often that I knew its exact measurements. My foot, from heel to toe, was eleven inches long. That made my room just over fifteen feet in length; for, when I measured the last foot, my toes turned up against the wall. It wasn't more than eight-feet broad, which meant that two people was the most it could comfortably accommodate. I was the only tenant but at times I had put up at least three friends—two on the floor, two on the bed. The plaster had been peeling off the walls and in addition the greasy stains and patches were difficult to hide, though I covered the worst ones with pictures cut out from magazines—Waheeda Rehman, the Indian actress, successfully blotted out one big patch and a recent Mr Universe displayed his muscles from the opposite wall. The biggest stain was all but concealed by a calendar that showed Ganesh, the elephant-headed god, whose blessings were vital to all good beginnings.

My belongings were few. A shelf on the wall supported an untidy pile of paperbacks, and a small table in one corner of the room supported the solid weight of my rejected manuscripts and an ancient typewriter which I had obtained on hire.

I was eighteen years old and a writer.

Such a combination would be disastrous enough anywhere, but in India it was doubly so; for there were not many papers to write for and payments were small. In addition, I was very inexperienced and though what I wrote came from the heart, only a fraction touched the hearts of editors. Nevertheless, I persevered and was able to earn about a hundred rupees a month, barely enough to keep body, soul and typewriter together. There wasn't much else I could do. Without that passport to a job—a university degree—I had no alternative but to accept the classification of 'self-employed'—which was impressive as it included doctors, lawyers, property dealers, and grain merchants, most of whom earned well over a thousand rupees a month.

'Haven't you realized that India is bursting with young people trying to pass exams?' asked a journalist friend. 'It's a desperate matter, this race for academic qualifications. Everyone wants to pass his exam the easy way, without reading too many books or attending more than half a dozen lectures. That's where a smart fellow like you comes in! Why would students wade through five volumes of political history when they can buy a few model-answer papers at any bookstall? They are helpful, these guess-papers. You can write them quickly and flood the market. They'll sell like hot cakes!'

'Who eats hot cakes here?'

'Well, then, hot chapattis.'

'I'll think about it,' I said; but the idea repelled me. If I was going to misguide students, I would rather do it by writing second-rate detective stories than by providing them with readymade answer papers. Besides, I thought it would bore me.

II

The string of the cot needed tightening. The dip in the middle of the bed was so bad that I woke up in the morning with a stiff back. But I was hopeless at tightening bed-strings and would have to wait until one of the boys from the tea shop paid me a visit. I was too tall for the cot, anyway, and if my feet didn't stick out at one end, my head lolled over the other.

Under the cot was my tin trunk. Apart from my clothes, it contained notebooks, diaries, photographs, scrapbooks, and other odds and ends that form a part of a writer's existence.

I did not live entirely alone. During cold or rainy weather, the boys from the tea shop, who normally slept on the pavement, crowded into the room. Apart from them, there were lizards on the walls and ceilings—friends these—and a large rat—definitely an enemy—who got in and out of the window and who sometimes carried away manuscripts and clothing.

June nights were the most uncomfortable. Mosquitoes emerged from all the ditches, gullies and ponds, to swarm over Pipalnagar. Bugs, finding it uncomfortable inside the woodwork of the cot, scrambled out at night and found their way under the sheet. The lizards wandered listlessly over the walls, impatient for the monsoon rains, when they would be able to feast off thousands of insects.

Everyone in Pipalnagar was waiting for the cool, quenching relief of the monsoon.

III

I woke every morning at five as soon as the first bus moved out of the shed, situated only twenty or thirty yards down the road. I dressed, went down to the tea shop for a glass of hot tea and some buttered toast, and then visited Deep Chand the barber, in his shop.

At eighteen, I shaved about three times a week. Sometimes I shaved myself. But often, when I felt lazy, Deep Chand shaved me, at the special concessional rate of two annas.

'Give my head a good massage, Deep Chand,' I said. 'My brain is not functioning these days. In my latest story there are three murders, but it is boring just the same.'

'You must write a good book,' said Deep Chand beginning the ritual of the head massage, his fingers squeezing my temples and tugging at my hair-roots. 'Then you can make some money and clear out of Pipalnagar. Delhi is the place to go! Why, I know a man who arrived in Delhi in 1947 with nothing but the clothes he wore and a few rupees. He began by selling thirsty travellers glasses of cold water at the railway station, then he opened a small tea shop; now he has two big restaurants and lives in a house as large as the Prime Minister's!'

Nobody intended to live in Pipalnagar forever. Delhi was the city most aspired to but as it was 200 miles away, few could afford to travel there.

Deep Chand would have shifted his trade to another town if he had had the capital. In Pipalnagar his main customers were small shopkeepers, factory workers and labourers from the railway station. 'Here I can charge only six annas for a haircut,' he lamented. 'In Delhi I could charge a rupee.'

IV

I was walking in the wheat fields beyond the railway tracks when I noticed a boy lying across the footpath, his head and shoulders hidden by wheat plants. I walked faster, and when I came near I saw that the boy's legs were twitching. He seemed to be having some kind of fit. The boy's face was white, his legs kept moving and his hands fluttered restlessly among the wheat stalks.

'What's the matter?' I said, kneeling down beside him but he was still unconscious.

I ran down the path to a Persian well, and dipping the end of my shirt in a shallow trough of water, soaked it well before returning to the boy. As I sponged his face the twitching ceased, and though he still breathed heavily, his face was calm and his hands still. He opened his eyes and stared at me, but he didn't really see me.

'You have bitten your tongue,' I said wiping a little blood from the corner of his mouth. 'Don't worry. I'll stay here with you until you are all right.'

The boy raised himself and, resting his chin on his knees he passed his arms around his drawn-up legs.

'I'm all right now,' he said.

'What happened?' I asked sitting, down beside him.

'Oh, it is nothing, it often happens. I don't know why. I cannot control it.'

'Have you been to a doctor?'

'Yes, when the fits first started, I went to the hospital. They gave me some pills that I had to take every day. But the pills made me so tired and sleepy that I couldn't work properly. So I stopped taking them. Now this happens once or twice a week. What does it matter? I'm all right when it's over and I do not feel anything when it happens.'

He got to his feet, dusting his clothes and smiling at me. He was a slim boy, long-limbed and bony. There was a little fluff on his cheeks and the promise of a moustache. He told me his name was Suraj, that he went to a night school in the city, and that he hoped to finish his high school exams in a few months' time. He was studying hard, he said, and if he passed he hoped to get a scholarship to a good college. If he failed, there was only the prospect of continuing in Pipalnagar.

I noticed a small tray of merchandise lying on the ground. It contained combs and buttons and little bottles of perfume. The tray was made to hang at Suraj's waist, supported by straps that went around his shoulders. All day he walked about Pipalnagar, sometimes covering ten or fifteen miles, selling odds and ends to people at their houses. He averaged about two rupees a day, which was enough for his food and other necessities; he managed to save about ten rupees a month for his school fees. He ate irregularly at little tea shops, at the stall near the bus stop, under the shady jamun and mango trees. When the jamun fruit was ripe, he would sit on a tree, sucking the sour fruit until his lips were stained purple. There was a small, nagging fear that he might get a fit while sitting on the tree and fall off, but the temptation to eat jamun was greater than his fear.

All this he told me while we walked through the fields towards the bazaar.

'Where do you live?' I asked. 'I'll walk home with you.'

'I don't live anywhere,' said Suraj. 'My home is not in Pipalnagar. Sometimes I sleep at the temple or at the railway station. In the summer months I sleep on the grass of the municipal park.'

'Well, wherever it is you stay, let me come with you.'

We walked together into the town, and parted near the bus stop. I returned to my room, and tried to do some writing while Suraj went into the bazaar to try selling his wares. We had agreed to meet each other again. I realized that Suraj was an epileptic, but there was nothing unusual about him being an orphan and a refugee. I liked his positive attitude to life. Most people in Pipalnagar were resigned to their circumstances, but he was ambitious. I also liked his gentleness, his quiet voice, and the smile that flickered across his face regardless of whether he was sad or happy.

V

The temperature had touched forty-three degrees Celsius, and the small streets of Pipalnagar were empty. To walk barefoot on the scorching pavements was possible only for labourers, whose feet had developed several hard layers of protective skin; and now even these hardy men lay stretched out in the shade provided by trees and buildings.

I hadn't written anything in two weeks, and though one or two small payments were due from a Delhi newspaper, I could think of no substantial amount that was likely to come my way in the near future. I decided that I would dash off a couple of articles that same night, and post them the following morning.

Having made this comforting decision, I lay down on the floor in preference to the cot. I liked the touch of things, the touch of a cool floor on a hot day; the touch of earth—soft, grassy grass was good, especially dew-drenched grass. Wet earth was soft, sensuous, as was splashing through puddles and streams.

I slept, and dreamt of a cool clear stream in a forest glade, where I bathed in gay abandon. A little further downstream was another bather. I hailed him, expecting to see Suraj but when the bather turned I found that it was my landlord's pot-bellied rent collector, holding an accounts ledger in his hands. This woke me up, and for the remainder of the day I worked feverishly at my articles.

Next morning, when I opened the door, I found Suraj asleep at the top of the steps. His tray lay at the bottom of the steps. He woke up as soon as I touched his shoulder.

'Have you been sleeping here all night?' I asked. 'Why didn't you come in?'

'It was very late,' said Suraj. 'I didn't want to disturb you.'

'Someone could have stolen your things while you were asleep.'

'Oh, I sleep quite lightly. Besides I have nothing of great value. But I came here to ask you a favour.'

'You need money?'

He laughed. 'Do all your friends mean money when they ask for favours? No, I want you to take your meal with me tonight.'

'But where? You have no place of your own and it would be too expensive in a restaurant.'

'In your room,' said Suraj. 'I shall bring the meat and vegetables and cook them here. Do you have a cooker?'

'I think so,' I said, scratching my head in some perplexity. 'I will have to look for it.'

Suraj brought a chicken for dinner—a luxury, one to be indulged in only two or three times a year. He had bought the bird for seven rupees, which was cheap. We spiced it and roasted it on a spit.

'I wish we could do this more often,' I said, as I dug my teeth into the soft flesh of a second chicken leg.

'We could do it at least once a month if we worked hard,' said Suraj.

'You know how to work. You work from morning to evening and then you work again.'

'But you are a writer. That is different. You have to wait for the right moment.'

I laughed. 'Moods and moments are for geniuses. No, it's really a matter of working hard, and I'm just plain lazy, to tell you the truth.'

'Perhaps you are writing the wrong things.'

'Perhaps, I wish I could do something else. Even if I repaired bicycle tyres, I'd make more money!'

'Then why don't you repair bicycle tyres?'

'Oh, I would rather be a bad writer than a good repairer of cycle tyres.' I brightened up, 'I could go into business, though. Do you know I once owned a vegetable stall?'

'Wonderful! When was that?'

'A couple of months ago. But it failed after two days.'

'Then you are not good at business. Let us think of something else.'

'I can tell fortunes with cards.'

'There are already too many fortune tellers in Pipalnagar.'

'Then we won't talk of fortunes. And you must sleep here tonight. It is better than sleeping on the roadside.'

VI

At noon when the shadows shifted and crossed the road, a band of children rushed down the empty street, shouting and waving their satchels. They had been at their desks from early morning, and now, despite the hot sun, they would have their fling while their elders slept on string charpoys beneath leafy neem trees.

On the soft sand near the riverbed, boys wrestled or played leapfrog. At alley corners, where tall buildings shaded narrow passages, the favourite game was gulli-danda. The gulli—a small piece of wood, about four inches long sharpened to a point at each end—is struck with the danda—a short, stout stick. A player is allowed three hits, and his score is the distance, in danda lengths, of his hits of the gulli. Boys who were experts at the game sent the gulli flying far down the road—sometimes into a shop or through a windowpane, which resulted in confusion, loud invective, and a dash for cover.

A game for both children and young men was kabaddi. This is a game that calls for good breath control and much agility. It is also known in different parts of India as hootoo-too, kho-kho and atya patya. Ramu, Deep Chand's younger brother, excelled at this game. He was the Pipalnagar kabaddi champion.

The game is played by two teams, consisting of eight or nine members each, who face each other across a dividing line. Each side in turn sends out one of its players into the opponent's area. This person has to keep on saying *'kabaddi, kabaddi'* very fast and without taking a second breath. If he returns to his side after touching an opponent, that opponent is 'dead' and out of the game. If however, he is caught and cannot struggle back to his side while still holding his breath, he is 'dead'.

Ramu, who was also a good wrestler, knew all the kabaddi holds, and was particularly good at capturing opponents. He had vitality and confidence, rare things in Pipalnagar. He wanted to go into the army after finishing school, a happy choice I thought.

VII

Suraj did not know if his parents were dead or alive. He had literally lost them when he was six. His father had been a farmer, a dark unfathomable man who spoke little, thought perhaps even less and was vaguely aware he had a son—a weak boy given to introspection and dawdling at the riverbank when he should have been helping in the fields.

Suraj's mother had been a subdued, silent woman, frail and consumptive. Her husband seemed to expect that she would not live long, but Suraj did not know if she was living or dead. He had lost his parents at Amritsar railway station in the days of

Partition, when trains coming across the border from Pakistan disgorged themselves of thousands of refugees or pulled into the station half-empty, drenched with blood and littered with corpses.

Suraj and his parents had been lucky to escape one of these massacres. Had they travelled on an earlier train (which they had tried desperately to catch), they might have been killed. Suraj was clinging to his mother's sari while she tried to keep up with her husband who was elbowing his way through the frightened bewildered throng of refugees. Suraj collided with a burly Sikh and lost his grip on the sari. The Sikh had a long curved sword at his waist, and Suraj stared up at him in awe and fascination—at the man's long hair, which had fallen loose, at his wild black beard, and at the bloodstains on his white shirt. The Sikh pushed him aside and when Suraj looked around for his mother, she was not to be seen. She was hidden from him by a mass of restless bodies, all pushing in different directions. He could hear her calling his name and he tried to force his way through the crowd in the direction of her voice, but he was carried on the other way.

At night, when the platform emptied, he was still searching for his mother. Eventually, the police came and took him away. They looked for his parents but without success, and finally they sent him to a home for orphans. Many children lost their parents at about the same time.

Suraj stayed at the orphanage for two years and when he was eight, and felt himself a man, he ran away. He worked for some time as a helper in a tea shop; but when he started having epileptic fits the shopkeepers asked him to leave, and the boy found himself on the streets, begging for a living. He begged for a year, moving from one town to the next and ended up finally in Pipalnagar. By then he was twelve and really too old to beg, but he had saved some money, and with it he bought a small stock of combs, buttons, cheap perfumes and bangles, and, converting himself into a mobile shop, went from door to door selling his wares.

Pipalnagar is a small town and there was no house which Suraj hadn't visited. Everyone knew him; some had offered him food and drink; and the children liked him because he often played on a small flute when he went on his rounds.

VIII

Suraj came to see me quite often and, when he stayed late, he slept in my room, curling up on the floor and sleeping fitfully. He would always leave early in the morning, before I could get him anything to eat.

'Should I go to Delhi, Suraj?' I asked him one evening.
'Why not? In Delhi, there are many ways of making money.'
'And spending it too. Why don't you come with me?'
'After my exams, perhaps. Not now.'
'Well, I can wait. I don't want to live alone in a big city.'
'In the meantime, write your book.'
'All right, I will try.'

We decided we could try to save a little money from Suraj's earnings and my own occasional payments from newspapers and magazines. Even if we were to give Delhi only a few days' trial, we would need money to live on. We managed to put away twenty rupees one week, but withdrew it the next when a friend, Pitamber, asked for a loan to repair his cycle rickshaw. He returned the money in three instalments but we could not save any of it. Pitamber and Deep Chand also had plans of going to Delhi. Pitamber wanted to own his own cycle rickshaw; Deep Chand dreamt of a swanky barber shop in the capital.

One day Suraj and I hired bicycles and rode out of Pipalnagar.

It was a hot, sunny morning and we were perspiring after we had gone two miles, but a fresh wind sprang up suddenly, and we could smell the rain in the air though there were no clouds to be seen.

'Let us go where there are no people at all,' said Suraj. 'I am a little tired of people. I see too many of them all day.'

We got down from our cycles and, pushing them off the road, took a path through a paddy field and then one through a field of young maize, and in the distance we saw a tree, a crooked tree, growing beside a well. I do not even today know the name of that tree. I had never seen its kind before. It had a crooked trunk, crooked branches and it was clothed in thick, broad, crooked leaves, like the leaves on which food is served in bazaars.

In the trunk of the tree was a large hole and when I sat my cycle down with a crash, two green parrots flew out of the hole, and went dipping and swerving across the fields.

There was grass around the well, cropped short by grazing cattle, so we sat in the shade of the crooked tree and Suraj untied the red cloth in which we brought food. We ate our bread and vegetable curry, and meanwhile the parrots returned to the tree.

'Let us come here every week,' said Suraj, stretching himself out on the grass. It was a drowsy day, the air was humid and he soon fell asleep. I was aware of different sensations. I heard a cricket singing in the tree; the cooing of pigeons which lived in the walls of the old well; the soft breathing of Suraj; a rustling in the leaves of the tree; the distant drone of the bees. I smelt the grass and the old bricks around the well, and the promise of rain.

When I opened my eyes, I saw dark clouds on the horizon. Suraj was still sleeping with his arms thrown across his face to keep the glare out of his eyes. As I was thirsty, I went to the well and, putting my shoulders to it, turned the wheel very slowly, walking around the well four times, while cool clean water gushed out over the stones and along the channel to the fields. I drank from one of the trays, and the water tasted sweet; the deeper the wells, the sweeter the water. Suraj was sitting up now, looking at the sky.

'It's going to rain,' he said.

We pushed our cycles back to the main road and began riding homewards. We were a mile out of Pipalnagar when it began to rain. A lashing wind swept the rain across our faces, but we exulted in it and sang at the top of our voices until we reached the bus stop. Leaving the cycles at the hire shop, we ran up the rickety, swaying steps to my room.

In the evening, as the bazaar was lighting up, the rain stopped. We went to sleep quite early, but at midnight I was woken by the moon shining full in my face—a full moon, shedding its light all over Pipalnagar, peeping and prying into every home, washing the empty streets, silvering the corrugated tin roofs.

IX

The lizards hung listlessly on the walls and ceilings, waiting for the monsoon rains, which bring out all the insects from their cracks and crannies.

One day, clouds loomed up on the horizon, growing rapidly into enormous towers. A faint breeze sprang up, bringing with it the first of the monsoon raindrops. This was the moment everyone was waiting for. People ran out of their houses to take in the fresh breeze and the scent of those first few raindrops on the parched, dusty earth. Underground, in their cracks, the insects were moving. Termites and white ants, which had been sleeping through the hot season, emerged from their lairs.

And then, on the second or third night of the monsoon, came the great yearly flight of insects into the cool brief freedom of the night. Out of every crack, from under the roots of trees, huge winged ants emerged, at first fluttering about heavily, on the first and last flight of their lives. At night there was only one direction in which they could fly—towards the light; towards the electric bulbs and smoky kerosene lamps throughout Pipalnagar. The street lamp opposite the bus stop, beneath my room, attracted a massive quivering swarm of clumsy termites, which gave the impression of one thick, slowly revolving body.

This was the hour of the lizards. Now they had their reward for those days of patient waiting. Plying their sticky pink tongues, they devoured the insects as fast as they came. For hours, they crammed their stomachs, knowing that such a feast would not be theirs again for another year. How wasteful nature is, I thought. Through the whole hot season the insect world prepares for the flight out of the darkness into light and not one of them survives its freedom.

Suraj and I walked barefooted over the cool, wet pavements, across the railway lines and the riverbed, until we were not far from the crooked tree. Dotting the landscape were old abandoned brick kilns. When it rained heavily, the hollows made by the kilns filled up with water. Suraj and I found a small tank where we could bathe and swim. On a mound in the middle of the tank stood a ruined hut, formerly inhabited by a watchman at the kiln. We swam and then wrestled on the young green grass. Though I was heavier than Suraj and my chest as sound as a new drum, he had a lot of power in his long, wiry arms and legs, and he pinioned me about the waist with his bony knees.

And then suddenly, as I strained to press his back to the ground, I felt his body go tense. He stiffened, his thigh jerked against me and his legs began to twitch. I knew that a fit was coming on, but I was unable to get out of his grip. He held me more tightly as the fit took possession of him.

When I noticed his mouth working, I thrust the palm of my hand in, sideways to prevent him from biting his tongue. But so violent was the convulsion that his teeth bit into my flesh. I shouted with pain and tried to pull my hand away, but he was unconscious and his jaw was set. I closed my eyes and counted slowly up to seven and then I felt his muscles relax and I was able to take my hand away. It was bleeding a little but I bound it in a handkerchief before Suraj fully regained consciousness.

He didn't say much as we walked back to town. He looked depressed and weak, but I knew it wouldn't take long for him to recover his usual good spirits. He did not notice that I kept my hand out of sight and only after he had returned from classes that night did he notice the bandage and asked what happened.

X

'Do you want to make some money?' asked Pitamber, bursting into the room like a festive cracker.

'I do,' I said.

'What do we have to do for it?' asked Suraj, striking a cautious note.

'Oh nothing, carry a banner and walk in front of a procession.'

'Why?'

'Don't ask me. Some political stunt.'

'Which party?'

'I don't know. Who cares? All I know is that they are paying two rupees a day to anyone who'll carry a flag or banner.'

'We don't need two rupees that badly,' I said. 'And you can make more than that in a day with your rickshaw.'

'True, but they're paying me *five*. They're fixing a loudspeaker to my rickshaw, and one of the party's men will sit in it and make speeches as we go along. Come on, it will be fun.'

'No banners for us,' I said. 'But we may come along and watch.'

And we did watch, when, later that morning, the procession passed along our street. It was a ragged procession of about a hundred people, shouting slogans. Some of them were children, and some of them were men who did not know what it was all about, but all joined in the slogan-shouting.

We didn't know much about it, either. Because, though the man in Pitamber's rickshaw was loud and eloquent, his loudspeaker was defective, with the result that his words were punctuated with squeaks and an eerie whining sound. Pitamber looked up and saw us standing on the balcony and gave us a wave and a wide grin. We decided to follow the procession at a discreet distance. It was a protest march against something or other; we never did manage to find out the details. The destination was the municipal office, and by the time we got there the crowd had increased to two or three hundred people. Some rowdies had now joined in, and things began to get out of hand. The man in the rickshaw continued his speech; another man standing on a wall was making a speech; and someone from the municipal office was confronting the crowd and making a speech of his own.

A stone was thrown, then another. From a sprinkling of stones, it soon became a shower of stones; and then some police constables, who had been standing by watching the fun, were ordered into action. They ran at the crowd where it was thinnest, brandishing stout sticks.

We were caught in the stampede that followed. A stone—flung no doubt at a policeman—was badly aimed and struck me on the shoulder. Suraj pulled me down a side street. Looking back, we saw Pitamber's cycle rickshaw lying on its side in the middle of the road, but there was no sign of Pitamber.

Later, he turned up in my room, with a cut over his left eyebrow which was bleeding freely. Suraj washed the cut, and I poured iodine over it—Pitamber did not flinch—and covered it with sticking plaster. The cut was quite deep and should have had stitches, but Pitamber was superstitious about hospitals, saying he knew very few people to come out of them alive. He was of course thinking about the Pipalnagar hospital.

So he acquired a scar on his forehead. It went rather well with his demonic good looks.

XI

'Thank god for the monsoon,' said Suraj. 'We won't have any more demonstrations on the roads until the weather improves!'

And, until the rain stopped, Pipalnagar was fresh and clean and alive. The children ran naked out of their houses and romped through the streets. The gutters overflowed, and the road became a mountain stream, coursing merrily towards the bus stop.

At the bus stop there was confusion. Newly arrived passengers, surrounded on all sides by a sea of mud and rainwater, were met by scores of tongas and cycle rickshaws, each jostling the other trying to cater to the passengers. As a result, only half-found conveyances, while the other half found themselves knee-deep in Pipalnagar mud.

Pipalnagar mud has a quality all its own—and it is not easily removed or forgotten. Only buffaloes love it because it is soft and squelchy. Two parts of it is thick sticky clay which seems to come alive at the slightest touch, clinging tenaciously to human flesh. Feet sink into it and have to be wrenched out. Fingers become webbed. Get it into your hair, and there is nothing you can do except go to Deep Chand and have your head shaved.

London has its fog, Paris its sewers, Pipalnagar its mud. Pitamber, of course, succeeded in getting as his passenger the most attractive girl to step off the bus, and showed her his skill and daring by taking her to her destination by the longest and roughest road.

The rain swirled over the trees and roofs of the town, and the parched earth soaked it up, giving out a fresh smell that came only once a year, the fragrance of quenched earth, that loveliest of all smells.

In my room I was battling against the elements, for the door would not close, and the rain swept into the room and soaked my cot. When finally I succeeded in closing the door, I discovered that the roof was leaking and the water was trickling down the walls, running through the dusty design I had made with my feet. I placed tins and mugs in strategic positions and, satisfied that everything was now under control, sat on the cot to watch the rooftops through my windows.

There was a loud banging on the door. It flew open, and there was Suraj, standing on the threshold, drenched. Coming in, he began to dry himself while I made desperate efforts to close the door again.

'Let's make some tea,' he said.

Glasses of hot, sweet milky tea on a rainy day…it was enough to make me feel fresh and full of optimism. We sat on the cot, enjoying the brew.

'One day, I'll write a book,' I said. 'Not just a thriller, but a real book, about real people. Perhaps about you and me and Pipalnagar. And then we'll be famous and our troubles will be over and new troubles will begin. I don't mind problems as long as they are new. While you're studying, I'll write my book. I'll start tonight. It is an auspicious time, the first night of the monsoon.

A tree must have fallen across the wires somewhere, because the lights would not come on. So I lit a small oil lamp, and while it spluttered in the steamy darkness, Suraj opened his book and, with one hand on the book, the other playing with his toe—this helped him to concentrate!—he began to study. I took the inkpot down from the shelf, and finding it empty, added a little rainwater to it from one of the mugs. I sat down beside Suraj and began to write, but the pen was no good and made blotches all over the paper. And, although I was full of writing just then, I didn't really know what I wanted to say.

So I went out and began pacing up and down the road. There I found Pitamber, a little drunk, very merry, and prancing about in the middle of the road.

'What are you dancing for?' I asked.

'I'm happy, so I'm dancing,' said Pitamber.

'And why are you happy?' I asked.

'Because I'm dancing,' he said.

The rain stopped and the neem trees gave out a strong, sweet smell.

XII

Flowers in Pipalnagar—did they exist? As a child I knew a garden in Lucknow where there were beds of phlox and petunias and another garden where only roses grew. In the fields around Pipalnagar was thorn apple—a yellow buttercup nestling among thorn leaves. But in the Pipalnagar bazaar, there were no flowers except one—marigold growing out of a crack on my balcony. I had removed the plaster from the base of the plant, and filled in a little earth which I watered every morning. The plant was healthy, and sometimes it produced a small orange marigold.

Sometimes Suraj plucked a flower and kept it in his tray, among the combs, buttons and scent bottles. Sometimes he gave the flower to passing child, once to a small boy who immediately tore it to shreds. Suraj was back on his rounds, as his exams were over.

Whenever he was tired of going from house to house, Suraj would sit beneath a shady banyan or pipal tree, put his tray aside, and take out his flute. The haunting notes travelled down the road in the afternoon stillness, drawing children to him. They would sit beside him and be very quiet when he played, because there was something melancholic and appealing about the tune. Suraj sometimes made flutes out of pieces of bamboo, but he never sold them. He would give them to the children he liked. He would sell almost anything, but not flutes.

Suraj sometimes played the flute at night, when he lay awake, unable to sleep; but even though I slept, I could hear the music in my dreams. Sometimes he took his flute with him to the crooked tree and played for the benefit of the birds. The parrots made harsh noises in response and flew away. Once, when Suraj was playing his flute to a small group of children, he had a fit. The flute fell from his hands. And he began to roll about in the dust on the roadside. The children became frightened and ran away, but they did not stay away for long. The next time they heard the flute, they came to listen as usual.

XIII

It was Lord Krishna's birthday, and the rain came down as heavily as it is said to have done on the day Krishna was born. Krishna is the best beloved of all the gods. Young mothers laugh or weep as they read or hear the pranks of his boyhood; young men pray to be as tall and as strong as Krishna was when he killed King Kamsa's elephant and wrestlers; young girls dream of a lover as daring as Krishna to carry them off in a war chariot; grown men envy the wisdom and statesmanship with which he managed the affairs of his kingdom.

The rain came so unexpectedly that it took everyone by surprise. In seconds, people were drenched, and within minutes, the streets were flooded. The temple tank overflowed, the railway lines disappeared, and the old wall near the bus stop shivered and silently fell—the sound of its collapse drowned in the downpour. A naked young man with a dancing bear cavorted in the middle of the vegetable market. Pitamber's rickshaw churned through the floodwater while he sang lustily as he worked.

Wading through knee-deep water down the road, I saw the roadside vendors salvaging whatever they could. Plastic toys, cabbages and utensils floated away and were seized by urchins. The water had risen to the level of the shop fronts and the floors were awash. Deep Chand and Ramu, with the help of a customer, were using buckets to bail the water out of their shop. The rain stopped as suddenly as it had begun and the sun came out. The water began to find an outlet, flooding other low-lying areas, and a paper boat came sailing between my legs.

Next morning, the morning on which the result of Suraj's examinations was due, I rose early—the first time I ever got up before Suraj—and went down to the news agency. A small crowd of students had gathered at the bus stop, joking with each other and hiding their nervousness with a show of indifference. There were not many passengers on the first bus, and there was a mad grab for newspapers as the bundle landed with a thud on the pavement. Within half-an-hour, the newsboy had sold all his copies. It was the best day of the year for him.

I went through the columns relating to Pipalnagar, but I couldn't find Suraj's roll number on the list of successful candidates. I had the number on a slip of paper, and I looked at it again to make sure I had compared it correctly with the others; then I went through the newspaper once more. When I returned to the room, Suraj was sitting on the doorstep. I didn't have to tell him he had failed—he knew by the look on my face. I sat down beside him, and we said nothing for some time.

'Never mind,' Suraj said eventually. 'I will pass next year.'

I realized I was more depressed than he was and that he was trying to console me.

'If only you'd had more time,' I said.

'I have plenty of time now. Another year. And you will have time to finish your book, and then we can go away together. Another year of Pipalnagar won't be so bad. As long as I have your friendship almost everything can be tolerated.'

He stood up, the tray hanging from his shoulders. 'What would you like to buy?'

XIV

Another year of Pipalnagar! But it was not to be. A short time later, I received a letter from the editor of a newspaper, calling me to Delhi for an interview. My friends insisted that I should go. Such an opportunity would not come again.

But I needed a shirt. The few I possessed were either frayed at the collar or torn at the shoulders. I hadn't been able to afford a new shirt for over a year, and I couldn't afford one now. Struggling writers weren't expected to dress well, but I felt in order to get the job I would need both a haircut and a clean shirt.

Where was I to go to get a shirt? Suraj generally wore an old red-striped T-shirt; he washed it every second evening, and by morning it was dry and ready to wear again; but it was tight even on him. He did not have another. Besides, I needed something white, something respectable!

I went to Deep Chand who had a collection of shirts. He was only too glad to lend me one. But they were all brightly coloured—pinks, purples and magentas... No editor was going to be impressed by a young writer in a pink shirt. They looked fine on Deep Chand, but he had no need to look respectable.

Finally, Pitamber came to my rescue. He didn't bother with shirts himself, except in winter, but he was able to borrow a clean white shirt from a guard at the jail, who'd got it from the relative of a convict in exchange for certain favours.

'This shirt will make you look respectable,' said Pitamber. 'To be respectable—what an adventure!'

XV

Freedom. The moment the bus was out of Pipalnagar, and the fields opened out on all sides, I knew that I was free, that I had always been free. Only my own weakness, hesitation, and the habits that had grown around me had held me back. All I had to do was sit in a bus and go somewhere.

I sat near the open window of the bus and let the cool breeze from the fields play against my face. Herons and snipe waded among the lotus roots in flat green ponds. Blue jays swooped around telegraph poles. Children jumped naked into the canals that wound through the fields. Because I was happy, it seemed to me that everyone else was happy—the driver, the conductor, the passengers, the farmers in the fields and those driving bullock-carts. When two women behind me started quarrelling over their seats. I helped to placate them. Then I took a small girl on my knee and pointed out camels, buffaloes, vultures and pariah dogs.

Six hours later, the bus crossed the bridge over the swollen Jamuna river, passed under the walls of the great Red Fort built by a Mughal emperor, and entered the old city of Delhi.

I found it strange to be in a city again, after several years in Pipalnagar. It was a little frightening too. I felt like a stranger. No one was interested in me.

In Pipalnagar, people wanted to know each other, or at least to know about one another. In Delhi, no one cared who you were or where you came from, like big cities almost everywhere. It was prosperous but without a heart.

After a day and a night of loneliness, I found myself wishing that Suraj had accompanied me; wishing that I was back in Pipalnagar. But when the job was offered to me—at a starting salary of three hundred rupees per month, a princely sum compared to what I had been making on my own—I did not have the courage to refuse it. After accepting the job—which was to commence in a week's time—I spent the day wandering through the bazaars, down the wide shady roads of the capital, resting under the jamun trees, and thinking all the time what I would do in the months to come.

I slept at the railway waiting room and all night long I heard the shunting and whistling of engines which conjured up visions of places with sweet names like Kumbakonam, Krishnagiri, Polonnarurawa. I dreamt of palm-fringed beaches and inland lagoons; of the echoing chambers of deserted cities, red sandstone and white marble; of temples in the sun; and elephants crossing wide slow-moving rivers...

XVI

Pitamber was on the platform when the train steamed into the Pipalnagar station in the early hours of a damp September morning. I waved to him from the carriage window, and shouted that everything had gone well.

But everything was not well here. When I got off the train, Pitamber told me that Suraj had been ill—that he'd had a fit on a lonely stretch of road the previous afternoon and had lain in the sun for over an hour. Pitamber had found him, suffering from heatstroke, and brought him home. When I saw him, he was sitting up on the string bed drinking hot tea. He looked pale and weak, but his smile was reassuring.

'Don't worry,' he said. 'I will be all right.'

'He was bad last night,' said Pitamber. 'He had a fever and kept talking, as in a dream. But what he says is true—he is better this morning.'

'Thanks to Pitamber,' said Suraj. 'It is good to have friends.'

'Come with me to Delhi, Suraj,' I said. 'I have got a job now. You can live with me and attend a school regularly.'

'It is good for friends to help each other,' said Suraj, 'but only after I have passed my exam will I join you in Delhi. I made myself this promise. Poor Pipalnagar—nobody wants to stay here. Will you be sorry to leave?'

'Yes, I will be sorry. A part of me will still be here.'

XVII

Deep Chand was happy to know that I was leaving. 'I'll follow you soon,' he said. 'There is money to be made in Delhi, cutting hair. Girls are keeping it short these days.'

'But men are growing it long.'

'True. So I shall open a barbershop for ladies and a beauty salon for men! Ramu can attend to the ladies.'

Ramu winked at me in the mirror. He was still at the stage of teasing girls on their way to school or college.

The snip of Deep Chand's scissors made me sleepy, as I sat in his chair. His fingers beat a rhythmic tattoo on my scalp. It was my last haircut in Pipalnagar, and Deep Chand did not charge me for it. I promised to write as soon as I had settled down in Delhi.

The next day when Suraj was stronger, I said, 'Come, let us go for a walk and visit our crooked tree. Where is your flute, Suraj?'

'I don't know. Let us look for it.'

We searched the room and our belongings for the flute but could not find it.

'It must have been left on the roadside,' said Suraj. 'Never mind. I will make another.'

I could picture the flute lying in the dust on the roadside and somehow this made me sad. But Suraj was full of high spirits as we walked across the railway lines and through the fields.

'The rains are over,' he said, kicking off his chappals and lying down on the grass. 'You can smell the autumn in the air. Somehow, it makes me feel light-hearted. Yesterday I was sad, and tomorrow I might be sad again, but today I know that I am happy. I want to live on and on. One lifetime cannot satisfy my heart.'

'A day in a lifetime,' I said. 'I'll remember this day—the way the sun touches us, the way the grass bends, the smell of this leaf as I crush it...'

XVIII

At six every morning the first bus arrives, and the passengers alight, looking sleepy and dishevelled, and rather discouraged by their first sight of Pipalnagar. When they have gone their various ways, the bus is driven into the shed. Cows congregate at the dustbin and the pavement dwellers come to life, stretching their tired limbs on the hard stone steps. I carry the bucket up the steps to my room, and bathe for the last time on the open balcony. In the villages, the buffaloes are wallowing in green ponds while naked urchins sit astride them, scrubbing their backs, and a crow or water bird perches on their glistening necks. The parrots are busy in the crooked tree, and a slim green snake basks in the sun on our island near the brick-kiln. In the hills, the mists have lifted and the distant mountains are fringed with snow.

It is autumn, and the rains are over. The earth meets the sky in one broad bold sweep.

A land of thrusting hills. Terraced hills, wood-covered and windswept. Mountains where the gods speak gently to the lonely. Hills of green grass and grey rock, misty at dawn, hazy at noon, molten at sunset, where fierce fresh torrents rush to the valleys below. A quiet land of fields and ponds, shaded by ancient trees and ringed with palms, where sacred rivers are touched by temples, where temples are touched by southern seas.

This is the land I should write about. Pipalnagar should be forgotten. I should turn aside from it to sing instead of the splendours of exotic places.

But only yesterdays are truly splendid... And there are other singers, sweeter than I, to sing of tomorrow. I can only write of today, of Pipalnagar, where I have lived and loved.

ONCE YOU HAVE LIVED WITH MOUNTAINS

It was while I was living in England in the jostle and drizzle of London, that I remembered the Himalayas at their most vivid. I had grown up amongst those great blue and brown mountains, they had nourished my blood, and though I was separated from them by thousands of miles of ocean, plain and desert, I could not forget them. It is always the same with mountains. Once you have lived with them for any length of time, you belong to them. There is no escape.

And so, in London in March, the fog became a mountain mist and the boom of traffic became the boom of the Ganges emerging from the foothills. I remembered a little mountain path which led my restless feet into a cool sweet forest of oak and rhododendron and then on to the windswept crest of a naked hilltop. The hill was called Cloud's End. It commanded a view of the plains on one side, and of the snow peaks on the other. Little silver rivers twisted across the valley below, where the rice fields formed a patchwork of emerald green. And on the hill itself the wind made a 'hoo-hoo-hoo' in the branches of the tall deodars where it found itself trapped. During the rains, clouds enveloped the valley but left the hills alone, an island in the sky. Wild sorrel grew among the rocks, and there were many flowers—convolvulus, clover, wild begonia, dandelion—sprinkling the hillside.

On a spur of the hill stood the ruins of an old building, the roof of which had long since disappeared and the rain had beaten the stone floors smooth and yellow. Moss, ferns and maidenhair grew from the walls. In a hollow beneath a flight of worn stone steps a wild cat had made its home. It was a beautiful grey creature, black-striped with pale great eyes. Sometimes it watched me from the steps or the wall, but it never came near.

No one lived on the hill, except occasionally a coal-burner in a temporary grass thatched hut. But villagers used the path for grazing their sheep and cattle on the grassy slopes. Each cow or sheep had a bell suspended from its neck to let the shepherd boy know its whereabouts.

The boy could then lie in the sun and eat wild strawberries without fear of losing his animals. I remembered some of the shepherd boys and girls. There was a boy who played the flute. Its rough, sweet, straightforward notes travelled clearly through the mountain air. He would greet me with a nod of his head, without taking the flute from his lips.

There was a girl who was nearly always cutting grass for fodder. She wore heavy bangles on her feet and long silver earrings. She did not speak much either, but she always had a wide smile on her face when she met me on the path. She used to sing to herself, or to the sheep, or to the grass, or to the sickle in her hand. And there was a boy who carried milk into town (a distance of about five miles) who would often fall into step with me to hold a long conversation. He had never been away from the hills or in a large city. He had never been on a train.

I told him about the cities and he told me about his village, how they made bread from maize, how fish were to be caught in the mountain streams, how the bears came to steal his father's pumpkins. Whenever the pumpkins were ripe, he told me, the bears would come and carry them off. These things I remembered—these, and the smell of pine needles, the silver of oak leaves and the red of maple, the call of the Himalayan cuckoo, and the mist, like a wet face-cloth, pressing against the hills.

Odd, how some little incident, some snatch of conversation comes back to one again and again in the most unlikely places. Standing in the aisle of a crowded tube train on a Monday morning, my nose tucked into the back page of someone else's newspaper, I suddenly had a vision of a bear making off with a ripe pumpkin! A bear and a pumpkin—and there, between Belsize Park and the Tottenham Court Road station, all the smells and sounds of the Himalayas came rushing back to me.

THE NIGHT TRAIN AT DEOLI

When I was at college I used to spend my summer vacations in Dehra, at my grandmother's place. I would leave the plains early in May and return late in July. Deoli was a small station about thirty miles from Dehra. It marked the beginning of the heavy jungles of the Indian Terai.

The train would reach Deoli at about five in the morning when the station would be dimly lit with electric bulbs and oil lamps, and the jungle across the railway tracks would just be visible in the faint light of dawn. Deoli had only one platform, an office for the stationmaster and a waiting room. The platform boasted a tea stall, a fruit vendor and a few stray dogs; not much else because the train stopped there for only ten minutes before rushing on into the forests.

Why it stopped at Deoli, I don't know. Nothing ever happened there. Nobody got off the train and nobody got on. There were never any coolies on the platform. But the train would halt there a full ten minutes and then a bell would sound, the guard would blow his whistle, and presently Deoli would be left behind and forgotten.

I used to wonder what happened in Deoli behind the station walls. I always felt sorry for that lonely little platform and for the place that nobody wanted to visit. I decided that one day

I would get off the train at Deoli and spend the day there just to please the town.

I was eighteen, visiting my grandmother, and the night train stopped at Deoli. A girl came down the platform selling baskets.

It was a cold morning and the girl had a shawl thrown across her shoulders. Her feet were bare and her clothes were old but she was a young girl, walking gracefully and with dignity.

When she came to my window, she stopped. She saw that I was looking at her intently, but at first she pretended not to notice. She had pale skin, set off by shiny black hair and dark, troubled eyes. And then those eyes, searching and eloquent, met mine.

She stood by my window for some time and neither of us said anything. But when she moved on, I found myself leaving my seat and going to the carriage door. I stood waiting on the platform looking the other way. I walked across to the tea stall. A kettle was boiling over on a small fire, but the owner of the stall was busy serving tea somewhere on the train. The girl followed me behind the stall.

'Do you want to buy a basket?' she asked. 'They are very strong, made of the finest cane...'

'No,' I said, 'I don't want a basket.'

We stood looking at each other for what seemed a very long time, and she said, 'Are you sure you don't want a basket?'

'All right, give me one,' I said, and took the one on top and gave her a rupee, hardly daring to touch her fingers.

As she was about to speak, the guard blew his whistle. She said something, but it was lost in the clanging of the bell and the hissing of the engine. I had to run back to my compartment. The carriage shuddered and jolted forward.

I watched her as the platform slipped away. She was alone on the platform and she did not move, but she was looking at me and smiling. I watched her until the signal box came in the way and then the jungle hid the station. But I could still see her standing there alone...

I stayed awake for the rest of the journey. I could not rid my mind of the picture of the girl's face and her dark, smouldering eyes.

But when I reached Dehra the incident became blurred and distant, for there were other things to occupy my mind. It was only when I was making the return journey, two months later, that I remembered the girl.

I was looking out for her as the train drew into the station, and I felt an unexpected thrill when I saw her walking up the platform. I sprang off the footboard and waved to her.

When she saw me, she smiled. She was pleased that I remembered her. I was pleased that she remembered me. We were both pleased and it was almost like a meeting of old friends.

She did not go down the length of the train selling baskets but came straight to the tea stall. Her dark eyes were suddenly filled with light. We said nothing for some time but we couldn't have been more eloquent.

I felt the impulse to put her on the train there and then, and take her away with me. I could not bear the thought of having to watch her recede into the distance of Deoli station. I took the baskets from her hand and put them down on the ground. She put out her hand for one of them, but I caught her hand and held it.

'I have to go to Delhi,' I said.

She nodded. 'I do not have to go anywhere.'

The guard blew his whistle for the train to leave, and how I hated the guard for doing that.

'I will come again,' I said. 'Will you be here?'

She nodded again and, as she nodded, the bell clanged and

the train slid forward. I had to wrench my hand away from the girl and run for the moving train.

This time I did not forget her. She was with me for the remainder of the journey and for long after. All that year she was a bright, living thing. And when the college term finished, I packed in haste and left for Dehra earlier than usual. My grandmother would be pleased at my eagerness to see her.

I was nervous and anxious as the train drew into Deoli, because I was wondering what I should say to the girl and what I should do. I was determined that I wouldn't stand helplessly before her, hardly able to speak or do anything about my feelings.

The train came to Deoli, and I looked up and down the platform but I could not see the girl anywhere.

I opened the door and stepped off the footboard. I was deeply disappointed and overcome by a sense of foreboding. I felt I had to do something and so I ran up to the stationmaster and said, 'Do you know the girl who used to sell baskets here?'

'No, I don't,' said the stationmaster. 'And you'd better get on the train if you don't want to be left behind.'

But I paced up and down the platform and stared over the railings at the station yard. All I saw was a mango tree and a dusty road leading into the jungle. Where did the road go? The train was moving out of the station and I had to run up the platform and jump for the door of my compartment. Then, as the train gathered speed and rushed through the forests, I sat brooding in front of the window.

What could I do about finding a girl I had seen only twice, who had hardly spoken to me, and about whom I knew nothing—absolutely nothing—but for whom I felt a tenderness and responsibility that I had never felt before?

My grandmother was not pleased with my visit after all, because I didn't stay at her place more than a couple of weeks. I felt restless and ill at ease. So I took the train back to the plains, meaning to ask further questions of the stationmaster at Deoli.

But at Deoli there was a new stationmaster. The previous man had been transferred to another post within the past week. The new man didn't know anything about the girl who sold baskets. I found the owner of the tea stall, a small, shrivelled-up man, wearing greasy clothes, and asked him if he knew anything about the girl with the baskets.

'Yes, there was such a girl here. I remember quite well,' he said. 'But she has stopped coming now.'

'Why?' I asked. 'What happened to her?'

'How should I know?' said the man. 'She was nothing to me.'

And once again I had to run for the train.

As Deoli platform receded, I decided that one day I would have to break journey there, spend a day in the town, make inquiries, and find the girl who had stolen my heart with nothing but a look from her dark, impatient eyes.

With this thought I consoled myself throughout my last term in college. I went to Dehra again in the summer and when, in the early hours of the morning, the night train drew into Deoli station, I looked up and down the platform for signs of the girl, knowing I wouldn't find her but hoping just the same.

Somehow, I couldn't bring myself to break journey at Deoli and spend a day there. (If it was all fiction or a film, I reflected, I would have got down and cleaned up the mystery and reached a suitable ending to the whole thing.) I think I was afraid to do this. I was afraid of discovering what really happened to the girl. Perhaps she was no longer in Deoli, perhaps she was married, perhaps she had fallen ill...

In the last few years I have passed through Deoli many times, and I always look out of the carriage window half-expecting to see the same unchanged face smiling up at me. I wonder what happens in Deoli, behind the station walls. But I will never break my journey there. It may spoil my game. I prefer to keep hoping and dreaming and looking out of the window up and down that lonely platform, waiting for the girl with the baskets.

I never break my journey at Deoli but I pass through as often as I can.

A HILL STATION'S VINTAGE MURDERS

There is less crime in the hills than in the plains, and so the few murders that do take place from time to time stand out as landmarks in the annals of a hill station.

Among the gravestones in the Mussoorie cemetery there is one which bears the inscription: 'Murdered by the hand he befriended.' This is the grave of Mr James Reginald Clapp, a chemist's assistant, who was brutally done to death on the night of 31 August 1909.

Miss Ripley-Bean, who has spent most of her eighty-seven years in this hill station, remembers the case clearly, though she was only a girl at the time. From the details she has given me, and from a brief account in *A Mussoorie Miscellany*, now out of print, I am able to reconstruct this interesting case and a couple of others which were the sensations of their respective 'seasons'.

Mr Clapp was an assistant in the chemist's shop of Messrs. J.B. & E. Samuel (no longer in existence), situated in one of the busiest sections of the Mall. At that time the adjoining cantonment of Landour was an important convalescent centre for British soldiers. Mr Clapp was popular with the soldiers, and he had befriended some of them when they had run short of money. He was a steady worker and sent most of his savings home, to his mother in Birmingham; she was planning to use the money to buy the house in which she lived.

At the time of the murder, Clapp was particularly friendly with a Corporal Allen, who was eventually to be hanged at the Naini Jail. The murder was brutal, the initial attack being launched with a soda-water bottle on the victim's head. Clapp's throat was then cut from ear to ear with his own razor, which was left behind in the room. The body was discovered on the floor of the shop the next morning by the proprietor, Mr Samuel, who did not live on the premises.

Suspicion immediately fell on Corporal Allen because he had left Mussoorie that same night, arriving at Rajpur, in the foothills (a seven-mile walk by the bridle path) many hours later than he was expected at a Rajpur boarding house. According to some, Clapp had last been seen in the corporal's company.

There was other circumstantial evidence pointing to Allen's guilt. On the day of the murder, Mr Clapp had received his salary, and this sum, in sovereigns and notes, was never traced. Allen was alleged to have made a payment in sovereigns at Rajpur. Someone had given Allen a biscuit tin packed with sandwiches for his journey down, and it was thought that perhaps the tin had been used by the murderer as a safe for the money. But no tin was found, and Allen denied having had one with him.

Allen was arrested at Rajpur and brought back to Mussoorie under escort. He was taken immediately to the victim's bedside, where the body still lay, the police hoping that he might confess his guilt when confronted with the body of the victim; but Allen was unmoved, and protested his innocence.

Meanwhile, other soldiers from among Mr Clapp's friends had collected on the Mall. They had removed their belts and were ready to lynch Allen as soon as he was brought out of the shop. The situation was tense, but further mishap was averted by the resourcefulness of Mr Rust, a photographer, who, being of the same build as the corporal, put on an army coat with a turned-up collar, and arranged to be handcuffed between two policemen. He remained with them inside the shop, in partial view of the mob, while the rest of the police party escorted the corporal out by a back entrance. Mr Rust did not abandon his disguise or leave the shop until word arrived that Allen was secure in the police station.

Corporal Allen was eventually found guilty, and was hanged. But there were many who felt that he had never really been proved guilty, and that he had been convicted on purely circumstantial evidence; and looking back on the case from this distance in time one cannot help feeling that the soldier may have been a victim of circumstances, and perhaps of local prejudice, for he was not liked by his fellows. Allen himself hinted that he was not in the vicinity of the crime that night but in the company of a lady whose integrity he was determined to shield. If this was true, it was a pity that the lady prized her virtue more than her friend's life, for she did not come forward to save him. The chaplain who administered to Allen during his last days in the 'condemned cell' was prepared to absolve the corporal and could not accept that he was a murderer.

One of the hill station's most sensational crimes was committed on 25 July 1927, at the height of the 'season' and in the heart of the town, in Zephyr Hall, then a boarding house. It provided a good deal of excitement for the residents of the boarding house.

Soon after midday, Zephyr Hall residents were startled into brisk activity when a woman screamed and a shot rang out from one of the rooms. Other shots followed in rapid succession.

Those boarders who happened to be in the public lounge or verandah dived for the safety of their rooms; but one unhappy resident, taking the precaution of coming around a corner with his hands held well above his head, ran straight into a levelled pistol. And the man with the gun, who had just killed his wife and wounded his daughter, was still able to see some humour in the situation, for he burst into laughter! The boarder escaped unhurt. But the murderer, Mr Owen, did not savour the situation for long. He shot himself long before the police arrived.

Ten years earlier, on 24 November 1917, another husband had shot his wife.

Mrs Fennimore, the wife of a schoolmaster, had got herself inextricably enmeshed in a defamation law suit, each hearing of which was more distasteful to Mr Fennimore than the previous one. Finally he determined on his own solution. Late at night he armed himself with a loaded revolver, moved to his wife's bedside, and, finding her lying asleep on her side, shot her through the back of the head. For no accountable reason he put the weapon under her pillow, and then completed his plan. Going to the lavatory, three rooms beyond his wife's bedroom, he leaned over his loaded rifle and shot himself.

THE BLUE UMBRELLA

I

'Neelu! Neelu!' cried Binya.

She scrambled barefoot over the rocks, ran over the short summer grass, up and over the brow of the hill, all the time calling 'Neelu, Neelu!' Neelu—'blue'—was the name of the blue-grey cow. The other cow, which was white, was called Gori, meaning 'fair one'. They were fond of wandering off on their own, down to the stream or into the pine forest, and sometimes they came back by themselves and sometimes they stayed away—almost deliberately, it seemed to Binya.

If the cows didn't come home at the right time, Binya would be sent to fetch them. Sometimes her brother, Bijju, went with her, but these days he was busy preparing for his exams and didn't have time to help with the cows.

Binya liked being on her own, and sometimes she allowed the cows to lead her into some distant valley, and then they would all be late coming home. The cows preferred having Binya with them, because she let them wander. Bijju pulled them by their tails if they went too far.

Binya belonged to the mountains, to this part of the Himalayas known as Garhwal. Dark forests and lonely hilltops held no terrors for her. It was only when she was in the market town, jostled by the crowds in the bazaar, that she felt rather nervous and lost. The town, five miles from the village, was also a pleasure resort for tourists from all over India.

Binya was probably ten. She may have been nine or even eleven, she couldn't be sure because no one in the village kept birthdays; but her mother told her she'd been born during a winter when the snow had come up to the windows, and that was just over ten years ago, wasn't it? Two years later, her father had died, but his passing had made no difference to their way of life. They had three tiny terraced fields on the side of the mountain, and they grew potatoes, onions, ginger, beans, mustard and maize: not enough to sell in the town, but enough to live on.

Like most mountain girls, Binya was quite sturdy, fair of skin, with pink cheeks and dark eyes and her black hair tied in a pigtail. She wore pretty glass bangles on her wrists, and a necklace of glass beads. From the necklace hung a leopard's claw. It was a lucky charm, and Binya always wore it. Bijju had one, too, only his was attached to a string.

Binya's full name was Binyadevi, and Bijju's real name was Vijay, but everyone called them Binya and Bijju. Binya was two years younger than her brother.

She had stopped calling for Neelu; she had heard the cowbells tinkling, and knew the cows hadn't gone far. Singing to herself, she walked over fallen pine needles into the forest glade on the spur of the hill. She heard voices, laughter, the clatter of plates and cups, and stepping through the trees, she came upon a party of picnickers.

They were holidaymakers from the plains. The women were dressed in bright saris, the men wore light summer shirts, and the children had pretty new clothes. Binya, standing in the shadows between the trees, went unnoticed; for some time she watched the picnickers, admiring their clothes, listening to their unfamiliar accents, and gazing rather hungrily at the sight of all their food. And then her gaze came to rest on a bright blue umbrella, a frilly thing for women, which lay open on the grass beside its owner.

Now Binya had seen umbrellas before, and her mother had a big black umbrella which nobody used anymore because the field rats had eaten holes in it, but this was the first time Binya had seen such a small, dainty, colourful umbrella and she fell in love with it. The umbrella was like a flower, a great blue flower that had sprung up on the dry brown hillside.

She moved forward a few paces so that she could see the umbrella better. As she came out of the shadows into the sunlight, the picnickers saw her.

'Hello, look who's here!' exclaimed the older of the two women. 'A little village girl!'

'Isn't she pretty?' remarked the other. 'But how torn and dirty her clothes are!' It did not seem to bother them that Binya could hear and understand everything they said about her.

'They're very poor in the hills,' said one of the men.

'Then let's give her something to eat.' And the older woman beckoned to Binya to come closer.

Hesitantly, nervously, Binya approached the group.

Normally she would have turned and fled, but the attraction was the pretty blue umbrella. It had cast a spell over her, drawing her forward almost against her will.

'What's that on her neck?' asked the younger woman.

'A necklace of sorts.'

'It's a pendant—see, there's a claw hanging from it!'

'It's a tiger's claw,' said the man beside her. (He had never seen a tiger's claw.) 'A lucky charm. These people wear them to keep away evil spirits.' He looked to Binya for confirmation, but Binya said nothing.

'Oh, I want one too!' said the woman, who was obviously his wife.

'You can't get them in shops.'

'Buy hers, then. Give her two or three rupees, she's sure to need the money.'

The man, looking slightly embarrassed but anxious to please his young wife, produced a two-rupee note and offered it to Binya, indicating that he wanted the pendant in exchange. Binya put her hand to the necklace, half-afraid that the excited woman would snatch it away from her. Solemnly, she shook her head.

The man then showed her a five-rupee note, but again Binya shook her head.

'How silly she is!' exclaimed the young woman.

'It may not be hers to sell,' said the man. 'But I'll try again. How much do you want—what can we give you?' And he waved his hand towards the picnic things scattered about on the grass.

Without any hesitation Binya pointed to the umbrella.

'My umbrella!' exclaimed the young woman. 'She wants my umbrella. What cheek!'

'Well, you want her pendant, don't you?'

'That's different.'

'Is it?'

The man and his wife were beginning to quarrel with each other.

'I'll ask her to go away,' said the older woman.

'We're making such fools of ourselves.'

'But I want the pendant!' cried the other, petulantly.

And then, on an impulse, she picked up the umbrella and held it out to Binya.

'Here, take the umbrella!'

Binya removed her necklace and held it out to the young woman, who immediately placed it around her own neck. Then

Binya took the umbrella and held it up. It did not look so small in her hands; in fact, it was just the right size.

She had forgotten about the picnickers, who were busy examining the pendant. She turned the blue umbrella this way and that, looked through the bright blue silk at the pulsating sun, and then, still keeping it open, turned and disappeared into the forest glade.

II

Binya seldom closed the blue umbrella. Even when she had it in the house, she left it lying open in a corner of the room. Sometimes Bijju snapped it shut, complaining that it got in the way. She would open it again a little later. It wasn't beautiful when it was closed.

Whenever Binya went out—whether it was to graze the cows, or fetch water from the spring, or carry milk to the little tea shop on the Tehri road—she took the umbrella with her. That patch of sky-blue silk could always be seen on the hillside.

Old Ram Bharosa (Ram the Trustworthy) kept the tea shop on the Tehri road. It was a dusty, un-metalled road. Once a day, the Tehri bus stopped near his shop and passengers got down to sip hot tea or drink a glass of curd. He kept a few bottles of Coca-Cola too, but as there was no ice, the bottles got hot in the sun and so were seldom opened. He also kept sweets and toffees, and when Binya or Bijju had a few coins to spare, they would spend them at his shop. It was only a mile from the village.

Ram Bharosa was astonished to see Binya's blue umbrella.

'What have you there, Binya?' he asked.

Binya gave the umbrella a twirl and smiled at Ram Bharosa. She was always ready with her smile, and would willingly have lent it to anyone who was feeling unhappy.

'That's a lady's umbrella,' said Ram Bharosa. 'That's only

for memsahibs. Where did you get it?'

'Someone gave it to me—for my necklace.'

'You exchanged it for your lucky claw!'

Binya nodded.

'But what do you need it for? The sun isn't hot enough, and it isn't meant for the rain. It's just a pretty thing for rich ladies to play with!'

Binya nodded and smiled again. Ram Bharosa was quite right; it was just a beautiful plaything. And that was exactly why she had fallen in love with it.

'I have an idea,' said the shopkeeper. 'It's no use to you, that umbrella. Why not sell it to me? I'll give you five rupees for it.'

'It's worth fifteen,' said Binya.

'Well, then, I'll give you ten.'

Binya laughed and shook her head.

'Twelve rupees?' said Ram Bharosa, but without much hope.

Binya placed a five-paise coin on the counter.

'I came for a toffee,' she said.

Ram Bharosa pulled at his drooping whiskers, gave Binya a wry look, and placed a toffee in the palm of her hand. He watched Binya as she walked away along the dusty road. The blue umbrella held him fascinated, and he stared after it until it was out of sight.

The villagers used this road to go to the market town. Some used the bus, a few rode on mules and most people walked. Today, everyone on the road turned their heads to stare at the girl with the bright blue umbrella.

Binya sat down in the shade of a pine tree. The umbrella, still open, lay beside her. She cradled her head in her arms, and presently she dozed off. It was that kind of day, sleepily warm and summery.

And while she slept, a wind sprang up.

It came quietly, swishing gently through the trees, humming softly. Then it was joined by other random gusts, bustling over the tops of the mountains. The trees shook their heads and came to life. The wind fanned Binya's cheeks. The umbrella stirred on the grass.

The wind grew stronger, picking up dead leaves and sending them spinning and swirling through the air. It got into the umbrella and began to drag it over the grass. Suddenly it lifted the umbrella and carried it about six feet from the sleeping girl. The sound woke Binya.

She was on her feet immediately, and then she was leaping down the steep slope. But just as she was within reach of the umbrella, the wind picked it up again and carried it further downhill.

Binya set off in pursuit. The wind was in a wicked, playful mood. It would leave the umbrella alone for a few moments but as soon as Binya came near, it would pick up the umbrella again and send it bouncing, floating, dancing away from her.

The hill grew steeper. Binya knew that after twenty yards it would fall away in a precipice. She ran faster. And the wind ran with her, ahead of her, and the blue umbrella stayed up with the wind.

A fresh gust picked it up and carried it to the very edge of the cliff. There it balanced for a few seconds, before toppling over, out of sight.

Binya ran to the edge of the cliff. Going down on her hands and knees, she peered down the cliff face. About a hundred feet below, a small stream rushed between great boulders. Hardly anything grew on the cliff face—just a few stunted bushes, and, halfway down, a wild cherry tree growing crookedly out of the rocks and hanging across the chasm. The umbrella had stuck in the cherry tree.

Binya didn't hesitate. She may have been timid with strangers, but she was at home on a hillside. She stuck her bare leg over the edge of the cliff and began climbing down. She kept her face to the hillside, feeling her way with her feet, only changing her handhold when she knew her feet were secure. Sometimes she held on to the thorny bilberry bushes, but she did not trust the other plants, which came away very easily.

Loose stones rattled down the cliff. Once on their way, the stones did not stop until they reached the bottom of the hill; and they took other stones with them, so that there was soon a cascade of stones, and Binya had to be very careful not to start a landslide.

As agile as a mountain goat, she did not take more than five minutes to reach the crooked cherry tree. But the most difficult task remained—she had to crawl along the trunk of the tree, which stood out at right angles from the cliff. Only by doing this could she reach the trapped umbrella.

Binya felt no fear when climbing trees. She was proud of the fact that she could climb them as well as Bijju. Gripping the rough cherry bark with her toes, and using her knees as leverage, she crawled along the trunk of the projecting tree until she was almost within reach of the umbrella. She noticed with dismay that the blue cloth was torn in a couple of places.

She looked down, and it was only then that she felt afraid. She was right over the chasm, balanced precariously about eighty feet above the boulder-strewn stream. Looking down, she felt quite dizzy. Her hands shook, and the tree shook too. If she slipped now, there was only one direction in which she could fall—down, down, into the depths of that dark and shadowy ravine.

There was only one thing to do; concentrate on the patch of blue just a couple of feet away from her. She did not look down or up, but straight ahead, and willing herself forward, she managed to reach the umbrella.

She could not crawl back with it in her hands. So, after dislodging it from the forked branch in which it had stuck, she let it fall, still open, into the ravine below.

Cushioned by the wind, the umbrella floated serenely downwards, landing in a thicket of nettles.

Binya crawled back along the trunk of the cherry tree. Twenty minutes later, she emerged from the nettle clump, her precious umbrella held aloft. She had nettle stings all over her legs, but she was hardly aware of the smarting. She was as immune to nettles as Bijju was to bees.

III

About four years previously, Bijju had knocked a hive out of an oak tree, and had been badly stung on the face and legs. It had been a painful experience. But now, if a bee stung him, he felt nothing at all: he had been immunized for life!

He was on his way home from school. It was two o'clock and he hadn't eaten since six in the morning. Fortunately, the kingora bushes—the bilberries—were in fruit, and already Bijju's lips were stained purple with the juice of the wild, sour fruit.

He didn't have any money to spend at Ram Bharosa's shop, but he stopped there anyway to look at the sweets in their glass jars.

'And what will you have today?' asked Ram Bharosa.

'No money,' said Bijju.

'You can pay me later.'

Bijju shook his head. Some of his friends had taken sweets on credit, and at the end of the month they had found they'd eaten more sweets than they could possibly pay for! As a result, they'd had to hand over to Ram Bharosa some of their most treasured possessions—such as a curved knife for cutting grass, or a small hand axe, or a jar for pickles, or a pair of earrings—and these had become the shopkeeper's possessions and were kept by him or sold in his shop.

Ram Bharosa had set his heart on having Binya's blue umbrella, and so naturally he was anxious to give credit to either of the children, but so far neither had fallen into the trap.

Bijju moved on, his mouth full of kingora berries. Halfway home, he saw Binya with the cows. It was late evening, and the sun had gone down, but Binya still had the umbrella open. The two small rents had been stitched up by her mother.

Bijju gave his sister a handful of berries. She handed him the umbrella while she ate the berries.

'You can have the umbrella until we get home,' she said. It was her way of rewarding Bijju for bringing her the wild fruit.

Calling 'Neelu! Gori!' Binya and Bijju set out for home, followed at some distance by the cows.

It was dark before they reached the village, but Bijju still had the umbrella open.

◆

Most of the people in the village were a little envious of Binya's blue umbrella. No one else had ever possessed one like it. The schoolmaster's wife thought it was quite wrong for a poor cultivator's daughter to have such a fine umbrella while she, a second-class BA, had to make do with an ordinary black one. Her husband offered to have their old umbrella dyed blue; she gave him a scornful look, and loved him a little less than before. The pujari, who looked after the temple, announced that he would buy a multi-coloured umbrella the next time he was in the town. A few days later he returned looking annoyed and grumbling that they weren't available except in Delhi. Most people consoled themselves by saying that Binya's pretty umbrella wouldn't keep out the rain, if it rained heavily; that it would shrivel in the sun, if the sun was fierce; that it would collapse in a wind, if the wind was strong; that it would attract lightning, if lightning fell near it; and that it would prove unlucky, if there was any ill luck going about. Secretly, everyone admired it.

Unlike the adults, the children didn't have to pretend. They were full of praise for the umbrella. It was so light, so pretty, so bright a blue! And it was just the right size for Binya. They knew that if they said nice things about the umbrella, Binya would smile and give it to them to hold for a little while—just a very little while!

Soon it was the time of the monsoon. Big black clouds kept piling up, and thunder rolled over the hills.

Binya sat on the hillside all afternoon, waiting for the rain. As soon as the first big drop of rain came down, she raised the umbrella over her head. More drops, big ones, came pattering down. She could see them through the umbrella silk, as they broke against the cloth.

And then there was a cloudburst, and it was like standing under a waterfall. The umbrella wasn't really a rain umbrella, but it held up bravely. Only Binya's feet got wet. Rods of rain fell around her in a curtain of shivered glass.

Everywhere on the hillside people were scurrying for shelter. Some made for a charcoal burner's hut, others for a mule-shed, or Ram Bharosa's shop. Binya was the only one who didn't run. This was what she'd been waiting for—rain on her umbrella—and she wasn't in a hurry to go home. She didn't mind getting her feet wet. The cows didn't mind getting wet either.

Presently, she found Bijju sheltering in a cave. He would have enjoyed getting wet, but he had his schoolbooks with him and he couldn't afford to let them get spoilt. When he saw Binya, he came out of the cave and shared the umbrella. He was a head taller than his sister, so he had to hold the umbrella for her, while she held his books.

The cows had been left far behind.

'Neelu, Neelu!' called Binya.

'Gori!' called Bijju.

When their mother saw them sauntering home through the driving rain, she called out: 'Binya! Bijju! Hurry up, and bring the cows in! What are you doing out there in the rain?'

'Just testing the umbrella,' said Bijju.

IV

The rains set in, and the sun only made brief appearances. The hills turned a lush green. Ferns sprang up on walls and tree trunks. Giant lilies reared up like leopards from the tall grass. A white mist coiled and uncoiled as it floated up from the valley. It was a beautiful season, except for the leeches.

Every day, Binya came home with a couple of leeches fastened to the flesh of her bare legs. They fell off by themselves just as soon as they'd had their thimbleful of blood, but you didn't know they were on you until they fell off, and then, later, the skin became very sore and itchy. Some of the older people still believed that to be bled by leeches was a remedy for various ailments. Whenever Ram Bharosa had a headache, he applied a leech to his throbbing temple.

Three days of incessant rain had flooded out a number of small animals who lived in holes in the ground. Binya's mother suddenly found the roof full of field rats. She had to drive them out; they ate too much of her stored-up wheat flour and rice. Bijju liked lifting up large rocks to disturb the scorpions who were sleeping beneath. And snakes came out to bask in the sun.

Binya had just crossed the small stream at the bottom of the hill when she saw something gliding out of the bushes and coming towards her. It was a long black snake. A clatter of loose stones frightened it. Seeing the girl in its way, it rose up, hissing, prepared to strike. The forked tongue darted out, the venomous head lunged at Binya.

Binya's umbrella was open as usual. She thrust it forward, between herself and the snake, and the snake's hard snout thudded twice against the strong silk of the umbrella. The reptile then turned and slithered away over the wet rocks, disappearing into a clump of ferns.

Binya forgot about the cows and ran all the way home to tell her mother how she had been saved by the umbrella. Bijju had to put away his books and go out to fetch the cows. He carried a stout stick, in case he met with any snakes.

◆

First the summer sun, and now the endless rain, meant that the umbrella was beginning to fade a little. From a bright blue it had changed to a light blue. But it was still a pretty thing, and tougher than it looked, and Ram Bharosa still desired it. He did not want to sell it; he wanted to own it. He was probably the richest man in the area—so why shouldn't he have a blue umbrella? Not a day passed without his getting a glimpse of Binya and the umbrella; and the more he saw the umbrella, the more he wanted it.

The schools closed during the monsoon, but this didn't mean that Bijju could sit at home doing nothing. Neelu and Gori were providing more milk than was required at home, so Binya's mother was able to sell a kilo of milk every day: half a kilo to the schoolmaster, and half a kilo (at reduced rate) to the temple pujari. Bijju had to deliver the milk every morning.

Ram Bharosa had asked Bijju to work in his shop during the holidays, but Bijju didn't have time—he had to help his mother with the ploughing and the transplanting of the rice seedlings. So, Ram Bharosa employed a boy from the next village, a boy called Rajaram. He did all the washing-up, and ran various errands. He went to the same school as Bijju, but the two boys were not friends.

One day, as Binya passed the shop, twirling her blue umbrella, Rajaram noticed that his employer gave a deep sigh and began muttering to himself.

'What's the matter, Babuji?' asked the boy.

'Oh, nothing,' said Ram Bharosa. 'It's just a sickness that has come upon me. And it's all due to that girl Binya and her wretched umbrella.'

'Why, what has she done to you?'

'Refused to sell me her umbrella! There's pride for you. And I offered her ten rupees.'

'Perhaps, if you gave her twelve...'

'But it isn't new any longer. It isn't worth eight rupees now. All the same, I'd like to have it.'

'You wouldn't make a profit on it,' said Rajaram.

'It's not the profit I'm after, wretch! It's the thing itself. It's the beauty of it!'

'And what would you do with it, Babuji? You don't visit anyone—you're seldom out of your shop. Of what use would it be to you?'

'Of what use is a poppy in a cornfield? Of what use is a rainbow? Of what use are you, numbskull? Wretch! I, too, have a soul. I want the umbrella, because—because I want its beauty to be mine!'

Rajaram put the kettle on to boil, began dusting the counter, all the time muttering: 'I'm as useful as an umbrella,' and then, after a short period of intense thinking, said: 'What will you give me, Babuji, if I get the umbrella for you?'

'What do you mean?' asked the old man.

'You know what I mean. What will you give me?'

'You mean to steal it, don't you, you wretch? What a delightful child you are! I'm glad you're not my son or my enemy. But look, everyone will know it has been stolen, and then how will I be able to show off with it?'

'You will have to gaze upon it in secret,' said Rajaram with a chuckle. 'Or take it into Tehri, and have it coloured red! That's your problem. But tell me, Babuji, do you want it badly enough to pay me three rupees for stealing it without being seen?'

Ram Bharosa gave the boy a long, sad look. 'You're a sharp boy,' he said. 'You'll come to a bad end. I'll give you two rupees.'

'Three,' said the boy.

'Two,' said the old man.

'You don't really want it, I can see that,' said the boy.

'Wretch!' said the old man. 'Evil one! Darkener of my doorstep! Fetch me the umbrella, and I'll give you three rupees.'

V

Binya was in the forest glade where she had first seen the umbrella. No one came there for picnics during the monsoon. The grass was always wet and the pine needles were slippery underfoot. The tall trees shut out the light, and poisonous-looking mushrooms, orange and purple, sprang up everywhere. But it was a good place for porcupines, who seemed to like the mushrooms, and Binya was searching for porcupine quills.

The hill people didn't think much of porcupine quills, but far away in southern India, the quills were valued as charms and sold at a rupee each. So, Ram Bharosa paid a tenth of a rupee for each quill brought to him, and he in turn sold the quills at a profit to a trader from the plains.

Binya had already found five quills, and she knew there'd be more in the long grass. For once, she'd put her umbrella down. She had to put it aside if she was to search the ground thoroughly.

It was Rajaram's chance.

He'd been following Binya for some time, concealing himself behind trees and rocks, creeping closer whenever she became absorbed in her search. He was anxious that she should not see him and be able to recognize him later.

He waited until Binya had wandered some distance from the umbrella. Then, running forward at a crouch, he seized the open umbrella and dashed off with it.

But Rajaram had very big feet. Binya heard his heavy footsteps and turned just in time to see him as he disappeared between the trees. She cried out, dropped the porcupine quills, and gave chase.

Binya was swift and sure-footed, but Rajaram had a long stride. All the same, he made the mistake of running downhill. A long-legged person is much faster going uphill than down. Binya reached the edge of the forest glade in time to see the thief scrambling down the path to the stream. He had closed the umbrella so that it would not hinder his flight.

Binya was beginning to gain on the boy. He kept to the path, while she simply slid and leapt down the steep hillside. Near the bottom of the hill the path began to straighten out, and it was here that the long-legged boy began to forge ahead again.

Bijju was coming home from another direction. He had a bundle of sticks which he'd collected for the kitchen fire. As he reached the path, he saw Binya rushing down the hill as though all the mountain spirits in Garhwal were after her.

'What's wrong?' he called. 'Why are you running?'

Binya paused only to point at the fleeing Rajaram.

'My umbrella!' she cried. 'He has stolen it!'

Bijju dropped his bundle of sticks, and ran after his sister. When he reached her side, he said, 'I'll soon catch him!' and went sprinting away over the lush green grass. He was fresh, and he was soon well-ahead of Binya and gaining on the thief.

Rajaram was crossing the shallow stream when Bijju caught up with him. Rajaram was the taller boy, but Bijju was much stronger. He flung himself at the thief, caught him by the legs, and brought him down in the water. Rajaram got to his feet and tried to drag himself away, but Bijju still had him by a leg. Rajaram overbalanced and came down with a great splash. He had let the umbrella fall. It began to float away on the current. Just then Binya arrived, flushed and breathless, and went dashing into the stream after the umbrella.

Meanwhile, a tremendous fight was taking place. Locked in fierce combat, the two boys swayed together on a rock, tumbled on to the sand, rolled over and over the pebbled bank until they were again thrashing about in the shallows of the stream. The magpies, bulbuls and other birds were disturbed, and flew away with cries of alarm.

Covered with mud, gasping and spluttering, the boys groped for each other in the water. After five minutes of frenzied struggle, Bijju emerged victorious.

Rajaram lay flat on his back on the sand, exhausted, while Bijju sat astride him, pinning him down with his arms and legs.

'Let me get up!' gasped Rajaram. 'Let me go—I don't want your useless umbrella!'

'Then why did you take it?' demanded Bijju. 'Come on—tell me why!'

'It was that skinflint Ram Bharosa,' said Rajaram. 'He told me to get it for him. He said if I didn't fetch it, I'd lose my job.'

VI

By early October, the rains were coming to an end. The leeches disappeared. The ferns turned yellow, and the sunlight on the green hills was mellow and golden, like the limes on the small tree in front of Binya's home. Bijju's days were happy ones as he came home from school, munching on roasted corn. Binya's umbrella had turned a pale milky blue, and was patched in several places, but it was still the prettiest umbrella in the village, and she still carried it with her wherever she went.

The cold, cruel winter wasn't far off, but somehow October seems longer than other months, because it is a kind month: the grass is good to be upon, the breeze is warm and gentle and pine-scented. That October, everyone seemed contented—everyone, that is, except Ram Bharosa.

The old man had by now given up all hope of ever possessing Binya's umbrella. He wished he had never set eyes on it. Because of the umbrella, he had suffered the tortures of greed, the despair of loneliness. Because of the umbrella, people had stopped coming to his shop!

Ever since it had become known that Ram Bharosa had tried to have the umbrella stolen, the village people had turned against him. They stopped trusting the old man, instead of buying their soap and tea and matches from his shop, they preferred to walk an extra mile to the shops near the Tehri bus stand. Who would have dealings with a man who had sold his soul for an umbrella? The children taunted him, twisted his name around. From 'Ram the Trustworthy' he became 'Trusty Umbrella Thief'.

The old man sat alone in his empty shop, listening to the eternal hissing of his kettle and wondering if anyone would ever again step in for a cup of tea. Ram Bharosa had lost his own appetite, and ate and drank very little. There was no money coming in. He had his savings in a bank in Tehri, but it was a terrible thing to have to dip into them! To save money, he had dismissed the blundering Rajaram. So, he was left without any company. The roof leaked and the wind got in through the corrugated tin sheets, but Ram Bharosa didn't care.

Bijju and Binya passed his shop almost every day. Bijju went by with a loud but tuneless whistle. He was one of the world's whistlers; cares rested lightly on his shoulders. But, strangely enough, Binya crept quietly past the shop, looking the other way, almost as though she was in some way responsible for the misery of Ram Bharosa.

She kept reasoning with herself, telling herself that the umbrella was her very own, and that she couldn't help it if others were jealous of it. But had she loved the umbrella too much? Had it mattered more to her than people mattered? She couldn't help feeling that, in a small way, she was the cause of the sad look on Ram Bharosa's face ('His face is a yard long,' said Bijju) and the ruinous condition of his shop. It was all due to his own greed, no doubt, but she didn't want him to feel too bad about what he'd done, because it made her feel bad about herself; and so she closed the umbrella whenever she came near the shop, opening it again only when she was out of sight.

One day towards the end of October, when she had ten paise in her pocket, she entered the shop and asked the old man for a toffee.

She was Ram Bharosa's first customer in almost two weeks. He looked suspiciously at the girl. Had she come to taunt him, to flaunt the umbrella in his face? She had placed her coin on the counter. Perhaps it was a bad coin. Ram Bharosa picked it up and bit it; he held it up to the light; he rang it on the ground. It was a good coin. He gave Binya the toffee.

Binya had already left the shop when Ram Bharosa saw the closed umbrella lying on his counter. There it was, the blue umbrella he had always wanted, within his grasp at last! He had only to hide it at the back of his shop, and no one would know that he had it, no one could prove that Binya had left it behind.

He stretched out his trembling, bony hand, and took the umbrella by the handle. He pressed it open. He stood beneath it, in the dark shadows of his shop, where no sun or rain could ever touch it.

'But I'm never in the sun or in the rain,' he said aloud. 'Of what use is an umbrella to me?'

And he hurried outside and ran after Binya.

'Binya, Binya!' he shouted. 'Binya, you've left your umbrella behind!'

He wasn't used to running, but he caught up with her, held out the umbrella, saying, 'You forgot it—the umbrella!'

In that moment it belonged to both of them.

But Binya didn't take the umbrella. She shook her head and said, 'You keep it. I don't need it anymore.'

'But it's such a pretty umbrella!' protested Ram Bharosa. 'It's the best umbrella in the village.'

'I know,' said Binya. 'But an umbrella isn't everything.'

And she left the old man holding the umbrella, and went tripping down the road, and there was nothing between her and the bright blue sky.

VII

Well, now that Ram Bharosa has the blue umbrella—a gift from Binya, as he tells everyone—he is sometimes persuaded to go out into the sun or the rain, and as a result he looks much healthier. Sometimes he uses the umbrella to chase away pigs or goats. It is always left open outside the shop, and anyone who wants to borrow it may do so; and so in a way it has become everyone's umbrella. It is faded and patchy, but it is still the best umbrella in the village.

People are visiting Ram Bharosa's shop again. Whenever Bijju or Binya stop for a cup of tea, he gives them a little extra milk or sugar. They like their tea sweet and milky.

A few nights ago, a bear visited Ram Bharosa's shop. There had been snow on the higher ranges of the Himalayas, and the bear had been finding it difficult to obtain food; so it had come lower down, to see what it could pick up near the village. That night it scrambled on to the tin roof of Ram Bharosa's shop, and made off with a huge pumpkin which had been ripening on the roof. But in climbing off the roof, the bear had lost a claw.

Next morning Ram Bharosa found the claw just outside the door of his shop. He picked it up and put it in his pocket. A bear's claw was a lucky find.

A day later, when he went into the market town, he took the claw with him, and left it with a silversmith, giving the craftsman certain instructions. The silversmith made a locket for the claw, then he gave it a thin silver chain. When Ram Bharosa came again, he paid the silversmith ten rupees for his work.

The days were growing shorter, and Binya had to be home a little earlier every evening. There was a hungry leopard at large, and she couldn't leave the cows out after dark.

She was hurrying past Ram Bharosa's shop when the old man called out to her.

'Binya, spare a minute! I want to show you something.'

Binya stepped into the shop.

'What do you think of it?' asked Ram Bharosa, showing her the silver pendant with the claw.

'It's so beautiful,' said Binya, just touching the claw and the silver chain.

'It's a bear's claw,' said Ram Bharosa. 'That's even luckier than a leopard's claw. Would you like to have it?'

'I have no money,' said Binya.

'That doesn't matter. You gave me the umbrella, I give you the claw! Come, let's see what it looks like on you.'

He placed the pendant on Binya, and indeed it looked very beautiful on her.

Ram Bharosa says he will never forget the smile she gave him when she left the shop.

She was halfway home when she realized she had left the cows behind.

'Neelu, Neelu!' she called. 'Oh, Gori!'

There was a faint tinkle of bells as the cows came slowly down the mountain path.

In the distance she could hear her mother and Bijju calling for her.

She began to sing. They heard her singing, and knew she was safe and near.

She walked home through the darkening glade, singing of the stars, and the trees stood still and listened to her, and the mountains were glad.

A LONG WALK FOR BINA

I

A leopard, lithe and sinewy, drank at the mountain stream, and then lay down on the grass to bask in the late February sunshine. Its tail twitched occasionally and the animal appeared to be sleeping. At the sound of distant voices it raised its head to listen, then stood up and leapt lightly over the boulders in the stream, disappearing among the trees on the opposite bank.

A minute or two later, three children came walking down the forest path. They were a girl and two boys, and they were singing in their local dialect an old song they had learnt from their grandparents.

> Five more miles to go!
> We climb through rain and snow.
> A river to cross...
> A mountain to pass...
> Now we've four more miles to go!

Their school satchels looked new, their clothes had been washed and pressed. Their loud and cheerful singing startled a spotted forktail. The bird left its favourite rock in the stream and flew down the dark ravine.

'Well, we have only three more miles to go,' said the bigger boy, Prakash, who had been this way hundreds of times. 'But first we have to cross the stream.'

He was a sturdy twelve-year-old with eyes like black currants and a mop of bushy hair that refused to settle down on his head. The girl and her small brother were taking this path for the first time.

'I'm feeling tired, Bina,' said the little boy.

Bina smiled at him, and Prakash said, 'Don't worry, Sonu, you'll get used to the walk. There's plenty of time.' He glanced at the old watch he'd been given by his grandfather. It needed constant winding. 'We can rest here for five or six minutes.'

They sat down on a smooth boulder and watched the clear water of the shallow stream tumbling downhill. Bina examined the old watch on Prakash's wrist. The glass was badly scratched and she could barely make out the figures on the dial. 'Are you sure it still gives the right time?' she asked.

'Well, it loses five minutes every day, so I put it ten minutes ahead at night. That means by morning it's quite accurate! Even our teacher, Mr Mani, asks me for the time. If he doesn't ask, I tell him! The clock in our classroom keeps stopping.'

They removed their shoes and let the cold mountain water run over their feet. Bina was the same age as Prakash. She had pink cheeks, soft brown eyes, and hair that was just beginning to lose its natural curls. Hers was a gentle face, but a determined little chin showed that she could be a strong person. Sonu, her younger brother, was ten. He was a thin boy who had been sickly as a child but was now beginning to fill out. Although he did not look very athletic, he could run like the wind.

II

Bina had been going to school in her own village of Koli, on the other side of the mountain. But it had been a primary school, finishing at Class 5. Now, in order to study in Class 6, she would have to walk several miles every day to Nauti, where there was a high school going up to Class 8. It had been decided that Sonu would also shift to the new school, to give Bina company. Prakash, their neighbour in Koli, was already a pupil at the Nauti school. His mischievous nature, which sometimes got him into trouble, had resulted in his having to repeat a year.

But this didn't seem to bother him. 'What's the hurry?' he had told his indignant parents. 'You're not sending me to a foreign land when I finish school. And our cows aren't running away, are they?'

'You would prefer to look after the cows, wouldn't you?' asked Bina, as they got up to continue their walk.

'Oh, school's all right. Wait till you see old Mr Mani. He always gets our names mixed up, as well as the subjects he's supposed to be teaching. At our last lesson, instead of maths, he gave us a geography lesson!'

'More fun than maths,' said Bina.

'Yes, but there's a new teacher this year. She's very young they say, just out of college. I wonder what she'll be like.'

Bina walked faster and Sonu had some trouble keeping up with them. She was excited about the new school and the prospect of different surroundings. She had seldom been outside her own village, with its small school and single ration shop. The day's routine never varied—helping her mother in the fields or with household tasks like fetching water from the spring or cutting grass and fodder for the cattle. Her father, who was a soldier, was away for nine months in the year and Sonu was still too small for the heavier tasks.

As they neared Nauti Village, they were joined by other children coming from different directions. Even where there were no major roads, the mountains were full of little lanes and shortcuts. Like a game of snakes and ladders, these narrow paths zigzagged around the hills and villages, cutting through fields and crossing narrow ravines until they came together to form a fairly busy road along which mules, cattle and goats joined the throng.

Nauti was a fairly large village, and from here a broader but dustier road started for Tehri. There was a small bus, several trucks and (for part of the way) a road roller. The road hadn't been completed because the heavy diesel roller couldn't take the steep climb to Nauti. It stood on the roadside halfway up the road from Tehri.

Prakash knew almost everyone in the area, and exchanged greetings and gossip with other children as well as with muleteers, bus drivers, milkmen and labourers working on the road. He loved telling everyone the time, even if they weren't interested.

'It's nine o'clock,' he would announce, glancing at his wrist. 'Isn't your bus leaving today?'

'Off with you!' the bus driver would respond, 'I'll leave when I'm ready.'

As the children approached Nauti, the small flat school buildings came into view on the outskirts of the village, fringed by a line of long-leaved pines. A small crowd had assembled on the one playing field. Something unusual seemed to have happened. Prakash ran forward to see what it was all about. Bina and Sonu stood aside, waiting in a patch of sunlight near the boundary wall.

Prakash soon came running back to them. He was bubbling over with excitement.

'It's Mr Mani!' he gasped. 'He's disappeared! People are saying a leopard must have carried him off!'

III

Mr Mani wasn't really old. He was about fifty-five and was expected to retire soon. But for the children, most adults over forty seemed ancient! And Mr Mani had always been a bit absent-minded, even as a young man.

He had gone out for his early morning walk, saying he'd be back by eight o'clock, in time to have his breakfast and be ready for class. He wasn't married, but his sister and her husband stayed with him. When it was past nine o'clock his sister presumed he'd stopped at a neighbour's house for breakfast (he loved tucking into other people's breakfast) and that he had gone on to school from there. But when the school bell rang at ten o'clock, and everyone but Mr Mani was present, questions were asked and guesses were made.

No one had seen him return from his walk and enquiries made in the village showed that he had not stopped at anyone's house. For Mr Mani to disappear was puzzling; for him to disappear without his breakfast was extraordinary.

Then a milkman returning from the next village said he had seen a leopard sitting on a rock on the outskirts of the pine forest. There had been talk of a cattle-killer in the valley, of leopards and other animals being displaced by the construction of a dam. But as yet no one had heard of a leopard attacking a man. Could Mr Mani have been its first victim? Someone found a strip of red cloth entangled in a blackberry bush and went running through the village showing it to everyone. Mr Mani had been known to wear red pyjamas. Surely he had been seized and eaten! But where were his remains? And why had he been in his pyjamas?

Meanwhile Bina and Sonu and the rest of the children had followed their teachers into the school playground. Feeling a little lost, Bina looked around for Prakash. She found herself facing a dark, slender young woman wearing spectacles, who must have been in her early twenties—just a little too old to be another student. She had a kind, expressive face and she seemed a little concerned by all that had been happening.

Bina noticed that she had lovely hands; it was obvious that the new teacher hadn't milked cows or worked in the fields!

'You must be new here,' said the teacher, smiling at Bina. 'And is this your little brother?'

'Yes, we've come from Koli Village. We were at school there.'

'It's a long walk from Koli. You didn't see any leopards, did you? Well, I'm new too. Are you in the Class 6?'

'Sonu is in the third. I'm in the 6th.'

'Then I'm your new teacher. My name is Tania Ramola. Come along, let's see if we can settle down in our classroom.'

♦

Mr Mani turned up at twelve o'clock, wondering what all the fuss was about. No, he snapped, he had not been attacked by a leopard; and yes, he had lost his pyjamas and would someone kindly return them to him?

'How did you lose your pyjamas, sir?' asked Prakash.

'They were blown off the washing line!' snapped Mr Mani.

After much questioning, Mr Mani admitted that he had gone further than he had intended, and that he had lost his way coming back. He had been a bit upset because the new teacher, a slip of a girl, had been given charge of the 6th, while he was still with the fifth, along with that troublesome boy Prakash, who kept on reminding him of the time! The Headmaster had explained that as Mr Mani was due to retire at the end of the year, the school did not wish to burden him with a senior class. But Mr Mani looked upon the whole thing as a plot to get rid of him. He glowered at Miss Ramola whenever he passed her. And when she smiled back at him, he looked the other way!

Mr Mani had been getting even more absent-minded of late—putting on his shoes without his socks, wearing his homespun waistcoat inside out, mixing up people's names and, of course, eating other people's lunches and dinners. His sister had made a mutton broth for the postmaster, who was down with 'flu', and had asked Mr Mani to take it over in a thermos. When the postmaster opened the thermos, he found only a few drops of broth at the bottom—Mr Mani had drunk the rest somewhere along the way.

When sometimes Mr Mani spoke of his coming retirement, it was to describe his plans for the small field he owned just behind the house. Right now, it was full of potatoes, which did not require much looking after; but he had plans for growing dahlias, roses, French beans, and other fruits and flowers.

The next time he visited Tehri, he promised himself, he would buy some dahlia bulbs and rose cuttings. The monsoon season would be a good time to put them down. And meanwhile, his potatoes were still flourishing.

IV

Bina enjoyed her first day at the new school. She felt at ease with Miss Ramola, as did most of the boys and girls in her class. Tania Ramola had been to distant towns such as Delhi and Lucknow—places they had only heard about—and it was said that she had a brother who was a pilot and flew planes all over the world. Perhaps he'd fly over Nauti some day!

Most of the children had of course seen planes flying overhead, but none of them had seen a ship, and only a few had been on a train. Tehri mountain was far from the railway and hundreds of miles from the sea. But they all knew about the big dam that was being built at Tehri, just forty miles away.

Bina, Sonu and Prakash had company for part of the way home, but gradually the other children went off in different directions. Once they had crossed the stream, they were on their own again.

It was a steep climb all the way back to their village. Prakash had a supply of peanuts which he shared with Bina and Sonu, and at a small spring they quenched their thirst.

When they were less than a mile from home, they met a postman who had finished his round of the villages in the area and was now returning to Nauti.

'Don't waste time along the way,' he told them. 'Try to get home before dark.'

'What's the hurry?' asked Prakash, glancing at his watch. 'It's only five o'clock.'

'There's a leopard around. I saw it this morning, not far from the stream. No one is sure how it got here. So don't take any chances. Get home early.'

'So, there really is a leopard,' said Sonu.

They took his advice and walked faster, and Sonu forgot to complain about his aching feet.

They were home well before sunset.

There was a smell of cooking in the air and they were hungry.

'Cabbage and roti,' said Prakash gloomily. 'But I could eat anything today.' He stopped outside his small slate-roofed house, and Bina and Sonu waved goodbye and carried on across a couple of ploughed fields until they reached their small stone house.

'Stuffed tomatoes,' said Sonu, sniffing just outside the front door.

'And lemon pickle,' said Bina, who had helped cut, sun and salt the lemons a month previously.

Their mother was lighting the kitchen stove. They greeted her with great hugs and demands for an immediate dinner. She was a good cook who could make even the simplest of dishes taste delicious. Her favourite saying was, 'Home-made bread is better than roast meat abroad,' and Bina and Sonu had to agree.

Electricity had yet to reach their village, and they took their meal by the light of a kerosene lamp. After the meal, Sonu settled down to do a little homework, while Bina stepped outside to look at the stars.

Across the fields, someone was playing a flute. 'It must be Prakash,' thought Bina. 'He always breaks off on the high notes.' But the flute music was simple and appealing, and she began singing softly to herself in the dark.

V

Mr Mani was having trouble with the porcupines. They had been getting into his garden at night and digging up and eating his potatoes. From his bedroom window—left open now that the mild April weather had arrived—he could listen to them enjoying the vegetables he had worked hard to grow. Scrunch, scrunch! katar, katar, as their sharp teeth sliced through the largest and juiciest of potatoes. For Mr Mani it was as though they were biting through his own flesh. And the sound of them digging industriously as they rooted up those healthy, leafy plants made him tremble with rage and indignation. The unfairness of it all!

Yes, Mr Mani hated porcupines. He prayed for their destruction, their removal from the face of the earth. But, as his friends were quick to point out, 'The creator made porcupines too,' and in any case you could never see the creatures or catch them, they were completely nocturnal.

Mr Mani got out of bed every night, torch in one hand, a stout stick in the other but, as soon as he stepped into the garden, the crunching and digging stopped and he was greeted by the most infuriating of silences. He would grope around in the dark, swinging wildly with the stick, but not a single porcupine was to be seen or heard. As soon as he was back in bed, the sounds would start all over again—scrunch, scrunch, katar, katar...

Mr Mani came to his class tired and dishevelled, with rings under his eyes and a permanent frown on his face. It took some time for his pupils to discover the reason for his misery, but when they did, they felt sorry for their teacher and took to discussing ways and means of saving his potatoes from the porcupines.

It was Prakash who came up with the idea of a moat or water ditch. 'Porcupines don't like water,' he said knowledgeably.

'How do you know?' asked one of his friends.

'Throw water on one and see how it runs! They don't like getting their quills wet.'

There was no one who could disprove Prakash's theory, and the class fell in with the idea of building a moat, especially as it meant getting most of the day off.

'Anything to make Mr Mani happy,' said the Headmaster, and the rest of the school watched with envy as the pupils of Class 5, armed with spades and shovels collected from all parts of the village, took up their positions around Mr Mani's potato field and began digging a ditch.

By evening the moat was ready, but it was still dry and the porcupines got in again that night and had a great feast.

'At this rate,' said Mr Mani gloomily, 'there won't be any potatoes left to save.'

But the next day, Prakash and the other boys and girls managed to divert the water from a stream that flowed past the village. They had the satisfaction of watching it flow gently into the ditch. Everyone went home in a good mood. By nightfall, the ditch had overflowed, the potato field was flooded, and Mr Mani found himself trapped inside his house. But Prakash and his friends had won the day. The porcupines stayed away that night!

♦

A month had passed, and wild violets, daisies and buttercups now sprinkled the hill slopes and, on her way to school, Bina gathered enough to make a little posy. The bunch of flowers fitted easily into an old ink well. Miss Ramola was delighted to find this little display in the middle of her desk.

'Who put these here?' she asked in surprise.

Bina kept quiet, and the rest of the class smiled secretively. After that, they took turns bringing flowers for the classroom.

On her long walks to school and home again, Bina became aware that April was the month of new leaves. The oak leaves were bright green above and silver beneath, and when they rippled in the breeze they were clouds of silvery green. The path was strewn with old leaves, dry and crackly. Sonu loved kicking them around.

Clouds of white butterflies floated across the stream. Sonu was chasing a butterfly when he stumbled over something dark and repulsive. He went sprawling on the grass. When he got to his feet, he looked down at the remains of a small animal.

'Bina! Prakash! Come quickly!' he shouted.

It was part of a sheep, killed some days earlier by a much larger animal.

'Only a leopard could have done this,' said Prakash.

'Let's get away, then,' said Sonu. 'It might still be around!'

'No, there's nothing left to eat. The leopard will be hunting elsewhere by now. Perhaps it's moved on to the next valley.'

'Still, I'm frightened,' said Sonu. 'There may be more leopards!'

Bina took him by the hand. 'Leopards don't attack humans!' she said.

'They will, if they get a taste for people!' insisted Prakash.

'Well, this one hasn't attacked any people as yet,' said Bina, although she couldn't be sure. Hadn't there been rumours of a leopard attacking some workers near the dam? But she did not want Sonu to feel afraid, so she did not mention the story. All she said was, 'It has probably come here because of all the activity near the dam.'

All the same, they hurried home. And for a few days, whenever they reached the stream, they crossed over very quickly, unwilling to linger too long at that lovely spot.

VI

A few days later, a school party was on its way to Tehri to see the new dam that was being built.

Miss Ramola had arranged to take her class, and Mr Mani, not wishing to be left out, insisted on taking his class as well. That meant there were about fifty boys and girls taking part in the outing. The little bus could only take thirty. A friendly truck driver agreed to take some children if they were prepared to sit on sacks of potatoes. And Prakash persuaded the owner of the diesel roller to turn it around and head it back to Tehri—with him and a couple of friends up on the driving seat.

Prakash's small group set off at sunrise, as they had to walk some distance in order to reach the stranded road roller. The bus left at 9 a.m. with Miss Ramola and her class, and Mr Mani and some of his pupils. The truck was to follow later.

It was Bina's first visit to a large town, and her first bus ride. The sharp curves along the winding, downhill road made several children feel sick. The bus driver seemed to be in a tearing hurry. He took them along at a rolling, rollicking speed, which made Bina feel quite giddy. She rested her head on her arms and refused to look out of the window. Hairpin bends and cliff edges, pine forests and snow-capped peaks, all swept past her, but she felt too ill to want to look at anything. It was just as well—those sudden drops, hundreds of feet to the valley below, were quite frightening. Bina began to wish that she hadn't come—or that she had joined Prakash on the road roller instead!

Miss Ramola and Mr Mani didn't seem to notice the lurching and groaning of the old bus. They had made this journey many times. They were busy arguing about the advantages and disadvantages of large dams—an argument that was to continue on and off for much of the day.

Meanwhile, Prakash and his friends had reached the roller. The driver hadn't turned up, but they managed to reverse it and get it going in the direction of Tehri. They were soon overtaken by both bus and truck but kept moving along at a steady chug. Prakash spotted Bina at the window of the bus and waved cheerfully. She responded feebly.

Bina felt better when the road levelled out near Tehri. As they crossed an old bridge over the wide river, they were startled by a loud bang which made the bus shudder. A cloud of dust rose above the town.

'They're blasting the mountain,' said Miss Ramola.

'End of a mountain,' said Mr Mani, mournfully.

While they were drinking cups of tea at the bus stop, waiting for the potato truck and the road roller, Miss Ramola and Mr Mani continued their argument about the dam. Miss Ramola maintained that it would bring electric power and water for irrigation to large areas of the country, including the surrounding area. Mr Mani declared that it was a menace, as it was situated in an earthquake zone. There would be a terrible disaster if the dam burst! Bina found it all very confusing. And what about the animals in the area, she wondered, what would happen to them?

The argument was becoming quite heated when the potato truck arrived. There was no sign of the road roller, so it was decided that Mr Mani should wait for Prakash and his friends while Miss Ramola's group went ahead.

◆

Some eight or nine miles before Tehri, the road roller had broken down, and Prakash and his friends were forced to walk. They had not gone far, however, when a mule train came along—five or six mules that had been delivering sacks of grain in Nauti. A boy rode on the first mule, but the others had no loads.

'Can you give us a ride to Tehri?' called Prakash.

'Make yourselves comfortable,' said the boy.

There were no saddles, only gunny sacks strapped on to the mules with rope. They had a rough but jolly ride down to the Tehri bus stop. None of them had ever ridden mules; but they had saved at least an hour on the road.

Looking around the bus stop for the rest of the party, they could find no one from their school. And Mr Mani, who should have been waiting for them, had vanished.

VII

Tania Ramola and her group had taken the steep road to the hill above Tehri. Half an hour's climbing brought them to a little plateau which overlooked the town, the river and the dam site.

The earthworks for the dam were only just coming up, but a wide tunnel had been bored through the mountain to divert the river into another channel. Down below, the old town was still spread out across the valley and from a distance it looked quite charming and picturesque.

'Will the whole town be swallowed up by the waters of the dam?' asked Bina.

'Yes, all of it,' said Miss Ramola. 'The clock tower and the old palace. The long bazaar, and the temples, the schools and the jail, and hundreds of houses, for many miles up the valley. All those people will have to go—thousands of them! Of course they'll be resettled elsewhere.'

'But the town's been here for hundreds of years,' said Bina. 'They were quite happy without the dam, weren't they?'

'I suppose they were. But the dam isn't just for them—it's for the millions who live further downstream, across the plains.'

'And it doesn't matter what happens to this place?'

'The local people will be given new homes somewhere else.' Miss Ramola found herself on the defensive and decided to change the subject. 'Everyone must be hungry. It's time we had our lunch.'

Bina kept quiet. She didn't think the local people would want to go away. And it was a good thing, she mused, that there was only a small stream and not a big river running past her village. To be uprooted like this—a town and hundreds of villages—and put down somewhere on the hot, dusty plains—seemed to her unbearable.

'Well, I'm glad I don't live in Tehri,' she said.

She did not know it, but all the animals and most of the birds had already left the area. The leopard had been among them.

◆

They walked through the colourful, crowded bazaar, where fruit sellers did business beside silversmiths, and pavement vendors sold everything from umbrellas to glass bangles. Sparrows attacked sacks of grain, monkeys made off with bananas, and stray cows and dogs rummaged in refuse bins, but nobody took any notice. Music blared from radios. Buses blew their horns. Sonu bought a whistle to add to the general din, but Miss Ramola told him to put it away. Bina had kept five rupees aside, and now she used it to buy a cotton headscarf for her mother.

As they were about to enter a small restaurant for a meal, they were joined by Prakash and his companions; but of Mr Mani there was still no sign.

'He must have met one of his relatives,' said Prakash. 'He has relatives everywhere.'

After a simple meal of rice and lentils, they walked the length of the bazaar without finding Mr Mani. At last, when they were about to give up the search, they saw him emerge from a by-lane, a large sack slung over his shoulder.

'Sir, where have you been?' asked Prakash. 'We have been looking for you everywhere.'

On Mr Mani's face was a look of triumph.

'Help me with this bag,' he said breathlessly.

'You've bought more potatoes, sir,' said Prakash.

'Not potatoes, boy. Dahlia bulbs!'

VIII

It was dark by the time they were all back in Nauti. Mr Mani had refused to be separated from his sack of dahlia bulbs, and had been forced to sit in the back of the truck with Prakash and most of the boys.

Bina did not feel so ill on the return journey. Going uphill was definitely better than going downhill! But by the time the bus reached Nauti it was too late for most of the children to walk back to the more distant villages. The boys were put up in different homes, while the girls were given beds in the school verandah.

The night was warm and still. Large moths fluttered around the single bulb that lit the verandah. Counting moths, Sonu soon fell asleep. But Bina stayed awake for some time, listening to the sounds of the night. A nightjar went tonk-tonk in the bushes, and somewhere in the forest an owl hooted softly. The sharp call of a barking deer travelled up the valley from the direction of the stream. Jackals kept howling. It seemed that there were more of them than ever before.

Bina was not the only one to hear the barking deer. The leopard, stretched full length on a rocky ledge, heard it too. The leopard raised its head and then got up slowly. The deer was its natural prey. But there weren't many left, and that was why the leopard, robbed of its forest by the dam, had taken to attacking dogs and cattle near the villages.

As the cry of the barking deer sounded nearer, the leopard left its lookout point and moved swiftly through the shadows towards the stream.

IX

In early June the hills were dry and dusty, and forest fires broke out, destroying shrubs and trees, killing birds and small animals. The resin in the pines made these trees burn more fiercely, and the wind would take sparks from the trees and carry them into the dry grass and leaves, so that new fires would spring up before the old ones had died out. Fortunately, Bina's village was not in the pine belt; the fires did not reach it. But Nauti was surrounded by a fire that raged for three days, and the children had to stay away from school.

And then, towards the end of June, the monsoon rains arrived and there was an end to forest fires. The monsoon lasts three months and the lower Himalayas would be drenched in rain, mist and cloud for the next three months.

The first rain arrived while Bina, Prakash and Sonu were returning home from school. Those first few drops on the dusty path made them cry out with excitement. Then the rain grew heavier and a wonderful aroma rose from the earth.

'The best smell in the world!' exclaimed Bina.

Everything suddenly came to life. The grass, the crops, the trees, the birds. Even the leaves of the trees glistened and looked new.

That first wet weekend, Bina and Sonu helped their mother plant beans, maize and cucumbers. Sometimes, when the rain was very heavy, they had to run indoors. Otherwise they worked in the rain, the soft mud clinging to their bare legs.

Prakash now owned a dog, a black dog with one ear up and one ear down. The dog ran around getting in everyone's way, barking at cows, goats, hens and humans, without frightening any of them. Prakash said it was a very clever dog, but no one else seemed to think so. Prakash also said it would protect the village from the leopard, but others said the dog would be the first to be taken—he'd run straight into the jaws of Mr Spots!

In Nauti, Tania Ramola was trying to find a dry spot in the quarters she'd been given. It was an old building and the roof was leaking in several places. Mugs and buckets were scattered about the floor in order to catch the drips.

Mr Mani had dug up all his potatoes and presented them to the friends and neighbours who had given him lunches and dinners. He was having the time of his life, planting dahlia bulbs all over his garden.

'I'll have a field of many-coloured dahlias!' he announced. 'Just wait till the end of August!'

'Watch out for those porcupines,' warned his sister. 'They

eat dahlia bulbs too!'

Mr Mani made an inspection tour of his moat, no longer in flood, and found everything in good order. Prakash had done his job well.

♦

Now, when the children crossed the stream, they found that the water level had risen by about a foot. Small cascades had turned into waterfalls. Ferns had sprung up on the banks. Frogs chanted.

Prakash and his dog dashed across the stream. Bina and Sonu followed more cautiously. The current was much stronger now and the water was almost up to their knees. Once they had crossed the stream, they hurried along the path, anxious not to be caught in a sudden downpour.

By the time they reached school, each of them had two or three leeches clinging to their legs. They had to use salt to remove them. The leeches were the most troublesome part of the rainy season. Even the leopard did not like them. It could not lie in the long grass without getting leeches on its paws and face.

One day, when Bina, Prakash and Sonu were about to cross the stream they heard a low rumble, which grew louder every second. Looking up at the opposite hill, they saw several trees shudder, tilt outwards and begin to fall. Earth and rocks bulged out from the mountain, then came crashing down into the ravine.

'Landslide!' shouted Sonu.

'It's carried away the path,' said Bina. 'Don't go any further.'

There was a tremendous roar as more rocks, trees and bushes fell away and crashed down the hillside.

Prakash's dog, who had gone ahead, came running back, tail between his legs.

They remained rooted to the spot until the rocks had stopped falling and the dust had settled. Birds circled the area, calling wildly. A frightened barking deer ran past them.

'We can't go to school now,' said Prakash. 'There's no way around.'

They turned and trudged home through the gathering mist.

In Koli, Prakash's parents had heard the roar of the landslide. They were setting out in search of the children when they saw them emerge from the mist, waving cheerfully.

X

They had to miss school for another three days, and Bina was afraid they might not be able to take their final exams. Although Prakash was not really troubled at the thought of missing exams, he did not like feeling helpless just because their path had been swept away. So he explored the hillside until he found a goat-track going around the mountain. It joined up with another path near Nauti. This made their walk longer by a mile, but Bina did not mind. It was much cooler now that the rains were in full swing.

The only trouble with the new route was that it passed close to the leopard's lair. The animal had made this area its own since being forced to leave the dam area.

One day Prakash's dog ran ahead of them barking furiously. Then he ran back whimpering.

'He's always running away from something,' observed Sonu. But a minute later he understood the reason for the dog's fear.

They rounded a bend and Sonu saw the leopard standing in their way. They were struck dumb—too terrified to run. It was a strong, sinewy creature. A low growl rose from its throat. It seemed ready to spring.

They stood perfectly still, afraid to move or say a word. And the leopard must have been equally surprised. It stared at them for a few seconds, then bounded across the path and into the oak forest.

Sonu was shaking. Bina could hear her heart hammering. Prakash could only stammer: 'Did you see the way he sprang? Wasn't he beautiful?'

He forgot to look at his watch for the rest of the day.

A few days later, Sonu stopped and pointed to a large outcrop of rock on the next hill.

The leopard stood far above them, outlined against the sky. It looked strong, majestic. Standing beside it were two young cubs.

'Look at those little ones!' exclaimed Sonu.

'So it's a female, not a male,' said Prakash.

'That's why she was killing so often,' said Bina. 'She had to feed her cubs too.'

They remained still for several minutes, gazing up at the leopard and her cubs. The leopard family took no notice of them.

'She knows we are here,' said Prakash, 'but she doesn't care. She knows we won't harm them.'

'We are cubs too!' said Sonu.

'Yes,' said Bina. 'And there's still plenty of space for all of us. Even when the dam is ready there will still be room for leopards and humans.'

XI

The school exams were over. The rains were nearly over too. The landslide had been cleared, and Bina, Prakash and Sonu were once again crossing the stream.

There was a chill in the air, for it was the end of September.

Prakash had learnt to play the flute quite well, and he played on the way to school and then again on the way home. As a result he did not look at his watch so often. One morning they found a small crowd in front of Mr Mani's house.

'What could have happened?' wondered Bina. 'I hope he hasn't got lost again.'

'Maybe he's sick,' said Sonu.

'Maybe it's the porcupines,' said Prakash.

But it was none of these things.

Mr Mani's first dahlia was in bloom, and half the village had turned up to look at it! It was a huge red double dahlia, so heavy that it had to be supported with sticks. No one had ever seen such a magnificent flower!

Mr Mani was a happy man. And his mood only improved over the coming week, as more and more dahlias flowered—crimson, yellow, purple, mauve, white—button dahlias, pompom dahlias, spotted dahlias, striped dahlias... Mr Mani had them all! A dahlia even turned up on Tania Ramola's desk—he got along quite well with her now—and another brightened up the Headmaster's study.

A week later, on their way home—it was almost the last day of the school term—Bina, Prakash and Sonu talked about what they might do when they grew up.

'I think I'll become a teacher,' said Bina. 'I'll teach children about animals and birds, and trees and flowers.'

'Better than maths!' said Prakash.

'I'll be a pilot,' said Sonu. 'I want to fly a plane like Miss Ramola's brother.'

'And what about you, Prakash?' asked Bina.

Prakash just smiled and said, 'Maybe I'll be a flute player,' and he put the flute to his lips and played a sweet melody.

'Well, the world needs flute players too,' said Bina, as they fell into step beside him.

The leopard had been stalking a barking deer. She paused when she heard the flute and the voices of the children. Her own young ones were growing quickly, but the girl and the two boys did not look much older.

They had started singing their favourite song again.

> Five more miles to go!
> We climb through rain and snow,
> A river to cross...
> A mountain to pass...
> Now we've four more miles to go!

The leopard waited until they had passed, before returning to the trail of the barking deer.

A FACE IN THE DARK

It may give you some idea of rural humour if I begin this tale with an anecdote that concerns me. I was walking alone through a village at night when I met an old man carrying a lantern. I found, to my surprise, that the man was blind. 'Old man,' I asked, 'if you cannot see, why do you carry a lamp?'

'I carry this,' he replied, 'so that fools do not stumble against me in the dark.'

This incident has only a slight connection with the story that follows, but I think it provides the right sort of tone and setting. Mr Oliver, an Anglo-Indian teacher, was returning to his school late one night, on the outskirts of the hill-station of Simla. The school was conducted on English public school lines and the boys, most of them from well-to-do Indian families, wore blazers, caps and ties. *Life* magazine, in a feature on India had once called this school the 'Eton of the East'.

Individuality was not encouraged; they were all destined to become 'leaders of men'.

Mr Oliver had been teaching in the school for several years. Sometimes it seemed like an eternity; for one day followed another with the same monotonous routine. The Simla bazaar, with its cinemas and restaurants, was about two miles from the school; and Mr Oliver, a bachelor, usually strolled into the town in the evening, returning after dark, when he would take a short cut through a pine forest.

When there was a strong wind, the pine trees made sad, eerie sounds that kept most people to the main road. But Mr Oliver was not a nervous or imaginative man. He carried a torch and, on the night I write of, its pale gleam—the batteries were running down—moved fitfully over the narrow forest path. When its flickering light fell on the figure of a boy, who was sitting alone on a rock, Mr Oliver stopped. Boys were not supposed to be out of school after 7 p.m., and it was now well past nine.

'What are you doing out here, boy?' asked Mr Oliver sharply, moving closer so that he could recognize the miscreant. But even as he approached the boy, Mr Oliver sensed that something was wrong. The boy appeared to be crying. His head hung down, he held his face in his hands, and his body shook convulsively. It was a strange, soundless weeping, and Mr Oliver felt distinctly uneasy.

'Well—what's the matter?' he asked, his anger giving way to concern. 'What are you crying for?' The boy would not answer or look up. His body continued to be racked with silent sobbing.

'Come on, boy, you shouldn't be out here at this hour. Tell me the trouble. Look up!'

The boy looked up. He took his hands from his face and looked up at his teacher. The light from Mr Oliver's torch fell on the boy's face—if you could call it a face.

He had no eyes, ears, nose, or mouth. It was just a round, smooth head—with a school cap on top of it. And that's where the story should end—as indeed it has for several people who have had similar experiences and dropped dead of inexplicable heart attacks. But for Mr Oliver it did not end there.

The torch fell from his trembling hand. He turned and

scrambled down the path, running blindly through the trees and calling for help. He was still running towards the school building when he saw a lantern swinging in the middle of the path. Mr Oliver had never before been so pleased to see the night-watchman. He stumbled up to the watchman, gasping for breath and speaking incoherently.

'What is it, Sir?' asked the watchman. 'Has there been an accident? Why are you running?'

'I saw something—something horrible—a boy weeping in the forest—and he had no face!'

'No face, Sir?'

'No eyes, nose, mouth—nothing.'

'Do you mean it was like this, Sir?' asked the watchman, and raised the lamp to his own face. The watchman had no eyes, no ears, no features at all—not even an eyebrow!

The wind blew the lamp out, and Mr Oliver had his heart attack.

LANDOUR BAZAAR

In most North Indian bazaars, there is a clock tower. And like most clocks in clock towers, this one works in fits and starts: listless in summer, sluggish during the monsoon, stopping altogether when it snows in January. Almost every year the tall brick structure gets a coat of paint. It was pink last year. Now it's a livid purple.

From the clock tower at one end to the mule sheds at the other, this old Mussoorie bazaar is a mile long. The tall, shaky three-storey buildings cling to the mountainside, shutting out the sunlight. They are even shakier now that heavy trucks have started rumbling down the narrow street, originally made for nothing heavier than a rickshaw. The street is narrow and damp, retaining all the bazaar smells—sweetmeats frying, smoke from wood or charcoal fires, the sweat and urine of mules, petrol fumes, all these mingle with the smell of mist and old buildings and distant pines.

The bazaar sprang up about 150 years ago to serve the needs of British soldiers who were sent to the Landour convalescent depot to recover from sickness or wounds. The old military hospital, built in 1827, now houses the Defence Institute of

Work Study.* One old resident of the bazaar, a ninety-year-old tailor, can remember the time, in the early years of the century, when the Redcoats marched through the small bazaar on their way to the cantonment church. And they always carried their rifles into church, remembering how many had been surprised in churches during the 1857 uprising.

Today, the Landour bazaar serves the local population, Mussoorie itself being more geared to the needs and interest of tourists. There are a number of silversmiths in Landour. They fashion silver nose-rings, earrings, bracelets and anklets, which are bought by the women from the surrounding Jaunpuri villages. One silversmith had a chest full of old silver rupees. These rupees are sometimes hung on thin silver chains and worn as pendants. I have often seen women in Garhwal wearing pendants or necklaces of rupees embossed with the profiles of Queen Victoria or King Edward VII.

At the other extreme there are the kabari shops, where you can pick up almost everything—a tape recorder discarded by a Woodstock student, or a piece of furniture from grandmother's time in the hill station. Old clothes, Victorian bric-a-brac, and bits of modern gadgetry vie for your attention.

The old clothes are often more reliable than the new. Last winter I bought a new pullover marked 'Made in Nepal' from a Tibetan pavement vendor. I was wearing it on the way home when it began to rain. By the time I reached my cottage, the pullover had shrunk inches and I had some difficulty getting out of it! It was now just the right size for Bijju, the milkman's twelve-year-old son, and I gave it to the boy. But it continued to shrink at every wash, and it is now being worn by Teju, Bijju's

---

*The Defence Institute of Work Study has been renamed the Institute of Technologic Management.

younger brother, who is eight.

At the dark windy corner in the bazaar, one always found an old man hunched up over his charcoal fire, roasting peanuts. He'd been there for as long as I could remember, and he could be seen at almost any hour of the day or night, in all weathers.

He was probably quite tall, but I never saw him standing up. One judged his height from his long, loose limbs. He was very thin, probably tubercular, and the high cheekbones added to the tautness of his tightly stretched skin.

His peanuts were always fresh, crisp and hot. They were popular with small boys, who had a few coins to spend on their way to and from school. On cold winter evenings, there was always a demand for peanuts from people of all ages.

No one seemed to know the old man's name. No one had ever thought of asking. One just took his presence for granted. He was as fixed a landmark as the clock tower or the old cherry tree that grew crookedly from the hillside. He seemed less perishable than the tree, more dependable than the clock. He had no family, but in a way all the world was his family because he was in continuous contact with people. And yet he was a remote sort of being; always polite, even to children, but never familiar. He was seldom alone, but he must have been lonely.

Summer nights he rolled himself up in a thin blanket and slept on the ground beside the dying embers of his fire. During winter he waited until the last cinema show was over, before retiring to the rickshaw coolies' shelter where there was protection from the freezing wind.

Did he enjoy being alive? I often wondered. He was not a joyful person; but then neither was he miserable. Perhaps he was one of those who do not attach overmuch importance to themselves, who are emotionally uninvolved in the life around them, content with their limitations, their dark corners; people on whom cares rest lightly, simply because they do not care at all.

I wanted to get to know the old man better, to sound him out on the immense questions involved in roasting peanuts all one's life; but it's too late now. He died last summer.

That corner remained very empty, very dark, and every time I passed it, I was haunted by visions of the old peanut vendor, troubled by the questions I did not ask; and I wondered if he was really as indifferent to life as he appeared to be.

Then, a few weeks ago, there was a new occupant of the corner, a new seller of peanuts. No relative of the old man, but a boy of thirteen or fourteen. The human personality can impose its own nature on its surroundings. In the old man's time it seemed a dark, gloomy corner. Now it's lit up by sunshine—a sunny personality, smiling, chattering. Old age gives way to youth; and I'm glad I won't be alive when the new peanut vendor grows old. One shouldn't see too many people grow old.

Leaving the main bazaar behind, I walk some way down the Mussoorie–Tehri road, a fine road to walk on, in spite of the dust from an occasional bus or jeep. From Mussoorie to Chamba, a distance of some thirty-five miles, the road seldom descends below 7,000 feet, and there is a continual vista of the snow ranges to the north and valleys and rivers to the south. Dhanaulti is one of the lovelier spots, and the Garhwal Mandal Vikas Nigam has a rest house here, where one can spend an idyllic weekend. Some years ago I walked all the way to Chamba, spending the night at Kaddukhal, from where a short climb takes one to the Surkhanda Devi temple.

Leaving the Tehri road, one can also trek down to the little Aglar river and then up to Nag Tibba, 9,000 feet, which has good oak forests and animals ranging from barking deer to Himalayan bear; but this is an arduous trek and you must be prepared to spend the night in the open or seek the hospitality of a village.

On this particular day I reach Suakholi and rest in a tea shop, a loose stone structure with a tin roof held down by stones. It serves the bus passengers, mule drivers, milkmen and others who use this road.

I find a couple of mules tethered to a pine tree. The mule drivers, handsome men in tattered clothes, sit on a bench in the shade of the tree, drinking tea from brass tumblers. The shopkeeper, a man of indeterminate age—the cold dry winds from the mountain passes having crinkled his face like a walnut—greets me enthusiastically, as he always does. He even produces a chair, which looks a survivor from one of Wilson's rest houses, and may even be a Sheraton. Fortunately, the Mussoorie kabaris do not know about it or they'd have snapped it up long ago. In any case, the stuffing has come out of the seat. The shopkeeper apologizes for its condition: 'The rats were nesting in it.' And then, to reassure me: 'But they have gone now.'

I would just as soon be on the bench with the Jaunpuri mule drivers, but I do not wish to offend Mela Ram, the tea shop owner; so I take his chair into the shade and lower myself into it.

'How long have you kept this shop?'

'Oh, ten...fifteen years, I do not remember.' He hasn't bothered to count the years. Why should he? Outside the towns in the isolation of the hills, life is simply a matter of yesterday, today and tomorrow. And not always tomorrow.

Unlike Mela Ram, the mule drivers have somewhere to go and something to deliver—sacks of potatoes! From Jaunpur to Jaunsar, the potato is probably the crop best suited to these stony, terraced fields. They have to deliver their potatoes in the Landour bazaar and return to their villages before nightfall; and soon they lead their pack animals away, along the dusty road to Mussoorie.

'Tea or lassi?' Mela Ram offers me a choice, and I choose the curd preparation, which is sharp, sour and very refreshing. The wind soughs gently in the upper branches of the pine trees, and I relax in my Sheraton chair like some eighteenth-century nawab who has brought his own furniture into the wilderness. I can see why Wilson did not want to return to the plains when he came this way in the 1850s. Instead, he went further and higher into the mountains and made his home among the people of the Bhagirathi Valley.

Having wandered some way down the Tehri road, it is quite late by the time I return to the Landour bazaar. Lights still twinkle on the hills, but shop fronts are shuttered and the little bazaar is silent. The people living on either side of the narrow street can hear my footsteps, and I hear their casual remarks, music, a burst of laughter.

Through a gap in the rows of buildings I can see Pari Tibba outlined in the moonlight. A greenish phosphorescent glow appears to move here and there about the hillside. This is the 'fairy light' that gives the hill its name Pari Tibba, Fairy Hill. I have no explanation for it, and I don't know anyone else who has been able to explain it satisfactorily; but often from my window I see this greenish light zigzagging about the hill.

A three-quarter moon is up, and the tin roofs of the bazaar, drenched with dew, glisten in the moonlight. Although the street is unlit, I need no torch. I can see every step of the way. I can even read the headlines on the discarded newspaper lying in the gutter.

Although I am alone on the road, I am aware of the life, pulsating around me. It is a cold night, doors and windows are shut; but through the many clinks, narrow fingers of light reach out into the night. Who could still be up? A shopkeeper going through his accounts, a college student preparing for his exams, someone coughing and groaning in the dark.

Three stray dogs are romping in the middle of the road. It is their road now, and they abandon themselves to a wild chase, almost knocking me down.

A jackal slinks across the road, looking to the right and left—he knows his road-drill—to make sure the dogs have gone. A field rat wriggles through a hole in a rotting plank on its nightly foray among sacks of grain and pulses.

Yes, this is an old bazaar. The bakers, tailors, silversmiths and wholesale merchants are the grandsons of those who followed the mad Sahibs to this hilltop in the 1930s and 40s of the last century. Most of them are plainsmen, quite prosperous, even though many of their houses are crooked and shaky.

Although the shopkeepers and tradesmen are fairly prosperous, the hill people—those who come from the surrounding Tehri and Jaunpur villages—are usually poor. Their small holdings and rocky fields do not provide them with much of a living, and men and boys have to often come into the hill station or go down to the cities in search of a livelihood. They pull rickshaws, or work in hotels and restaurants. Most of them have somewhere to stay.

But as I pass along the deserted street under the shadow of the clock tower, I find a boy huddled in a recess, a thin shawl wrapped around his shoulders. He is wide awake and shivering.

I pass by, my head down, my thoughts already on the warmth of my small cottage only a mile away. And then I stop. It is almost as though the bright moonlight has stopped me, holding my shadow in thrall.

If I am not for myself,
Who will be for me?
And if I am not for others,
What am I?

And if not now, when?

The words of an ancient sage beat upon my mind. I walk back to the shadows where the boy crouches. He does not say anything, but he looks up at me, puzzled and apprehensive. All the warnings of well-wishers crowd in upon me—stories of crime by night, of assault and robbery, 'ill met by moonlight'.

But this is not northern Ireland or Lebanon or the streets of New York. This is Landour in the Garhwal Himalayas. And the boy is no criminal. I can tell from his features that he comes from the hills beyond Tehri. He has come here looking for work and has yet to find any.

'Have you somewhere to stay?' I ask.

He shakes his head; but something about my tone of voice has given him confidence, because now there is a glimmer of hope, a friendly appeal in his eyes.

I have committed myself. I cannot pass on. A shelter for the night—that's the very least one human should be able to expect from another.

'If you can walk some way,' I offer, 'I can give you a bed and blanket.'

He gets up immediately, a thin boy, wearing only a shirt and part of an old tracksuit. He follows me without any hesitation. I cannot now betray his trust. Nor can I fail to trust him.